DARK
BREAKS
THE DAWN

DARK
BREAKS
THE DAWN

— BOOK ONE —

SARA B. LARSON

Scholastic Press
New York

Library of Congress Cataloging-in-Publication Data
Names: Larson, Sara B., author.
Title: Dark breaks the dawn / Sara B. Larson.
Description: First edition. | New York : Scholastic Press, 2017. | Series: Dark breaks the dawn ; book 1 | Summary: It is her eighteenth birthday, and Princess Evelayn of Éadrolan, the Light Kingdom has finally come into her full magical powers, which include shapeshifting, but she still has to be trained, and with her mother, the queen, away fighting the war with the Dark Kingdom of Dorjhalon, she must rely on two dark Draíolons, Lord Tanvir and Kelwyn, to prepare her—and with the corrupt King Bain plotting an attack she will need her powers much sooner than anyone foresaw.
Identifiers: LCCN 2016031955 | ISBN 9781338068696
Subjects: LCSH: Magic—Juvenile fiction. | Shapeshifting—Juvenile fiction. | Princesses—Juvenile fiction. | Nobility—Juvenile fiction. | Light and darkness—Juvenile fiction. | CYAC: Magic—Fiction. | Shapeshifting—Fiction. | Princesses—Fiction. | Nobility—Fiction. | Light and darkness—Fiction.
Classification: LCC PZ7.L323953 Dar 2017 | DDC 813.6 [Fic]—dc23
LC record available at https://lccn.loc.gov/2016031955

10 9 8 7 6 5 4 3 2 1   17 18 19 20 21

Printed in the U.S.A.   23
First edition, June 2017

Book design by Abby Denning

This one is for Elisse—my favorite ballet studio owner in the whole world. You've always supported me, cheered for me, and read for me (often more than once) at the drop of a hat and at lightning speed. Chasing our dreams together hasn't always been easy, but it has been worth it.

DARK
BREAKS
THE DAWN

An eon of peace, a world of joy,

Until it was shattered, by one foul boy,

A youngling at sixteen, Drystan his name,

For the first blood spilt, came his dark fame.

Banished he was, with followers in tow,

Power taken, as the final blow.

But cursed we were, immortality lost,

For the deeds he did, this was the cost.

Take heed, and follow not his path,

Or curse be restored, and removed, that we hath.

Peace is required, for life to thrive,

Those who seek power, from our shores we must drive.

Balance is required, such a thin knife,

That binds us all, and gives us life.

—DRAÍOLON NURSERY RHYME

ONE

THE JEWELED FOREST BLURRED INTO A TAPESTRY OF color as Evelayn sprinted away from the castle. She whipped past the trees and bushes as though she was made from the wind that pushed at her back. The sentries unlucky enough to have been assigned to guard her—or, more accurately, to trail her—on these early morning runs were already falling behind, their harsh breathing cutting across the gray-tinged stillness of dawn.

Good, she couldn't help but think, as she kicked up her heels and pushed herself even harder. What she really wanted right now was to be *alone,* something nearly impossible to achieve. Inside the castle, on the grounds, even with just her sentries, she knew her duty. She knew the part she had to play. The queen had taught her well.

But she'd jerked awake this morning after yet another nightmare, only to realize that nothing had changed. Evelayn had found it harder than ever to don the mask that she was usually so adept at summoning. *The queen must always appear calm, unruffled. Your subjects will look to you; your actions will determine theirs.* Her mother's words, and Evelayn had lived by them her whole life. After all, she would be the queen one day. Hopefully in the *very* distant future.

But what kind of queen would she be without her full power?

Evelayn's lungs burned hot for a moment, her throat went raw with suppressed emotion. Her sentries were no longer visible—or audible—but still she struggled for control. It was all she knew; it was her only defense against the rising panic.

Because it was her eighteenth birthday and *nothing had changed*.

She hadn't planned on running today, but after pacing in her room for a few minutes, Evelayn couldn't stand the silence or the tightness in her belly any longer. She'd pulled her lavender-streaked hair into a ponytail, yanked on her soft, supple running boots, and splashed water on her pale face. Evelayn had tried not to scowl at the dark circles beneath her violet eyes when she caught a glimpse of herself in the mirror. Too many sleepless nights, worrying about the war. Worrying about her mother.

Queen Ilaria had promised she'd return from the warfront for Evelayn's birthday and the ceremony that was to take place that night. Evelayn could only hope her mother was going to keep that promise. She didn't want to see another Draíolon, didn't want to talk to anyone, except her mother.

Without even realizing it, she'd run north of the castle, skirting the city of Solas, heading for the high ground that would enable her to watch for her mother's arrival. It was a longer run than normal, and Tyne, her lady-in-waiting, would certainly be concerned, upset even, if she came to Evelayn's room and found it empty . . . but certainly she was at least allowed *this*, wasn't she? A brief escape as she tried to come to grips with the fact that her full power hadn't manifested—that something was wrong with her. The future queen of Éadrolan.

The morning had grown lighter above her when Evelayn glanced up; in fact, she realized that if she squinted, the first rays of the sunrise were beginning to streak across the sky to the east, above the treetops. And then, in the infinitesimal break between one heartbeat and the next, something slammed into her. It felt as though her body had turned to flame, scorching her from within.

For the first time in her entire life her conduit stone burned in her breastbone.

Evelayn instinctively skidded to a halt, throwing out her hands to protect herself, expecting only the small burst of light she'd been capable of creating since she was a youngling. But instead, a ball of flame erupted from her right hand and a jet of light from the left. The light tore through the lush earth, leaving behind a black gash, and the fireball exploded against a nearby tree with an earth-shattering *boom*.

Evelayn slapped her hands over her ears with a howl of pain and blinked her eyes rapidly to clear the sudden tears from the onslaught of light and color and scent and *everything*. Until that moment she had existed in a world trapped by the pale, watery shades of dawn and had suddenly been thrust into the light of noon-day sun at Summer Solstice. Slowly the initial heat and shock of it all ebbed away, but the changes remained.

The blanket she'd always known was there, subduing her senses, had been pulled away. But no matter how many times she'd been taught about the block placed on all younglings' magic, no matter how often she'd been told what to expect on her eighteenth birthday, nothing could have prepared her for this. *This* was what Éadrolan truly looked like? Smelled like? Sounded like? She'd known it would be different, but *this* . . .

Evelayn slowly turned in a circle, letting her hands drop to her sides, allowing the sounds—there were *so many sounds*—to wash over her, to fill her. She inhaled deeply, trying to identify the myriad scents she'd never noticed before. Beneath the acrid smell of the tree she'd burnt, the perfume of the flowers surrounding her was so much headier than she'd ever realized; the musk of the earth beneath her feet was so much denser, more complex . . . And the colors. *Oh, the colors.* Details she hadn't known were physically possible to see until that moment blurred as tears filled her eyes. This time, Evelayn didn't fight them. She'd never been so overwhelmed in her whole life, except perhaps when her mother had returned from that first battle nearly a decade ago without her father. But that had been a stunned, bone-deep grief. *This* was . . . disbelief mingled with indescribable awe.

An unfamiliar scent—something citrusy and spicy all at once— caught her attention moments before she realized the soft thumping sounds she could hear were a Draíolon running through the forest. Evelayn spun in dismay just as a male burst through the trees to the north of her, his amber eyes flickering to the still-smoking tree and the black gash in the ground before returning to hers.

"Where are they? Who did this? Are you hurt?" His rapid succession of questions made her flinch and the concern on his face grew even more pronounced. "I can help you—I've just come from the warfront and I know quite a bit about tending to wounds. Where are you injured?"

Evelayn's dismay churned into an even darker emotion—mortification. "No," she managed to get out. She stumbled back when he moved toward her. With her heightened senses she noticed things about him she never would have seen so quickly before. The traces of gold in his amber eyes that matched the hint of gold in his skin, the richness of his bark-brown hair. And the sudden tang on the air that she was fairly certain was coming from him, as it mingled with the citrusy scent she'd already perceived.

"No? You're not hurt? Or no, you don't want my help?" He paused with his arm slightly outstretched.

Evelayn fought to keep her hands still at her sides, refusing to give him the satisfaction of seeing her wipe her still-damp cheeks. Her blood ran hot with humiliation. He obviously didn't realize who she was, based on how he'd addressed her—or rather, the lack of propriety in his address. Perhaps she could escape before he discovered her identity and realized this disoriented wreck of a girl was—

"I must insist on lending my assistance. I've seen this many times—you're in shock. If you will allow me—"

"I'm not hurt," Evelayn cut him off, drawing upon every ounce of training to don her most imperious voice and regal expression . . . despite the mess she certainly must have appeared to be. "Thank you for your offer, but I will bid you a good morning and let you continue on your way."

The Draíolon male's eyes narrowed and she had the suspicion he didn't believe her for one second. Before he could protest yet again, Evelayn whirled, prepared to dash away, just as she noticed her sentries finally heading toward her, their eyes wide as they took in, first, the destruction and then the strange male. They must have been truly lost to have only found her now, but it couldn't have been worse timing.

"Your Highness, *what* ha—"

"Let's head back, shall we?" Evelayn called out loudly the moment her sentry spoke, hoping to drown out his words. But her newly acute hearing didn't miss the sharp intake of breath behind her.

Evelayn waited no longer. With a silent prayer that the Draíolon who had errantly attempted to come to her aid would never tell another soul how he'd witnessed the crown princess of Éadrolan lose all control in the forest that morning, she kicked up her heels and sprinted past her sentries yet again.

It wasn't until she'd made it back to the castle that she realized she'd never reached the lookout point to see if her mother had kept her promise or not.

TWO

E VELAYN HAD ONLY BEEN BACK IN HER ROOM FOR A FEW
moments, trying to compose herself, when she heard the
whisper-soft movement of Tyne's hushed footsteps coming
down the hall. Before her lady-in-waiting even opened the door,
Evelayn caught the faint scent of roses and the mouthwatering aroma
of her breakfast.

Tyne's brief knock at her door seemed abnormally loud, making
Evelayn jump.

"Good morning, Princess," Tyne said as she bustled into the room
from the adjoining chamber. There was a glimmer—a depth—to the
rose color of her skin that Evelayn had never noticed before. Tyne bore a
tray laden with a mug of mint tea, a bowl of fresh fruit, and a berry scone
drizzled with honey—Evelayn's favorite. She gave the princess a quick
once-over, her eybrows lifting at Evelayn's sweat-and-tear-streaked appearance. But all she said was, "How does it feel to come into your full power?"

Evelayn hesitated for a moment, not sure how to put it into words,
then finally said, "Different."

Tyne shot her a conspiratorial smile as Evelayn finished unlacing her boots, pulled them off, and padded over to the table by the large eastern-facing window where her lady-in-waiting had set down the tray.

"You'll grow accustomed to it soon—then you'll wonder how you ever lived in such a dulled state before." Tyne bustled over to pull back the curtains, letting the sunshine stream in. Evelayn flinched at the onslaught of light.

"If you say so," she murmured, cutting off a piece of the scone.

"You'll notice the difference during training, as well. General Kelwyn said to tell you he's not giving you the day off."

Evelayn groaned as she lifted the cup of tea and took a sip. "Of course not. Because that might be perceived as preferential treatment, correct?"

Tyne just gave her a look.

"Fine. I'll go to training." She took another small bite of the scone, not looking up from the plate when she quietly asked, "Will I get to see my mother today?"

There was a long pause and then: "I hope so."

Which meant Queen Ilaria still hadn't returned to the castle from the warfront, just as Evelayn had feared. A flutter of nerves threatened to upset the bit of breakfast she'd already eaten, but she just nodded, still staring down at her food. "Thank you, Tyne. That will be all for now."

"But, Your Highness, your dress—"

"That's all for now," Evelayn repeated.

"Of course. Call for me when you're ready."

Only after she heard the click of the door shutting did Evelayn glance over her shoulder to make sure she was truly alone. And then she stood up and crossed to the other window, the one that faced north, where far away on the border of Éadrolan and Dorjhalon—the Light and Dark kingdoms—war raged. A war that had lasted for over a decade, with heavy casualties on both sides, including Evelayn's father, the king of Éadrolan.

She looked out toward the horizon, past the castle grounds, past the Dawn Temple, where the priestesses who weren't at the border upholding the wards that protected them from invasion lived and trained, past the city that was built to the northwest of the castle, where so many of the royal court and nobles dwelled, to the glimmering forest that stretched all the way to the border. Somewhere out there, her mother was fighting alongside her armies, trying to stop King Bain.

Evelayn had begged her not to go on the most recent campaign, since her birthday was coming up, but the queen had sworn she'd be back in time to celebrate with her. Her mother had never missed one of her birthdays before, and this was such an important one. The ball honoring Evelayn coming into her full power was to take place that night—it was to be the social event of the year, possibly even the century. It had been longer than that since a true royal had turned eighteen and had a celebration, not since Queen Ilaria's own, 105 years ago.

"You promised," Evelayn whispered to the clear glass that allowed her to watch her people hurrying about their busy lives below, while she stood in her room, fighting back tears, afraid that there could only be one reason her mother would break her word.

The midday sun was hot enough to make a Dark Draíolon sweat, since they thrived on the cooler weather of fall and winter, but Evelayn welcomed the warmth and the extra boost of power it meant for her and her people, as she walked out to the practice fields where Kelwyn waited with a couple of other Draíolon. When they saw her approaching, they all bowed—which she hated. But every time she told them to stop doing it, Kel would lecture her on proper decorum for someone of her station.

"Many happy wishes for this special day, my princess," he said as he and the other two Draíolon straightened.

She had to squint in the sun, still becoming accustomed to her heightened senses. Evelayn recognized the first Draíolon—a female Light Sentry whose name she believed was Dela; they'd been at a few training sessions together. But when she turned to meet the bemused gaze of the male Draíolon, her heart stuttered in her chest, her pleasant smile nearly slipping from her face. In the full light of day, his skin was the color of sunshine, and now his hair was tied back from his face, but it was those same inquisitive amber eyes she immediately recognized. The combination of citrus and spice mingled with Kelwyn's crisp scent of verbena and mint and the female sentry's lilac.

What was the Draiolon from the forest doing here at the castle— at her *training*?

"Thank you," Evelayn responded, turning back to Kelwyn, lifting her chin slightly, and adopting the mask she used whenever she wanted to hide what she was truly thinking. Years of practice served her well in that moment, as she could still feel the male Draíolon's eyes on her. *Please let him keep our encounter this morning to himself,* she sent up a silent plea before asking, "What will we be working on today?"

"Have you attempted to access your power yet this morning?" Kel returned her question with one of his own.

"A little." Evelayn didn't dare look at the male when she answered, not wanting to admit to any of them what had happened in the forest at dawn. She hadn't tried anything since, choosing instead to wait until the last possible moment to call for Tyne to help her pin up her long hair and lace up the back of her training outfit—supple leather pants and boots, a soft, close-fitting white shirt, and an over-vest made of the same leather as the pants. Usually, only Dark Draíolon favored wearing leather and other warmer clothing, while the Light Draíolon mainly stuck to flowing fabrics; but when it came to training they, too, wore leathers to protect their bodies. "What are we going to work on today?" she repeated, trying to move past the subject of how she'd spent her morning.

Kel studied her for a long moment as she struggled not to squirm beneath his searching gaze. Royalty didn't squirm—even when being scrutinized by someone as intimidating as Kelwyn. She noticed flecks of brown in his moss-green eyes that she'd never noticed before, the same color of newly tilled earth as his skin and hair. He and her father had trained together as younglings before Kel joined the Light Sentries and Drystan had become king of Éadrolan. Kel had been her father's closest friend and most trusted sentry, so there was no question who the queen wanted to train her daughter, despite Kel's wish to remain on the front lines of the war. But she'd insisted, so Kel was at the castle, training the princess for the next few months, while Evelayn's mother led her troops into battle against King Bain—most likely causing her to miss her daughter's birthday.

But *that* was a dangerous line of thought, fraut with fear and possible heartbreak, so Evelayn cut it off before it could fully form.

"We're going to have you utilize your new abilities to begin target practice," Kel finally answered, though his eyes were still slightly narrowed. "I want to give you the opportunity to feel just how much power you have access to now, and this is one of the best ways to do that." Kel gestured to the two other Draíolon. "You remember Dela, and I've also asked Tanvir, High Lord of the Delsachts and an incredibly proficient marksmale, to join us today to help me."

Evelayn knew she should be focusing entirely on Kelwyn, but instead she couldn't tear her attention away from Tanvir. He was a *High Lord*? What had he been doing in the forest this morning—and why was he helping with her training?

"It's a pleasure to meet you, *Your Highness*." She hoped she was the only one who noticed the hint of wryness in his tone as Lord Tanvir stepped forward, the scent of citrus and spice growing stronger with his proximity. He bowed to her a second time. When he rose, their eyes met again and this time a little thrill ran through Evelayn's body. There was something about the directness of his gaze that was disconcerting and enticing all at once.

But she'd met plenty of attractive nobles before, and very few of them had remained attractive to her once she'd had the chance to get to know them better—and they'd had the chance to show their *eagerness* to be Bound to the next queen of Éadrolan. Normally, she would be considered far too young for such a thing . . . if she'd been anyone other than the only living daughter of the king and queen. Her sister had died during birth, her mother had never conceived again before the king was killed, and she'd never been willing to be Bound again afterward. Evelayn was the only heir to the crown—and the power—of the Light Kingdom. Which meant there was quite a bit of pressure for her to be Bound and produce another heir as soon as possible.

So it wasn't hard for her to nod at him coolly, despite the slight increase in her pulse, and murmur, "The pleasure is all mine, Lord Tanvir."

"Please, just call me Tanvir," he quickly requested. "I still haven't become accustomed to being addressed so formally."

"You'll find that you and *Lord* Tanvir have much in common— including the tendency to despise formal titles and formal manners." Kel shook his head, but the look he gave Tanvir was more fond than annoyed.

"It's true, I generally can't abide any formality," Tanvir agreed. "Though I admit myself surprised to hear that the princess shares the same vice."

Again, there was that wry turn to his words, forcing her to recall that morning . . . and the complete lack of formality of their first "meeting"—if it could even be called that. "If that's the case, then it is truly a surprise that you were chosen to assist in my training." Evelayn was better at keeping her own agitation from her voice, maintaining her cool demeanor instead, even though she loathed having decisions that directly affected her made without her knowledge or consent. Such as summoning a High Lord from the front lines of the war to assist in her training. "Kelwyn has worked so hard to impress upon me the necessity of proper decorum, after all."

"Lord Tanvir was a leader in my battalion and impressed me with his skill and ability. But he is also young and has only recently inherited his title. *And* this is his first time at court. He will soon learn." Kelwyn gave her a look that clearly indicated that she should help persuade the High Lord of the Delsachts that Kelwyn was right.

Evelayn acknowledged his unspoken request with a slight dip of her head, all the while turning over in her mind what little she'd discovered about the mysterious Draíolon. He was attractive, had only recently become High Lord, which must mean his father had passed away not long ago—a blow she could well relate to—and he was apparently young. One curse—or blessing—of the Draíolon's long lifespan was the challenge of ascertaining age when meeting someone for the first time. It was rather difficult when they looked mature by the time they came into their full power at eighteen, and then didn't show any signs of aging until late into their second century, sometimes even third.

"Let's get started," Kelwyn finally announced, much to Evelayn's relief. "I asked Lord Tanvir to come help demonstrate what I wish you to do, and to assist in your training. As I said, he was considered one of the best marks in our armies, before he was called back to his family's holdings to take up the mantle of High Lord. You will soon see why."

Ah, so *that* was why he'd come—or at least one of the reasons. He was being presented at court as a new High Lord.

Kelwyn turned to Dela, whose mauve hair was pulled back in a severe braid. "Will you fetch the targets and place them in center field, please?"

"Of course." Dela turned to walk away after flashing a smile at Evelayn, her teeth shockingly white against the pale cerulean color of her skin.

When she had finished her task, four wooden targets cut in the shape of Draíolon males and females stood across the large field from them. They seemed *really* far away but Evelayn kept her face impassive, refusing to give any sign that she was nervous or uncertain. Kel nodded at Dela and then turned to Evelayn.

"Up until today we've only worked on minor skills," he began, "but now that you have come into your full power you are capable of so much more. Not only will I expect you to be able to hit those targets, I want your aim to be perfect. Many Draíolon struggle with that. They can achieve *distance* with their attacks, but they struggle with *precision*. As the princess—and someday the queen—you must be the exemplar in every way, including this." Kel gestured at Lord Tanvir. "If you please, go ahead and take out the first target."

Lord Tanvir nodded, all trace of amusement wiped away, replaced by a collected concentration that started in the narrowing of his eyes and extended all the way through the suddenly tense lines of his body. He was a predator ready to pounce, his muscles tightened in preparation. Evelayn studied him, analyzing his stance, the way he rolled his shoulders back and down, the sudden sharp scent of what she could only describe as anticipation in the air, how he lifted his hand and exhaled slowly . . .

And then a blast of light—very similar to the lightning that sometimes tore through the sky—rent a hole in the first target, right where the heart would be, had it been a real male. A tendril of dark smoke drifted up into the otherwise clear morning sky. The smell of singed wood and ozone filled the air, burning her nose.

"Excellent. Now again—but this time, aim to injure the target, not to kill."

Lord Tanvir repeated the entire process, but this time he struck the target in the bicep, just above the elbow, barely leaving the rest of the arm attached.

"Do you see that, Your Highness? The control and precision. He makes it look easy, but as you will soon find out, it is anything but. You must take into account tiny fluctuations in the wind, the amount of force to use for any distance, and many other factors. And of course this is all compounded if your target is moving. But let's not get ahead of ourselves." Kelwyn raised his voice and gestured at Dela. "Get ready, I'm going to have the princess try now."

Dela nodded while Evelayn struggled not to scowl. Most Draíolon had the same skills—Light could manipulate and summon heat, sunshine, and light, while Dark could manipulate cold, shadow, and darkness. But occasionally some would exhibit an extra ability. Dela's particular affinity was with water—she could control and direct it. A rare and useful skill, especially if one was expecting to put out a fire, for example.

"I want you to face the target fully. This is not so very different from what we've already been practicing—though it requires more power and more control, as you have learned in your lessons the last few years. You are probably feeling somewhat off-balance with all of the additional input you're receiving from your heightened senses, but you will soon learn to control them and pay attention only to what is necessary."

Evelayn did as he instructed, squaring her feet and settling into her stance as she'd watched Lord Tanvir do. She tried to block out everything else—all the extra scents and sounds that tempted to distract her. This was nothing like the minor skills she'd worked on with the limited access she'd had to the Light Power before now. Shooting a jet of light at a target hundreds of feet away was much more difficult than creating a spark to start a fire or summoning a ball of light to hover above her hand to light a darkened hallway. Yes, she'd studied tome upon massive tome about gaining her full Light Power and how to wield it, but that wasn't the same as actually *using* it—as she'd learned that morning.

But she did her best to keep her face expressionless, refusing to give any sign that she was nervous or uncertain.

"When you reach for your power, you will feel the difference—you'll sense the well of power you now have access to. You must learn to call only as much as you need, not too much or too little. If you summon too much you will take from others who might need it and you run the risk of injuring yourself or others unintentionally. And if you don't summon enough you will fail at your task and waste the power you called upon."

Evelayn nodded, even though Kelwyn was only repeating what she'd heard a hundred times before.

"Clear your mind and focus."

She stared at the target across the field and took a deep breath. *Not too much, not too little,* Evelayn coached herself as she lifted her hand. *Aim with precision.*

She called upon the power that had always been there, deep inside her. Only it wasn't the same at all—it was like comparing the trickling of a tiny stream to the rush of a torrential waterfall. The tidal wave surged within her and out of her hand in a blast of light that exited her body with such force it knocked her backward off her feet, to land unceremoniously on the ground, breathless and embarrassed.

But also *exhilarated*.

That morning she'd been too overwhelmed, too shocked, to truly take in what she had access to now. But this time, she'd felt it—she'd felt *all* of it. There was *so much* power. Far more than she had ever imagined. And despite her ignominious start, Evelayn couldn't keep herself from laughing with a surprised joy that filled her entire body.

"Are you all right, Princess?" Lord Tanvir was there, holding out his hand to help her up. But she ignored it, climbing to her feet on her own.

"Quite all right." She grinned, even though Dela was standing across the field, directing a jet of water from the bucket at her feet up into the tree where Evelayn's first attempt had gone high and wide, setting a branch on fire.

Kelwyn smiled back at her, for once not lecturing her on proper behavior. "Isn't it marvelous?"

"I had no idea," Evelayn agreed, still slightly breathless. "Let's do it again."

"Of course, Your Highness," Kelwyn agreed. "But first, let's discuss what you did wrong."

THREE

CEREN PACED THE LENGTH OF THE LUNCHEON ROOM despite the irritated looks her mother kept flashing her from where she sat, eating with a large group of the royal court. They looked like a brightly arrayed flock of birds gathered around the table that ran from one end of the room to the other. But Ceren had finished her meal long ago and there was still no sign of Evelayn. It was unusual for the princess to miss a meal, especially on a day like today; but if the quiet mutterings at both breakfast and luncheon were true, the queen hadn't returned from the warfront yet, and Ceren knew how excited Evelayn had been at the prospect of seeing her mother. She'd been more excited about *that* than the fact that she would be coming into her full power.

Ceren was certain Evelayn's full power had come with the breaking of the dawn, but the queen hadn't, and she also was certain that the queen's continued absence had probably devastated her friend. However, rather than letting her go search for Evelayn, Ceren's mother had forced her to come to luncheon with the rest of the court, claiming that Evelayn would send for her if she wanted company.

The noise of the conversations flowed over her as she marched back and forth, her own one-person rebellion, so that she only caught snippets here and there.

"—they say that ten more from the same battalion died of their wounds the next day—"

"—can't honestly believe that color of fabric is attractive, can she? Yellow is never a good idea with green skin—"

"—noticed a difference, but Prinlor claims that he's felt his power diminishing slightly every year that this war continues and—"

"—her infant is already talking and she thinks that means she's going to be—"

Ceren could barely keep from scowling at the ridiculousness of it all. The mundane mixed with the vital, neither seeming to have greater import to the members of the court. *As if a fashion faux pas is just as troubling as the death count from the warfront,* she thought caustically. Which was all too easy for them to discuss as they ate their fruit salad, vegetable soup, and fresh rolls in the comfort and safety of the castle, far from the horrors Ceren imagined existed on the borders of their kingdom where so many priestesses and Light Draíolon fought to keep the wards up and the Dark Draíolon out.

When the door opened and a page entered the room, holding a tray with a white card, Ceren nearly closed her eyes to pray it would be for her, but there was no need. He searched the room and, as soon as he spotted her, brought her the tray. She recognized Evelayn's writing and the tightness that she hadn't even realized was squeezing her heart released slightly.

My dearest Ceren,
Please attend me in my private quarters for luncheon.
I apologize if you have already lunched, but pray that
you will still indulge my request.
Yours,
Princess Evelayn of Éadrolan

"If you will please excuse me, the princess requests my presence." Ceren curtsied in the general direction of her mother and then hurried to follow the page out before anyone could ask her to deliver a message to Evelayn or otherwise delay her.

A few minutes later Ceren burst into Evelayn's outer chamber to find the princess sitting at her table, with more food than one person could ever hope to eat spread in front of her. The sunlight reflected off the hint of lavender in her pale blonde hair, which was intricately arranged around the small diadem for the ball that night. But she still only wore a day dress, not the elaborate gown the castle seamstresses had been working on for weeks in preparation for the celebration.

"Ceren!" Evelayn turned at the sound of the door with a smile on her face, which released the tightness in Ceren's chest even more as she hurried forward to embrace her friend.

"Happy birthday, Ev," Ceren said as she took a seat across the table from her. "I'm so sorry about your mother . . ."

She almost immediately regretted bringing it up when worry clouded Evelayn's face momentarily, but then she shrugged and picked up the roll she'd been eating before Ceren's arrival and took another bite. "There's nothing to be done about it now. She must have had pressing business to attend to at the warfront. I only hope she's safe."

I'm sure she is. The words were right there, ready to be spoken, but Ceren merely nodded, knowing that with this war, there were no guarantees. She remembered all too well the day Evelayn had learned that her father had been killed in battle. But surely the queen was still alive—they still had their power, after all. "I'm sure she would have come if it were at all possible."

"I suppose this means my aunt Rylese will have to escort me to the ball now." Evelayn made a face. Ceren didn't know King Drystan's older sister very well, but she knew Evelayn was often irritated with Rylese for lecturing her and treating her like she was still a youngling.

Ceren reached for a few grapes. Now that she was with Evelayn her appetite had returned. "Maybe she'll treat you differently now that you've come into your full power?"

"Maybe," Evelayn echoed unconvincingly, but then her violet eyes lit up. "Which reminds me—Why didn't you tell me?"

"Tell you what?"

"About the power! About how *incredible* it is." Evelayn's food lay forgotten as she leaned forward. Her conduit stone—the diamond that she'd been born with, embedded about an inch below the center of her collarbone, just like her mother—flashed in the sunlight. "That's why I missed luncheon. I just couldn't bring myself to stop training. By the end I summoned my first sun-sword, and I was even hitting the targets consistently. Not as well as Lord Tanvir, but considering it's only my first day, I think they were impressed."

"Lord who? And I *did* tell you, it's just not the same as actually *feeling* it."

"Lord Tanvir—the new High Lord of the Delsachts. I'd never seen him before I ran into him in the forest this morning—well, *technically*, he tried to come to my rescue, which was absurd—but then he was at my training today, and he's an excellent marksmale—"

"Wait—what?" Ceren cut in. "You ran into him in the forest? When he tried to *rescue* you? From what? Or who?"

"Myself, I suppose. Though he didn't know that. He said he was good with wounds from being on the warfront. And, as I said, he's a very good marksmale; apparently that is why Kelwyn asked him to help with my training, because of how skilled he is." Evelayn continued, talking so fast Ceren couldn't help but laugh, resigning herself to questioning her friend for details later, when she'd calmed down a bit. This was the Evelayn she knew and loved—the one almost no one else ever saw. When other Draíolon were around, she was demure, collected; she tried to be the perfect princess everyone expected her to be. But in private, she was still the same girl Ceren had grown up with. The girl who had raced through the castle halls, and explored the forest for hours with her, heedless of their dresses—until their mothers saw the damage they'd done and halfheartedly scolded them.

But everything had changed when King Bain had suddenly sent an army across the border and attacked the city of Ristra when they were eight.

Evelayn was in the middle of describing the look on Lord Tanvir's and General Kelwyn's faces after she hit the target on her third try, when the door opened and Tyne bustled in.

"Good afternoon, Miss Ceren." Tyne nodded toward her and then turned to Evelayn. "I apologize for intruding, Your Highness, but I must get to work if I'm to have you ready in time for tonight."

Evelayn sighed, most of the happiness and exuberance draining from her face to be replaced by the polite mask she wore in public—when she was concealing her true emotions. "Of course. Ceren, if you'll excuse us."

Ceren nodded and stood up. "I'll see you tonight?"

"Of course," Evelayn repeated with a half smile.

Ceren curtsied, conscious of Tyne's presence, and left her friend behind to be transformed into a royal princess ready to attend her coming-of-age ball.

FOUR

AUNT RYLESE HADN'T LEFT EVELAYN'S SIDE ON THE dais even though the princess had already been presented to the glittering mass of Draíolon and had eaten the first piece of the five-tiered cake, as was tradition to start the celebration. The cake had been as light as air and the buttercream frosting was perfection, decorated with beautiful fruits that were so vibrant in color they'd almost looked like jewels, but it had turned to ash in Evelayn's mouth and lead in her belly as she looked out over the gathered crowd and forced a smile. The earlier exhilaration of training had long since left her and what remained was an aching hollowness. A strange sensation of being completely alone even though she was surrounded by hundreds of younglings and adults, males and females, including Aunt Rylese, who had been kind enough to lecture her for only five minutes about what was expected of her, rather than the usual fifteen or more.

But Evelayn's last hope that her mother would somehow make it back in time had died when she'd had to take Aunt Rylese's elbow and allow her to escort Evelayn onto the dais to the cheers of the royal court and all the other Draíolon who had come for the ball, while her senses were assaulted by all the scents and sounds and colors of so many gathered in one room.

The dancing had begun an hour ago and the cake was now down to the last layer, but still Aunt Rylese stood there, glaring at anyone who dared try to approach the princess. Her idea of decorum seemed to amount to Evelayn's becoming an ornament of sorts—an object to be viewed, not a living being to be included in her own party. Her mother would have made sure she was dancing, eating, *enjoying* herself.

"Sighing will make you seem bored, Evelayn. You don't want your subjects to be concerned that you aren't having a good time," Aunt Rylese scolded. "This is your special night!"

"I'm *not* having a good time," Evelayn retorted, unable to keep the bitterness from her voice any longer. "Honestly, I'm quite miserable. I will stay for another fifteen minutes and then I will retire to my rooms for the night. I have a headache."

She didn't have to look at her aunt to know that her earth-colored eyes—the same color that her father's had been—were probably wide with astonishment. "You can't possibly leave that early, what will your subjects think—"

"I don't know that I care what they think at this point. It's my 'special night' as you said, shouldn't someone care what *I* think—or how *I* feel?"

Aunt Rylese put a hand on her arm, probably meaning to be soothing, but it only irritated Evelayn further. "Of course we care, darling, but you must consider what's proper. You are not like the other females in Éadrolan, be they noble or not. You are a *princess*. The *only* princess, and you must act in accordance with—"

"Do you think I'm not aware of that?" Evelayn cut her off yet again, this time glancing over to see her aunt blanch at her audacity. Part of her felt guilty for causing Rylese distress; though she was annoying, she meant well enough. But the other part, the part of her that had responded with exhilaration earlier today at the sudden increase in her power, felt only the need to escape—to leave behind the limitations and restraints of her position, at least until the morning. The dress the seamstresses had designed for her special night had been inspired by a butterfly, made of layers of iridescent lavender, white, and palest blue fabrics that hugged her curves and swooped up to attach to her arms—giving the appearance of wings if she stretched them. How she wished to be a butterfly right then. Or even better, to have mastered the ability to shift into her swan form, so she could fly away from the crowd and the emptiness inside that hollowed her out.

It was her birthday, and Evelayn was going to spend the last hour or two as she wished, *where* she wished, not trapped at a party held in her honor that apparently had nothing to do with her.

"If you'll excuse me—" She was turning away even as she spoke, hurrying down the stairs toward the crowded Great Hall before her aunt could stop her. Suddenly, she was enveloped in noise and sound and heat and *life*. All around her Draíolon danced and laughed and ate and danced some more. Dresses and evening clothes of every color filled her vision, along with the many varied hair and skin tones that distinguished her people—colors of the earth and all living things that were a part of spring and summer. Their scents combined in a heady blend that was almost overwhelming. But all too soon her subjects noticed the princess there among them, and the dancing and laughing and joviality slowly ground to an uncomfortable halt, as if they weren't sure what to do with her standing there.

"Please don't stop." She signaled the musicians to continue, and tried to smile despite the sudden harsh pulse of her blood in her ears. A vein at her temple throbbed against the jewels and glitter Tyne had so painstakingly applied to create a swirling masterpiece down either side of her face earlier that night. But though the music started again, only a couple of Draíolon resumed dancing. Everyone else stood in small clumps and groups, watching her, some whispering, some silent. Evelayn wasn't prone to blushing, but she could feel her neck growing hot as the awkwardness continued to build. Where was Ceren? She would know what to do. Evelayn turned around, searching the crowd for her friend's vibrant red hair, but she was nowhere to be seen. Perhaps Aunt Rylese had been correct after all—perhaps her place really was just to watch, to adorn her own party from afar.

The scent of citrus and spice tickled her nose a moment before a voice asked, "If I may be so bold, would you care to dance, Your Highness?"

Evelayn spun around to see Lord Tanvir bowing low, his hand extended. Her relief was instantaneous. "I would be honored, my lord." She placed her hand in his and his fingers closed around hers, his skin warm and slightly rougher than her own.

"The honor is all mine, I assure you." He straightened and there was that glint again in his striking amber eyes as their gazes met and he pulled her in toward his body so he could circle her waist with his other arm, placing his hand on the small of her back. Her breath caught as he expertly guided her across the floor in time to the music, her feet following his automatically. Within moments the other Draíolon apparently decided it was acceptable to continue celebrating, and Evelayn and Lord Tanvir were soon surrounded by other dancing couples.

"Thank you," she finally said when it seemed that everything had returned to normal.

Lord Tanvir lifted one eyebrow. "Whatever do you mean?"

"I believe you know."

He gave her a little smile, his hand flexing against her back. "My gallant attempt to assist you in the forest this morning?" Evelayn just gave him a look and he laughed. "No, that definitely is not what you meant. I take it that you have no desire to explain what happened to that poor tree before I arrived, either?"

"None," she agreed.

"Well, then I am left to assume that you are thanking me for asking you to dance. To which my reply is that any time I can come to the aid of a fellow despiser of the formal conventions of our society is an opportunity I'd be loath to miss."

Despite herself, Evelayn smiled back at him. "Ah yes, I forgot. I was supposed to be setting an example for you, so that you might come to see the error of your uncouth ways, *Lord* Tanvir."

"A task at which you have failed miserably, because you look much happier right now than you have the entire evening, Your Highness. Flaunting the proper decorum for a princess seems to suit you."

Evelayn wasn't sure if she should laugh or chastise him, but when their eyes met and she saw the teasing glint in his, the laughter won, taking her by surprise.

"My aunt would be mortified to hear that."

"Then we won't tell her. Besides, she looks imperious enough for the both of you."

Evelayn laughed again as she snuck a glance up at the dais. She wasn't surprised to see Aunt Rylese's hands clenched in her skirts, her expression a strange cross between irritation and what she probably meant to be a pleasant, *proper* smile.

"She means well," Evelayn felt compelled to explain.

"As do many interfering and opinionated people. That doesn't mean you must listen to them or do as they bid." He spun her deeper into the crowd, farther away from the dais.

"She's my aunt."

"And you are the crown princess of Éadrolan. I think your authority supersedes hers."

Evelayn fell quiet for a moment, uncomfortable with the reminder of who she was—the reminder of the fact that of course he saw her that way. She was amusing *and* powerful to him, that was all. It had been silly to think for even a moment that perhaps he could truly understand her.

When the music ended, Lord Tanvir didn't let her go right away.

"Have I offended you in some way, Your Highness?" He was only a few inches taller than she; their eyes were nearly on the same level, but she wouldn't let herself meet his searching gaze.

"Of course not, Lord Tanvir. Thank you again for the dance." She gently pulled back and he immediately let go, as if only then realizing the song had finished. "If you'll excuse me."

He bent forward into a deep bow, looking up at her from that position, and seemed about to say something else, but she turned and pushed through the crowd toward the doors that would let her escape the Great Hall.

FIVE

THE MEETING, WHICH WAS SUPPOSED TO HAVE BEEN "quick," had long since become interminable. Lorcan was sure he'd been sitting in the same chair listening to the same arguments for the better part of the entire afternoon. Only the members of his father's closest circle of advisors and generals were included. This was the meeting that no one else was supposed to know about. The plan King Bain had presented was both daring and dangerous. Only the handful of Draíolon gathered could know about it if they wanted to pull it off. But if it worked . . .

"It's just too great a risk for you, Your Majesty," General Maedre insisted, the same thing he'd been insisting all day. He had been a part of the inner circle for less than a year. "Yes, it's unexpected. But it leaves you open to attack—or worse. *If* you manage to make it through the Undead Forest unscathed, you *might* succeed in killing her, but then you would be susceptible—you'd be trapped in the midst of their army!"

"You forget that if he succeeds and kills Queen Ilaria, her people will be rendered powerless immediately. They won't be able to hurt him," Lorcan's mother, Queen Abarrane, pointed out.

"What say you, Caedmon? You've been quiet all afternoon." King Bain turned to the newest general to be promoted to his inner circle after General Virlin was killed in battle a few weeks prior.

Caedmon looked up at the king, his eyes going to the blood-red conduit stone in the king's forehead—the exact same oval, ruby stone that Lorcan and Lothar had been born with, though theirs were cold and powerless for now—and then to Bain's questioning gaze.

Lorcan studied Caedmon as he considered the king's query. The general had a special affinity for snow and had taken on many characteristics of it—skin so white it practically glittered and irises so pale the only true color visible in his eyes were his pupils. Though all Dark Draíolon smelled of fall or winter, Caedmon's scent was sharper than most; a blast of ice assaulted Lorcan's nose whenever the other male walked into the room. He was known to be intelligent and lethal, but Lorcan always felt a little bit uncomfortable when Caedmon turned his disconcerting gaze to him.

"I believe that it is a great risk," Caedmon finally responded, slowly, thoughtfully, "but has the chance of great victory. If you are willing to take such a risk, and if everything goes according to the plan, it has a good likelihood of success because it would be so unexpected. You should consider that though the Light Draíolon will be powerless should you succeed, they will still have strength in numbers. Even you cannot hope to defeat them with only the few Dark Draíolon you will have with you."

Everyone was silent for a long while, digesting his response.

"So I will retreat immediately, gather my army, and then lead one final attack before her daughter can regain the power for her people. I'd have three days, which is more than enough time."

Everyone around the table nodded, except for Maedre and Caedmon.

"You disagree, Maedre?"

Lorcan stiffened at the latent fury in his father's voice and the sudden acrid scent of his anger. Bain was notorious for his mood swings—going from seemingly calm to a raging inferno in moments. But General Maedre didn't back down.

"If you consider time to retreat and gather your army and then the time it would take to reach Solas, it would be longer than three days to lead a full attack on Éadrolan and seize control of their kingdom."

King Bain's eyes narrowed, and Lorcan noticed his brother, Lothar, flinching in preparation for the anger that was sure to come. Instead, Bain merely asked, "How old is the young princess again?"

"I believe she just turned eighteen today," Lothar supplied, which wasn't surprising, since he was forever reading and studying, rather than spending every spare moment training as Lorcan did.

King Bain barked out a laugh. "So she barely came into her full power today and you think she could possibly complete the ceremony to reclaim the Light Power in time? Pardon me if I don't share your concern." He laughed again and everyone else nervously joined him— everyone except General Maedre.

"Still," he persisted, "it would be foolish not to take into account the possibility that she *could* succeed, even though it would be quite remarkable—"

"Are you calling me *foolish*?" King Bain roared, cutting him off. This time even Lorcan flinched.

Before General Maedre could respond, Bain lifted his hand and shot a blast of dark-flame at him, tearing a hole through his chest. The general's eyes widened in disbelief for a split second before he slumped over in his chair, dead.

"Anyone else here believe me to be foolish?"

Everyone was silent, shocked at the sudden violence—everyone except Bain's queen and sons, who had seen him lose his temper many times and knew how unwise it was to push him.

"Good. Abarrane, call for someone to come dispose of that." King Bain stood up, the signal that he was dismissing the meeting. "What a nuisance. Now I will have to find a replacement for him before I can proceed with my plan."

"I have a few suggestions, if I may, sire." Obrecht, Bain's most trusted and longest-surviving general, spoke as he rose.

"Excellent. Let's hope you choose more wisely this time." King Bain didn't even glance at the body as he exited the room.

SIX

T HE FOREST WAS QUIET AND DARK AS EVELAYN CARE-
fully walked along the trail leading to the lake where her
swans lived. Behind her the noise of the party faded until
there was nothing to hear except the soft *shoosh* of her breathing, the
swish of her skirts as she walked, the cadence of insects' nighttime
songs . . . and the almost-silent footfalls of the sentries who were dis-
creetly following her.

They were always there, though not always seen. But she'd never
been able to hear them as clearly as she could now.

She'd waited all day to come, hoping her mother would show up
so they could go together. But her birthday would be over in less than
an hour; Queen Ilaria wasn't coming. Only something terrible would
have kept her away, and it was all Evelayn could do not to let the fear of
what that terrible thing might be overwhelm her. She'd come to the
lake—the place where she had always found solace—to distract herself
by attempting to shift, though the thought of doing it by herself the
first time was daunting, to say the least.

There was no one else who could instruct her how to do it. Only true royals—those with conduit stones and who could claim the power of their kingdom—had the ability to shift. Which meant only Queen Ilaria was capable of it in Éadrolan. Even if she'd had a brother, Evelayn would still be the only other, because the power passed through the female line in Éadrolan. In Dorjhalon the royal males were the ones born with conduit stones, so the king and his two sons were the only Draíolon in their kingdom capable of shifting.

Evelayn didn't have to be near the swans to shift, but she wanted to do it there, on the banks of the lake, where she'd come so many times before. Where she'd first imprinted, and realized the swans she loved so much were to be her destiny once she came into her full power.

Normally, she would have had to summon light to be able to safely make the trek through the forest, but with her sharpened eyesight, Evelayn could see almost perfectly in the dark. She carefully picked her way down the path until suddenly the trees opened up to the night sky above and the lake below. And there on the glass-like water glided the flock of swans, their white feathers a beacon in the darkness.

Evelayn walked over to the log she thought of as hers, where she'd spent countless hours with her father, her mother, and by herself. Carefully gathering the exquisite gown into her arms, she sat down and took a deep breath, inhaling the sultry night air, more fragrant than it had ever been before, with the perfume of summer flowers, the freshness of the thriving greenery, and the musk of the rich soil beneath it all. Though they had kept their distance, Evelayn could scent the sentries as well—one of clove and fig, and the other of sunflowers and rain—and something else, beneath the surface, nuances that she'd never experienced before. She knew from what others had told her that they were emotions, feelings, and that she would soon learn how to recognize what they meant.

If she had to guess right now, Evelayn was fairly certain the faint sourness meant both sentries were bored, possibly even irritated. And if they could scent her, they probably knew she was upset, and full of trepidation.

She was sure to get an earful from Aunt Rylese for her behavior— first going down into the crowd, then dancing, then disappearing without a formal good night to her guests—but if it meant a few stolen moments of peace, it would be worth it. She could still feel the phantom heat on the small of her back from Lord Tanvir's hand, where he'd led her through the dance and had nearly succeeded in getting past her defenses. She was the world's greatest fool to have thought he was different from the rest of the nobility. All any of them wanted was the chance to become king, to father the next queen of Éadrolan. She was nothing more than a means to an end for any of them.

"Stop moping," she whispered to herself, "and get on with it."

It took a moment before she could follow her own advice. But finally, with a deep, fortifying breath, she stood back up and squared her shoulders. She knew how this was supposed to work in theory, but of course had never been able to practice before. Evelayn hated to do it in front of the sentries watching from the shadows of the forest behind her. But at least she knew her clothes would return when she shifted back into her Draíolon form. At least, they always had for her mother. Hopefully there wasn't some trick to it. If so, then these sentries would get a lot more than what they bargained for when they were assigned to guard her for the night.

Supposedly, all she had to do was picture the animal she had imprinted on—in her case, a swan—and then will herself to change form, using her conduit stone to channel additional power. It sounded so simple. But as she stood on the sandy bank, picturing a swan in her mind while staring at the swans on the lake . . . nothing happened.

The minutes dragged past while Evelayn tried everything she could think of to make herself shift, and though a hint of power rose through her body, that was it. She began to feel more and more foolish. Perhaps she needed to call upon the power first and then focus on changing?

"Somehow I knew I'd find you here."

The shock of hearing her mother's voice froze Evelayn in place momentarily. And then she spun to see the queen of Éadrolan standing at the edge of the forest, her violet hair pulled back into a bun, still clad in her battle attire, dusty and visibly exhausted. But it was *her*.

She'd come.

And suddenly, it didn't matter that she'd missed the ceremony and the ball and the entire day—all that mattered was that she was *there*. She was healthy, and whole, and she'd made it back before Evelayn's birthday ended. She'd kept her promise.

Tears burned in Evelayn's eyes, blurring her vision, as she picked up her skirts and bolted toward her mother.

The moment Queen Ilaria's arms were around her, squeezing her close, a tightness Evelayn hadn't even realized existed released from within her. She sagged into her mother's embrace like one would sink into a feather mattress, letting her familiar scent—still there beneath the dirt and grime—wash over and through her. There was so much to say, but nothing came out except a breathless, *"You're here."*

"I told you I would be. Even if I had to move the skies above and the earth below, I wasn't going to break my promise." Queen Ilaria's voice was soft and melodic, often misleading people into believing *she* was soft as well. But underneath her beautiful exterior and quiet voice was a ruler with steel running through her veins. She and Evelayn were the same height and had been for years, yet Evelayn still felt smaller somehow when she was with her mother. "But I am *so* sorry I missed everything . . . the ceremony and the ball. Things at the warfront—" She shook her head, letting go of Evelayn to step back and study her. "Was it wonderful?"

Evelayn shrugged. "It was . . . fine." Before her mother could press her further, she continued, "But I can't shift. I've been trying and it won't happen."

Her mother gave her a look, but let the not-so-subtle evasion go. "It's a little bit tricky at first, but you'll catch on quickly. I know you will. Come on, I'll show you."

Evelayn followed her mother down to the log near the shoreline and listened as she explained yet again how to call up the power, and how to bend it to her will—allowing her to transform. Then she demonstrated, shifting into her animal form—a sleek leopard. The predators were extremely rare, and it had only been chance that Ilaria had seen one the day of her eighth birthday. Chance, or perhaps fate. She'd told Evelayn many times about the pull she'd immediately felt to the powerful creature, and Evelayn had spent many nights dreaming of what animal she'd imprint on.

At first Evelayn had been embarrassed to admit she felt drawn to her swans—they weren't powerful like a leopard, or fast like a hawk (which it was rumored Prince Lorcan had imprinted on for his eighth birthday). Both her parents had been alive then, and they'd reassured her that there must be a reason she'd felt drawn to the beautiful birds and to trust in herself and the forces guiding her.

Now, as Evelayn stood on the banks beside her mother's leopard form and closed her eyes to focus, following the directions the queen had given her, she knew she had to will away her doubts. Her mother had been adamant that any hint of fear or uncertainty would keep her from being able to shift. She had to want it absolutely; she had to be completely certain and confident in her choice and her desire to change. And she did want it—so badly, her hands were fisted at her sides from the effort of concentrating.

But then one of the swans trumpeted in alarm. Evelayn opened her eyes just in time to see the entire flock open their magnificent wings and take flight, hurrying away from the lake—and the leopard sitting on the bank.

A rush of power swooshed around her, but it came from outside, not within. There was a swirl of white mist and then her mother stood before her in her battle clothes once more.

"I'm sorry," her mother said. "I didn't mean to scare them away."

Evelayn shrugged, trying not to let her disappointment show. "It wasn't working anyway."

"Perhaps you are trying *too* hard. It's not something that can be forced, or else more Draíolon would be capable of doing it. It's an instinct, born into you along with your conduit stone. Relax and *believe.*"

Focus, concentrate completely, drive out all doubts, but don't try *too* hard . . . so very simple, right? "I'm tired. Maybe I should wait and try again another time."

Sometimes when Evelayn balked at practice or training or lectures, it was the queen of Éadrolan who responded, commanding her to continue. But tonight it was her mother who gently responded, "All right. There's always tomorrow."

And though they both knew that was a lie—there were no guarantees—the princess and the queen turned and walked back to the castle arm in arm, leaving the dark, empty lake behind them.

SEVEN

G ENERAL KELWYN PACED BACK AND FORTH ACROSS the lawn while Tanvir watched and tried to quell the uncomfortable twist of nerves in his gut. He'd replayed the dance with Princess Evelayn over and over in his mind, keeping himself up for hours the night before, wondering what he'd said that had shuttered her expression and turned her fingers cold in his before she fled her own party. He hadn't been able to parse it out. All he knew was that he had blundered somehow.

And now the princess was late to her morning training.

"She's never late," he heard Dela mutter. He'd only helped once, so he hadn't been sure, but Dela's comment confirmed what he suspected. Evelayn's absence wasn't normal.

"The queen was called back to the warfront this morning," Tanvir supplied, repeating what the entire castle had been abuzz about ever since Queen Ilaria had arrived in the middle of the night but then left before dawn. "Maybe it has something to do with that?"

"Possibly. Perhaps you should—"

Whatever General Kelwyn had been about to suggest was cut off by the princess emerging from the trees, striding toward them with her chin slightly lifted as if daring any of them to comment on her tardiness. She was outfitted in her training leathers, revealing the litheness of her body that was concealed by the dresses she usually wore. Her lavender-streaked flaxen hair was pulled back into a simple braid today, the coronet missing, and her face washed clean of the tiny jewels and makeup that had created glittering wings on either side of her stunning eyes the night before. But even without all that, she could never be mistaken for a commoner or a mere sentry arriving to train. Something about her commanded attention—demanded veneration. It wasn't just because she was attractive, although she *was* blindingly beautiful. It was in her *presence*.

And of course, there was the conduit stone. All of Evelayn's clothes were either cut low enough to show it, or had a hole cut out around the stone so it was always visible.

As Tanvir watched the princess draw closer, something inside him tightened. Though her expression didn't show it, unhappiness clung to her like her shadow, darkening her now-familiar subtle sunshine and floral scent. Her violet eyes were red-rimmed but when their gazes met, something sparked in hers—a challenge.

Instead of risking saying the wrong thing again, he merely bowed. "Your Highness," he murmured, trying not to remember the way she'd smiled up at him—laughed even—last night. Before he'd somehow managed to wipe all the happiness from her expression.

"What are we working on today?" she addressed Kelwyn, turning her back to Tanvir.

What had he done that had earned her ire so completely?

"I thought we'd begin with working on our defensive strategies— particularly if you were to find yourself powerless for any reason or outnumbered. The only hope of protection if you were under attack without your power is to use a Scíath," Kelwyn said, glancing at Tanvir speculatively before returning his full focus to the princess.

Evelayn nodded, all business. Tanvir felt the loss of her attention acutely, even though he'd had it for only a brief moment. But it gave him the opportunity to observe her unnoticed—she was too busy avoiding looking at him.

So he watched . . . watched and learned. As she listened to Kelwyn. As she learned how to wield a Scíath—the coveted shield, forged in Rúnda by the few priestesses who lived there, that was capable of protecting the bearer from any attack, Light or Dark. The silvery disc, nearly as big as her entire torso, flashed in the sunlight as she ducked and blocked blast after blast from Kelwyn.

He watched as they switched places and she practiced honing her power, succeeding far more quickly than any other Draíolon he'd ever trained beside. As they moved on to hand-to-hand combat, summoning sun-swords and sun-daggers made of lightning and white-flame, created by the power she wielded. As she worked on fighting with regular knives, swords, and a bow and arrows. Kelwyn insisted she know how to battle with more than her power—just in case.

"Now, fight Lord Tanvir. He has a different style than me. After him, you'll spar with Dela."

Though sweat beaded along her hairline, Evelayn merely nodded, turning to face Tanvir. She was younger than he, but Tanvir knew not to underestimate her. She'd spent her whole life training, preparing to someday take her mother's place as queen and the conduit for all the power in the Light Kingdom. Somehow, until that moment as he faced her, preparing to spar, he hadn't ever wondered what it would be like to *be* the princess—the pressure, the expectations, the—

And that's when it hit him, just as she lifted the knives she held in either hand, sinking slightly into a fighting stance. He knew what he'd said wrong last night.

"On my mark," General Kelwyn said, lifting his hand.

Tanvir quickly pulled out his own daggers, forcing himself to focus. Later—he would right the wrong step he'd taken later. But for now, he would fight the princess.

General Kelwyn's hand fell.

Tanvir's burnt-gold eyes were trained on hers, his body tense, prepared, waiting for her attack. This wouldn't be like sparring with General Kelwyn, or Ceren, or anyone else for that matter. This was a dance of a different sort from the one they'd shared the night before, but as Evelayn made the first move and he nimbly dodged her swipe and then spun around to slash his own blade at her, it was clear that this was still a dance—a give and take, two partners locked on to each other— however, this time with deadly intent.

And Evelayn intended to win.

They moved faster and faster, learning each other's style, getting closer and closer to an actual hit. It was difficult to control her newly discovered power, to hold it at bay, to rely only on her speed and strength as she always had before her birthday. The blades were dulled so that they wouldn't slice through the leathers they wore, but Evelayn's body still sang with adrenaline, her blood pumping through her muscles as she twisted and lunged and ducked.

Often, her sparring partners were careful with her, holding back because they were nervous, afraid to hurt the princess. Those wins felt cheap, as if she'd been handed her victory.

But not today—not with Tanvir. He held nothing back, giving her the honor of fighting her as an equal. And he was *good*. So quick she could barely keep up.

She had to use all of her heightened senses to anticipate his attacks as they swung and lunged and swiped faster and faster and faster still. Though he nearly gained the upper hand, almost landing a killing slice against her ribs before she managed to roll away, sparring with him was intoxicating.

She did as she had been taught—channeling all the anger and hurt she'd had to crush when she'd woken for her morning run and found the note from her mother, and using it as a third, unseen weapon. She knew it wasn't her mother's fault she'd been called back to the warfront so quickly, but that didn't lessen the frustration of her situation. Fueled by that anger, Evelayn forced herself to keep going, to move beyond the burning of her muscles that begged for a break. When Tanvir lunged forward yet again, this time going for a debilitating torso wound, Evelayn used his momentum to hook his arm, swing herself around his body, and drag her blade across his back.

"Point to Princess Evelayn!" Kel called out. But not a killing blow.

She moved to disentangle her arm, but instead, in that one moment of hesitation when she'd allowed herself a pause of triumph, Tanvir dropped one of his blades to grab her wrist, squeezing so hard it compressed a nerve that forced her hand to convulse and drop her own knife. Simultaneously, he wrenched her forward so he could spin her in front of him, his arm now firmly wrapped around both of hers, and then, so fast she didn't even have a chance to struggle, his blade angled against her throat, ready to slit it.

A killing strike. Evelayn exhaled angrily even as her stomach sank.

"Lord Tanvir takes the match," Kel announced unnecessarily.

But Tanvir didn't move yet, his arm still holding her close and his blade still touching her skin, both of them breathing heavily. Her irritation at losing faded as she became aware of the heat of him pressing through her leathers, of a heady musk that suddenly colored his scent, sparking a responding warmth deep within her. A different kind than she'd ever felt before, it called for *more*, beckoned her to move even closer to the hard length of his body.

And then suddenly, he let go, stepping back. Evelayn stumbled forward, shocked at her own thoughts. Shocked that he'd beat her so quickly. Shocked that for a moment, she'd forgotten about her mother leaving, the war, not being able to shift, or anything beyond Lord Tanvir's arm around her and his muscled chest and abdomen against her back.

"Can you tell me what went wrong?" Kel asked her.

Evelayn glanced at Lord Tanvir to see him watching her, his amber eyes hooded, clutching his daggers at his sides. "I lost focus for a split second when you announced I had taken a point and he capitalized on it."

General Kelwyn nodded. "Any distraction—no matter how brief—can prove fatal on the battlefield, Your Highness. Whether you are fighting with your magic or with your hands." He gestured for Dela to come forward so he could demonstrate how Evelayn should have avoided Tanvir's attack.

The rest of the training continued on as normal, but Evelayn made sure to stay as far away from Lord Tanvir as possible. Of course her body had reacted to his nearness; he was one of the most attractive Draíolon she'd ever met. And yes, he hadn't held back, hadn't treated her like she was too fragile to give her a fair fight. And true, she'd forgotten about her grief and pain for a brief moment . . .

But none of that meant anything.

Did it?

EIGHT

As they were walking back to the castle to clean up for luncheon, Lord Tanvir fell into step beside her.

"Might I have a private word with you, Your Highness?"

Evelayn barely squashed the dismay that rose at his request. There was only one reason a male ever requested to speak to her in private. "I do not think I am properly attired for that kind of conversation."

"I don't see anything wrong with what you're wearing . . ."

Evelayn stopped and faced him, allowing Kel and Dela to outpace them so they wouldn't be overheard. "I'd prefer not to be—"

"I wish to apologize." Lord Tanvir cut her off, saving her from the humiliation she would have brought upon herself if she'd completed that sentence: *proposed to while I'm covered in sweat.*

"Apologize?" she echoed instead.

"Yes. I never meant to imply that I see you only as only an extension of your crown when I said your authority supersedes your aunt's. I merely meant to assure you that you were perfectly capable of choosing to do as you wished last night. I wanted to see you smile again. But I realize now that you might have interpreted my comment as a marker of interest in your power—your position—and not *you*. And for that, I am very sorry."

Evelayn employed every bit of training she had honed to keep herself from staring. That he had so completely read her mind, that he somehow understood *exactly* what she'd been thinking—it was not only surprising, it was . . . a relief. That's what made the tightly coiled muscles between her shoulder blades release slightly. Relief that maybe her first assessment of Lord Tanvir had been correct after all—that he wasn't like all the other males who had sought her out.

"And," he continued, "I am also sorry that your mother was called away again so soon. Duty is an unforgiving taskmaster and often comes with a steep price, especially for those left behind." He spoke as if he truly *understood*, as someone who had paid that price; not like so many who just used the words as a way to start a conversation. *So sorry your mother had to leave you again and may never return. But did you see Lady Oria's dress last night? It caused such a scandal.* A shadow crossed his face, a darkness made of sadness and pain and fear that called to her own.

Careful, Evelayn warned herself. *Just because he knows what to say and how to say it, doesn't guarantee he means it. He could just be a fantastic actor.* The silence stretched out as she warred with herself, wavering between answering with her usual diplomatic niceties or actually giving him a true answer—speaking to him as she would a friend. Which meant speaking to him like he was Ceren, for she was Evelayn's only true friend.

Before she could decide, his eyes shuttered and his face settled into a mask of neutrality. "Thank you for letting me speak my mind, Your Highness. I won't take up any more of your time." Lord Tanvir bowed stiffly to her and turned to walk away, when she finally found her voice.

"My lord . . ." The words were slightly hoarse. "Please don't go."

He paused and then faced her once more, his expression still guarded.

"Thank you." She took a hesitant step toward him, all too aware of each breath he took and the way he watched her, like he could see so much more than just her face. Remembering all too vividly the feel of his arm around her, his body pressed against her back when he had beat her during training. "And I am also sorry for my behavior last night—for jumping to conclusions."

"Does this mean I'm forgiven?" He lifted his brows, a spark of hope softening his amber eyes, and Evelayn found herself smiling again. He had quite a talent for getting her to smile.

"I believe it does, my lord."

He smiled back at her, and it was like the sun bursting on the horizon, bringing light to a new day.

Careful, tread slowly, that voice in her mind warned her still. But as they headed back to the castle, Evelayn didn't just walk beside Lord Tanvir, she tumbled forward into something new and exciting, foreign and terrifying. If only her mother were there to talk with—to ask her if this was what it had felt like when she'd met her father. A pang of regret darkened Evelayn's mood instantaneously.

Lord Tanvir glanced down at her and his smile slipped. She hadn't taken care to guard her expression. But then he smiled once more, this time a smug little grin.

"I've heard rumors of how fast you can run," he said. Which was not at all what she had expected him to say.

"That is the rumor," she agreed cautiously. All Draíolon were fast, but she *was* considered the fastest at the castle. At least, she had yet to be bested in a footrace.

"I quite enjoy running myself."

"Is that why were you out so early yesterday?"

"Indeed," Tanvir agreed. "So . . . would you care to race me?"

"Now?"

He nodded.

"Like this?" She gestured to her training leathers.

"What better outfit to wear than one that is already sweaty and dirty? Would you prefer a dress and dancing slippers?"

Evelayn glared. "Did you just call your crown princess *dirty*?"

"I believe I did." Tanvir grinned, unrepentant. "First one to the southeast door wins."

A surge of adrenaline washed through Evelayn's limbs, making her itch to take off, even though only a few minutes ago she'd been thinking about how tired she was after the training session. "And what does the winner get?"

"I didn't take you for the betting type." Lord Tanvir's eyes lit up with a wicked gleam.

"It makes my impending victory that much sweeter," Evelayn baited him. She couldn't believe her own daring. She'd never spoken to a male Draíolon this way before. It sent a thrill through her when he took a step closer and bent toward her.

Lord Tanvir lowered his voice. "Then I better make sure it's worth it."

Evelayn held his gaze. "If I win, you have to run with me for a week."

His eyebrows lifted again. "That doesn't sound like a punishment to me."

"If you come, the sentries won't have to trail me, slowing me down or getting left behind and lost."

"Ah," Tanvir said knowingly. "Well, if I win, I get to take you on a private picnic to a place of my choosing."

It was Evelayn's turn to raise her eyebrows. "That doesn't sound like a punishment to me, either."

He flashed that same grin, full of sunshine and heat, at her. "Then we have no reason to bemoan losing. Are we agreed?"

"Yes."

She'd barely spoken the word when he shouted, "Then go!" and took off at a dead run.

Cheater, she wanted to yell, but instead she saved her breath and shot after him.

At first her legs protested being pushed further, but a familiar calm quickly descended over her. When Evelayn ran, everything seemed clearer. The world sharpened around her; her breathing settled into a rhythm along with her heartbeat. And now with her new abilities, she was even faster than she had been before—her body seemed to have new amounts of strength and endurance. The trees blurred as she raced toward Tanvir, quickly gaining on him, despite his head start. They shot past General Kelwyn and Dela, who cried out in surprise, jumping out of their way.

He was fast—faster than many of the sentries assigned to guard her who lagged behind on her runs—but she was faster. She was sure of it. The castle loomed ahead, but she'd already come up on him so that they ran side by side for a moment, breath for breath, stride for stride, flying through the forest. They sprinted so quickly she could barely see individual trees or bushes or flowers; instead they blurred together into a glimmering tapestry of color and scents that filled her lungs and sent her blood singing through her veins.

Tanvir glanced over at her just as they exited the forest and streaked toward the castle. She winked at him. His eyes widened in surprise, and she couldn't help but laugh as she kicked her heels up even higher and pulled away from him, leaving him several body lengths behind her as she slammed to a halt, slapping her hand against the door.

Evelayn spun to face Tanvir just as he reached the door, a triumphant grin on her face.

"Looks like you get to go running with me tomorrow," she crowed.

"Looks like I need the extra conditioning," he replied, one hand on his side, breathing heavily, but a smile still on his face.

"Your Highness!"

Evelayn barely refrained from jumping when Tyne somehow materialized at her side, a stern look pulling her eyebrows down. "I've been looking for you, Your Highness. We must hurry if you are to be ready in time for the council meeting. With your mother away again, you must sit in her place. And then we must finish preparing the baskets to take to the families of the wounded. You cannot be late, if you are to return in time for supper."

The exultation of winning slid away, as did Evelayn's smile. No more running and laughing and teasing. It was time for her to become the proper, refined young princess of Éadrolan again.

Lord Tanvir nodded at Tyne, and then turned to Evelayn, a knowing look in his glowing eyes. "I will be eagerly awaiting the morning, Your Highness."

And that's when she realized what he'd done—how effectively he'd distracted her from her unhappiness. She didn't understand how he could have known a race would lift her spirits, but he had. And she was indebted to him for the brief distraction. Evelayn lifted her hand to him, something she rarely offered anyone.

He gently took it, the callused skin of his fingers brushing against the soft pad of the underside of her hand, sending a delicious shiver through her.

"I will send word of when and where to meet me, my lord." Evelayn managed to keep her voice even, despite the thump of her heart, which seemed to originate from where Tanvir touched her rather than her chest.

He bowed and released her. "Until tomorrow then."

"Until tomorrow."

Lord Tanvir turned and strode away, and only then did Evelayn realize a great many eyes were on them, watching their exchange. She quickly schooled her features into a mask of blankness, void of emotion of any kind, and gestured for Tyne to lead her back into the castle.

But as she followed her lady-in-waiting to her room, Evelayn's fingers curled in on the spot on her hand that still pulsed with the memory of Tanvir's touch.

NINE

THE TRAINING ROOMS WERE FULL OF DARK DRAÍOLON, the air thick with their sweat and shouts, as Lorcan strode toward the one isolated room where only the most elite were allowed to train in privacy. That's where his father and Lothar were waiting for him.

He opened the heavy door, and once it shut behind him, it closed off all noise, leaving behind a silence as heavy as the stare his father leveled at him, his silver eyes ominously dark.

"You're late."

Lorcan held up the missive in his left hand. "There was a messenger from the warfront."

The anger on King Bain's face tempered to speculation. He strode forward and snatched the sealed parchment from his son, then turned his back to open it. Lothar waited on the other side of the massive room, already stripped down to just his pants to spar with Lorcan. Their father preferred for them to train without protective clothing—to truly feel any mistakes they made. King Bain had the block on both princes' power removed when they were only fourteen and twelve so they could train longer than other Draíolon. Their bodies bore the reminders of the many errors they'd both made throughout their lives, the scars a map of their growing skill and their father's fury.

Lorcan stripped off his own vest and shirt, trying to quell his curiosity while the king read the letter with the unfamiliar seal. He didn't want his father to scent it and use it to manipulate him. He didn't risk asking either, knowing it would only goad his father into keeping the information from him, unless the king deemed it *necessary* that he know what the message held.

"What are you waiting for?" Bain suddenly snapped. "Get started."

Lorcan swallowed his angry retort and refocused his irritation into the power that flowed through his body. Lothar nodded at him from across the room, and Lorcan stalked forward. Their father wanted a show, so a show he would get.

Lothar attacked first—a blast of black, flaming shadow that Lorcan deflected with the shield he conjured, also made of shadow. Darkness versus darkness. It wasn't the same as fighting a Light Draíolon, but it was better than nothing. Lorcan went on the attack next, shooting two quick blasts at his brother—the first a snaking tendril of darkness to wrap around his ankles, the second a thicker band that would entrap his arms while Lothar was distracted trying to escape the snare on his feet. Lothar barely managed to twist out of the way, blocking the second but tripping and falling to the ground from the bindings around his ankles.

Lorcan hesitated for a split second before attacking again, allowing Lothar to break the bonds on his feet and jump back up, prepared to defend himself once again.

Lorcan's bare back exploded with pain. He arched away from it instinctively, almost falling to his knees. He barely managed to stay upright and swallow the bellow of agony that threatened to escape. It was one of his father's favorite tricks: turning the shadows into a whip that sliced through leather, skin, and even bone if wielded strongly enough.

"You're going easy on him."

Teeth clenched so tightly they ground together, Lorcan whirled to face his father, even as he felt his own blood slipping down his spine, soaking into the waistband of his pants. The king's silver eyes were cold, his mouth tight with disappointment.

"Do not ever give your enemy the chance to break free, to stand up. You attack and attack and *attack*." The letter crumpled as the king clenched his hand into a fist.

He's not my enemy. Lorcan bit back the words and merely nodded, knowing it would only mean more punishments if he said or did anything but agree, comply, *obey*.

"Again. And this time, don't hold back or else *I* will show you what it means to spar."

Lorcan turned back to face his brother, hoping Lothar could read the regret in his eyes. And then he attacked.

An hour later the king finally grew bored of watching his sons slashing at each other and lifted his hand.

"That's enough for today. Go get cleaned up and join me in the council room in one hour. The time has come. We depart in the morning."

"Where will we be going?" Lothar risked asking, picking up his shirt and using it to mop the blood off his chest from the wound Lorcan had inflicted on him just minutes earlier.

The king's silver eyes glittered with malice as he lifted the creased vellum. "To kill a queen."

Though Lorcan burned with the need to know what the message was—who it was from—he didn't let his gaze drop to the letter. "It was good news then, I take it?"

"Very." The king glanced between his sons, and after his gaze raked over the many wounds Lothar was nursing, he finally smiled, a cold, cruel twist of his lips. "Lorcan, you will meet me in my rooms in thirty minutes. I have a few things to discuss with you in private before we meet with everyone else."

Lorcan stiffened but then quickly bent forward into a shallow bow, the wound on his back, which had already begun to close, pulling at the movement. "As you wish, Father."

The king nodded, not even looking at Lothar again before turning and leaving the room.

Once the door was shut and the brothers were alone, Lorcan hurried over to Lothar's side.

"Here, let me help."

But Lothar twisted away from him. "I'm fine."

Lorcan watched in silence as Lothar continued wiping the blood from his body, revealing all the injuries he'd received at Lorcan's hands.

Many were already closed or closing, aided by the ability all royals had to heal faster than other Draíolon, who healed quite quickly themselves. But there were two particularly bad ones that looked like he might need to bandage. "You know how much I hate doing this to you," Lorcan's voice was a low growl, some of the fury he'd had to bite down in his father's presence seeping into his words.

"Father would have done worse." Lothar wouldn't look up as he finished tying a strip of leather around his abdomen, holding together one of the deeper slices, where Lorcan had turned the darkness he wielded into a whip and lashed through his brother's skin and muscle, nearly splitting him open to his organs. He was just as good at it as their father, and it made him sick to think he'd done that. But there was also an underlying pride in knowing he was faster, stronger, more skilled than his brother—and *that* only made his guilt worse.

"You'd better hurry if you want to be presentable in less than thirty minutes." Lothar turned away from Lorcan to pick up the rest of his belongings off the ground.

I'm sorry. The words were there, nearly spoken, the scent of his remorse bitter even in his own nose, but instead Lorcan turned and walked out silently, leaving Lothar alone in the training room, the floor stained with their blood.

"Lorcan."

He whirled around to see his mother standing a few feet away in the shadows, as if she had been waiting for some time. Her white hair was arranged in an intricate, useless style around the crown that gleamed, even all the way down here, in the lower levels of the palace where the only light came from the fires and candles lit all around the training rooms. Her crimson dress enhanced the obsidian darkness of her skin. He'd inherited so much of his looks from her; only his silver eyes were a testament to the king's paternity.

"Mother?"

Her eyes darted to his torso, to the few fresh wounds Lothar had managed to land and the many scars he bore from all the times before, and then back up again. "A meeting has been called," she said quietly.

"Yes. Father said it is time. He received a message." Lorcan spoke carefully, aware of the possibility that listening ears could be hovering nearby.

Abarrane, the Queen of Dorjhalon, nodded. "Stay strong, my son." Her gaze flickered to the scar that bisected his left bicep, a particularly terrible wound his father had inflicted on him with a shadow-sword when he was still a youngling. "Soon *you* will be the one to leave *your* mark."

When she met his probing gaze again, her eyes were so full of loathing and fury it made his own mirrored emotions that he worked so hard to suppress rise up, pulsing hot in his veins.

And then the door groaned open behind them. She quickly composed her expression into a calm, impenetrable mien before Lothar emerged.

"As my mother wills it," Lorcan murmured with a bow, and hurried away before his brother could stop him.

TEN

I DIDN'T REALIZE YOU WERE CAPABLE OF RISING BEFORE THE sun," Evelayn teased when the door creaked open behind her, already able to recognize the different footfalls and unique scents of many of her attendants and members of the court.

"It proves my dedication to you," Ceren responded, flouncing over to the princess's bed and throwing herself dramatically across it. "We never got a chance to talk yesterday, and I know you have training and meetings all day today . . . so I made the ultimate sacrifice."

Evelayn laughed as she finished braiding her hair and bent to pull on the soft leather boots she preferred to run in. "It wasn't *that* important . . . but your *sacrifice* is duly noted."

Ceren sat back up, her flame-red hair sticking out on one side, wearing only her nightgown with a navy blue dressing gown hastily tied over it. If her mother knew she'd snuck through the castle at dawn looking such a mess, she would have probably dragged her daughter all the way back to her room to beat her soundly. "Not important?" She gave Evelayn a knowing look. "Well, then I guess I'll just go back to—"

"He's coming again this morning." The words burst out before Ceren could finish her sentence.

Her friend smiled fiendishly. "Of course he is. Oh, he is *truly* smitten if he's willing to keep chasing you through the forest every morning."

Hope sprang up, but Evelayn shook her head. "He claims it is good conditioning. To keep him in shape for when he must return to the warfront, after he puts the Delsachts' holdings and affairs all in order."

"He's only saying that because he's afraid if he moves too quickly, he'll scare you off," Ceren disagreed. "Everyone knows how hard it is for you to open up. Well, to anyone besides me." She grinned again, smug in her position as the princess's only true friend.

"Everyone?" Evelayn echoed, the hope turning cold in her breast.

"Trust me." Ceren stood up and walked forward to take Evelayn's shoulders in her hands. "I've seen the way he looks at you—the way he constantly finds ways to be near you. Now go, before he wonders where you are." She pulled Evelayn in for a quick hug and then pushed her toward the door.

"Aren't you coming?"

"No." Ceren turned and crawled under the sheets. "Your bed is far more comfortable than mine. I'm going to go back to sleep until you return and tell me how right I am."

"But your mother . . . "

Ceren just closed her eyes, ignoring Evelayn, who shook her head with a little laugh and shut the door quietly, leaving Ceren to rest while she hurried through the quiet castle to meet Lord Tanvir.

֍

"Are you certain? You said they never found her body . . . maybe she survived?"

Tanvir grimaced, his gaze on the ground, making Evelayn wish she hadn't asked. They sat side by side on a mossy boulder, the breeze that wafted through the trees already turning warm with the heat of the rising sun. His hairline was still damp, even though they'd been resting for a few minutes, catching their breath before they made the long run back to the castle. They'd gone farther than ever this morning. Another few minutes and they would have reached Diasla, a small city between the castle and the Sliabán Mountains.

She hadn't expected him to continue running with her after his week was up, but on the morning of the eighth day, he'd shown up again. And then the next. And now it had been almost two weeks, and he still met her every morning, just as dawn broke, to dash through the trees and paths of Éadrolan, letting the cool morning air fill their lungs and their feet fly over the earth. She hardly dared let herself think of Ceren's claim—that it was because he truly cared about her. *Her*, not just her crown.

"Yes, it's certain. It was . . . a bloodbath. She was on the right flank and that entire division was hewn down so viciously, it was impossible to identify many of the bodies." Tanvir gripped his knees so hard, his knuckles were white. "She never showed up after we retreated. And the Dark Draíolon don't take prisoners."

The bright sunshine breaking through the treetops above them seemed at odds with the horrors of Tanvir's memories. She didn't say anything, because *I'm sorry* wasn't enough. Instead, with Ceren's words ringing in her mind, Evelayn hesitantly reached out, her pulse a flutter against the thin skin of her throat, letting her hand hover for just a moment before placing it over his. Aunt Rylese would be shocked at her daring, but Aunt Rylese wasn't here, and she didn't know what else to do. She'd never known the love of a sibling, but she understood the devastation that etched deep lines in Tanvir's face as he spoke of the day his sister died—only a few months before his father also passed away and he was suddenly called back from the warfront to become High Lord of the Delsachts.

He turned his hand over and laced their fingers together.

She wanted to reassure him that her mother would triumph, that soon the war would end, but she knew he'd see through the lie, as he saw through nearly everything she said or did. Even if Ilaria somehow managed to defeat Bain, what would happen next? He couldn't be trusted to continue to lead the Dorjhalon kingdom; he would have to be executed so that the power could transfer to one of his sons. But would either of them rule in peace—or had they been poisoned by their father's greed and shortsightedness?

"How old were you when your father died?"

Evelayn kept her eyes on their intertwined fingers. "I was eight."

"Your mother had only been queen for a few years, hadn't she?"

She nodded. "My grandmother Odessa ruled for over three hundred years and finally passed away when I was five. I don't remember her very well, but they say I am a lot like her—strong-willed and outspoken. She was a force to be reckoned with, at least according to my instructors."

"I've heard the stories. But I'm not sure that you are like her, at least not *that* much."

"Well, I'm certainly not as soft-spoken as my mother."

Tanvir shrugged. "You've got me there."

Evelayn raised her eyebrows.

"I'm just agreeing with you." He lifted his free hand up in supplication. "So," he continued quickly, "your mother had only been queen for a few years when Bain attacked for the first time."

"Yes. No one truly believed that Bain was behind the attack though. It seemed beyond comprehension that a king would risk destroying the balance of our two kingdoms."

"I remember my father talking about the same thing with his men. I was only fourteen so he wouldn't allow me in the meetings, but I would sit outside the door and eavesdrop. He said it was history repeating itself, because no one believed in the legend of Drystan anymore."

Drystan.

The name was a two-sided jolt. Her father's name and the name from the rhyme younglings were told at bedtime to frighten them into behaving.

The original Drystan had supposedly been the first to shed blood on the soil of Lachalonia—cursing the Draíolon to lose their immortality—and had then been banished with his followers. Supposedly, he'd only been sixteen, and that was why the Draíolon, both Light and Dark, had sworn an oath to bind their youngling's power until they were eighteen ever since, to keep them from making such huge mistakes while they were still too immature to handle their abilities. Her father hadn't believed it—claiming that it was just a story to keep them in line. And possibly because he shared the same name.

But her mother believed. Evelayn had always wondered which one was right. Peace had existed for so long, it seemed unimaginable that anyone would ever kill another Draíolon. Until the day of the initial attack.

"I remember feeling frightened for the first time in my life after word reached the castle, and I remember my parents telling me there was nothing to worry about. They tucked me into bed and promised they'd be back in a few days." Evelayn paused, the memory of pain rising up, still sharp when summoned. "My mother came back alive. My father didn't."

Tanvir's hand tightened on hers.

They sat in silence for a long moment, until the caw of a raven in a nearby tree shattered the quiet.

"We should head back," Tanvir suddenly said, letting go of her hand and standing up. "We'll be late for breakfast and training, and then you'll be forced to run with the sentries again."

Evelayn glanced up and saw that the sun had risen much higher than she'd realized, protected as they were in the shade of the trees. Tanvir had already begun to run away, and she hurried to catch up. She was still faster than he was if she pushed herself, but not by much anymore. The forest blurred around them as they sped back to the castle.

They were almost halfway there when Tanvir suddenly stopped, throwing out his arm so that Evelayn crashed into it and skidded to a halt as well. And then she noticed it, too—the brisk scent of snow, of winter, even though the early-summer morning had already grown hot.

A Dark Draíolon was nearby.

Evelayn's body went cold. How was that even possible? Half the priestesses were at the warfront on the border of the two kingdoms, maintaining the wards that kept the Dark Draíolon from being able to enter Éadrolan.

"He's to our left, upwind. He might not know we're here yet, since he's positioned badly," Tanvir murmured so quietly she could hear him only because they were standing so close together. "If we veer right and then cut back, we could avoid him and warn General Kelwyn."

"If he doesn't know we're here, we should circle around and see if we can follow him. Find out how he made it in to Éadrolan," Evelayn argued in a whisper.

"My first duty is to keep you safe. We're going back to the castle." Tanvir's voice had gone cold, as firm as steel.

"I'm the crown princess, and I order you—"

Before she could finish, Tanvir suddenly tackled her. They crashed into the ground, his full weight on top of her. Pain exploded across the back of her head and her elbows where she landed hard against the rocks and dirt. A blast of shadowflame detonated against the tree right next to them, tearing a massive, smoking hole through the trunk.

"It's an ambush." Tanvir's lips brushed her ear as he continued to press her into the ground, using his body to shield her. His words sent a fission of terror down Evelayn's spine. "Get behind me, and when I say so, you run like hellfire back to the castle."

He rolled off her into a crouch and sent a blast of lightning in the direction of the second Draíolon they hadn't scented. He straightened to his full height when Evelayn jumped to her feet.

"I'm not leaving you here alone!"

She felt a surge of magic from behind and this time *she* shoved *Tanvir* forward, out of the way of yet another blast of shadowflame. It barely missed them, singeing a black mark across the arm of Tanvir's tunic.

"Back to back!" she shouted, whirling so that he was behind her. Tension limned Tanvir's body, but he did as she commanded, turning so that their spines pressed together. She summoned her sun-sword, sparking with lightning and writhing with white-flame, and readied herself, staring into the forest, searching for any sign of movement, scenting the air for the hint of snow and ice that didn't belong.

She felt Tanvir move, and a surge of magic, and then there was a cry of pain from somewhere off in the forest. He truly had excellent aim, just as Kel had said.

There.

Evelayn's eyes narrowed, but she didn't give any sign that she'd seen the Draíolon slip from one tree to the next a few hundred paces to her right. Her heart thumped in her chest as she gripped her sword, preparing herself. Sweat slipped down her spine, but a strange kind of calm descended over her—similar to when she was running. Her mind cleared and all her focus honed in on her enemy, stalking silently toward them.

When he spun out from the tree he'd been hiding behind and shot a blast of shadowflame at her, it seemed like time slowed to a crawl. She felt the power surging toward her, saw the jet of blackness slicing through the air with blinding speed, but she easily lifted her sword and deflected it with a deafening crash of light meeting shadow that reverberated all the way up both of her arms.

The Draíolon's eyes met hers for the space of a breath. Then he turned and ran.

Evelayn hesitated for only a moment.

And then she sprinted after him.

ELEVEN

TANVIR'S PULSE POUNDED IN HIS EARS, BUT THE FAMILIAR battle-stillness he'd honed on the warfront made his hands steady as he took careful aim and blasted the Dark Draíolon hiding directly ahead of him in the forest. He rarely missed, and this was no exception. The male was flung through the air to land in a bed of ferns and vibrant scarlet flowers. He didn't get up.

The forest was eerily quiet as Tanvir stretched out his senses, searching for any hint of the others before they could attack again and hurt him or the princess. If she died now—

He cut off the thought viciously. He wouldn't let that happen.

And then she suddenly stiffened. A split second later there was a deafening boom that vibrated through her into him—a massive collision of power. Tanvir forced himself to keep his back to the princess, knowing he'd leave them both vulnerable if he turned.

But then she was gone.

Heedless of the danger, he whirled about, to see the princess sprinting into the forest, brandishing a sun-sword made of flame and lightning, rushing after a retreating male.

"Evelayn!" he shouted in horror. She didn't even pause. Tanvir took off after them, summoning his own sun-sword. Somewhere nearby there was at least one other Draíolon who could now attack from behind. But he couldn't just let her go tearing after the enemy alone. The princess was still untried, untrained.

Though his blood thundered through his veins, Tanvir's body felt strangely cold as he bolted through the forest, dodging tree branches and bushes, trying to keep Evelayn and the male in his sights. She was quickly gaining on the Dark Draíolon. By the Light, she was just so *fast*. Though he tried not to show it, it took every ounce of his strength and willpower to keep up with her each morning.

With a cry that sent a shiver down his spine, and without breaking stride, Evelayn suddenly swiped her sun-sword at the male, sending a lash of lightning at his legs. He screamed in pain and tumbled to the forest floor, the princess crashing to a halt so that her sword was pointed at his chest.

Tanvir scented the third Dark Draíolon an instant before the jet of shadowflame exploded from behind a tree to his left. He twisted to face his attacker as he threw himself to the ground, bringing his sword up out of pure instinct. Pain seared across his shoulder and left arm, and the scent of burned flesh filled his nose as the female Draíolon leapt at him, swinging a sword made of writhing darkness and black flame. Tanvir barely brought his own sword up in time to deflect the hit. The two weapons clashed with a thunderous boom that shook the forest floor. Tanvir used his free hand to blast a jet of light at the

Dark Draíolon, and in the moment it took her to dodge the attack, he'd launched himself back to his feet, simultaneously slashing his sword through the air.

She tried to dodge him again, but he was too fast—the sword sliced through flesh and bone, nearly cutting her arm off. With a howl of agony, her shadow-sword disappeared and she fell to her knees. Tanvir shot another blast, but this time she didn't try to avoid it, welcoming the release from the suffering. The bolt of light struck her in the chest, tearing through her body, and she crumpled into a heap.

Tanvir whirled to see Evelayn still holding the sword to the male's throat. Her emotions were thick on the air—triumph mixed with a lingering tang of fear. But the male wasn't someone who had been defeated. Tanvir could scent the foul musk of his smugness—as well as the lust rushing through his blood—and he bared his teeth with a low growl.

"—through the wards?"

He caught the end of her question as he raced toward them. The male noticed him one beat too late. The Dark Draíolon lifted his hand—to do what, Tanvir didn't know and didn't care. Again he leapt the final few feet, driving his sword down through the male's chest.

"Tanvir!"

Evelayn's shocked exclamation shook some of the red haze from his eyes. He turned to her, his heart slamming against his ribs. "Are you hurt?"

"I wanted him *alive*," was her tight response.

Tanvir stiffened. "Could you not scent his intentions? He was just biding his time. I *saved* you."

She stared down at the Dark Draíolon, his ice-blue eyes open and staring, his pale-blue hair and frost-white skin speckled with his own blood from the death wound Tanvir had inflicted.

"The others?" she asked without looking up.

Tanvir remained quiet.

Evelayn sighed heavily and her sun-sword winked out. "I guess we'll never find out how they got here or what they were doing." She finally lifted her head, but he couldn't read the expression on her face or in her violet eyes. She was upwind from him, so he couldn't scent her emotions, either. But when she wiped her hands on her leather pants, he noticed they were trembling.

"Evelayn, I'm—"

Ignoring the pain in his already-healing shoulder, he reached out, but she jerked away before he could touch her. "We'd better hurry back and report this. I'm sure General Kelwyn will want to investigate the bodies at least."

Without another word or glance in his direction, the princess turned and sprinted away from the body—and, he was afraid, from him.

TWELVE

EVELAYN PUSHED HERSELF AS HARD AS SHE COULD, thinking that perhaps if she ran fast enough she could somehow outrun the memory of Tanvir killing that Draíolon. That maybe the pounding of her feet could force away the trembling in her hands and the nausea that twisted her gut. She knew he'd only been protecting her—she'd also scented the male's disgusting intentions. And all three Draíolon had tried to kill them. But she'd never seen anyone cut down in front of her before. She'd never seen someone alive one moment and dead the next, his eyes open, unseeing, his mouth twisted in a scream that never escaped.

She'd hobbled him when she'd used her power to cut through his legs—that alone had been enough to make her sick. She'd planned on having him questioned at the castle. She *was* mad that now there was no possible way to know why they'd come, how they'd found her and Tanvir, and how they'd managed to get past the wards and travel so far into Éadrolan without being detected.

Evelayn heard Tanvir behind her, keeping a few paces back instead of drawing alongside her. When they returned to the castle . . . when she could bathe, and change out of these sweaty, blood-splattered clothes, and try to calm down . . . then she would find Tanvir and apologize. She could compose herself enough to thank him for protecting her. But for now, she just wanted to run and run until she ran out of forest, all the way to her room, where she could be alone.

As the sun arced ever higher in the sky, the trees began to thin and then, rising above the thick emerald leaves and creeping vines, there were the glittering white and gold turrets of her castle. The Light Sentries guarding the wall hadn't noticed her sprinting through the forest toward them yet when someone grabbed her arm, yanking her to a stop.

"How *dare* you—" she whirled to face Tanvir.

"Please." He cut her off, his gaze darting past her to the sentries beyond and then back again. "Let me apologize. The last thing I wanted was to make you angry."

Evelayn opened her mouth to command him to let her go, but something in his burning amber eyes stopped her.

He was breathing hard, his hair damp with sweat again. "They were attacking us—attacking *you*. I've been on too many battlefields, seen too many friends and family die. The way he was looking at you—the way he *smelled*—"

"Tanvir." His name was little more than a whisper, but he immediately fell silent. As quickly as it came, her anger dissolved at his words, at the unmasked anguish on his face. She'd lost it over a stranger dying in front of her—a stranger who had tried to kill her first—and he had held it together, even though he was no doubt haunted by the memories of his mother *and* father dying, his battalion . . . his *sister*, who had been murdered so brutally her body hadn't even been identifiable to bury and mourn.

A breeze rustled the leaves beside them, lifting a few tendrils of her sweaty hair from her neck. The sun was hot on her back where it broke through the branches above them as they stood there, Tanvir's fingers still wrapped around her arm, so close she could feel the heat from his body. His scent filled her nose—the mixture of spice and citrus that was uniquely his, but also the underlying scents that she was still struggling to understand. Possibly desperation . . . sorrow . . . and something else . . . the same rich, heady musk she'd noticed once before that made her belly tighten.

His eyes darkened slightly when she took a hesitant half step toward him, lifting her hand to touch his cheek—

A shockwave of power—not of her making—hit Evelayn, almost knocking her to the ground, yanking her out of Tanvir's grip. The usually cold conduit stone embedded in her breastbone flared white-hot for one terrifying moment. Evelayn stumbled back a step, involuntarily reaching up to touch the stone in her chest. It had gone cold again, along with the rest of her body.

"What *was* that?"

A horrific, pulsing terror seized Evelayn. Empty. *She was empty.*

"Blast that tree," she commanded urgently, pointing.

Tanvir gave her a strange look, confusion pulling his brows down. "Just *do it.*"

He lifted his hand and . . . nothing happened.

All the breath left Evelayn's lungs, as if someone had punched her with a fist made of ice.

"No," she whispered, shaking her head and taking another step back. *"No."*

"Evelayn?" His voice wavered.

Her eyes burned with the fire of sudden tears. *"NO!"* Evelayn shouted this time, flinging her hands out. Tanvir flinched, but nothing happened. There was no power to draw upon. Finally, the concern on his face deepened into shock and sorrow, as comprehension dawned. And still she fought against it—the horrible truth of what that surge of heat in her conduit stone and subsequent loss of power meant.

Evelayn dropped to her knees, tears spilling out onto her cheeks. And then she crumpled forward, curling into a ball on the grass, the hot sunshine pouring over her as she shuddered with sobs. "Mother," she moaned against the fist she had pressed to her mouth.

Because there was only one thing that could have happened to take away the Light Draíolons' power.

Their queen was dead.

THIRTEEN

ALL AROUND HER, THE OTHER LIGHT DRAÍOLON WERE in a state of panic. The air was thick with fright, grief, and shock. Some were shouting, others sobbing. But it all faded to a dull roar as Ceren shoved through the huddled groups of nobility and servants, trying to escape the morning room where she had gone to wait for Evelayn to return.

She'd been pacing the floor near the dormant fireplace when it happened.

And now she was desperate to find Evelayn. Tears burned near the surface, but Ceren forced herself to swallow them. She didn't have time to break down right now. She had to find Evelayn. Their power was gone, which could mean only one thing—King Bain had killed Queen Ilaria. Only a royal had the power to kill another royal.

It meant her friend was now an orphan.

She'd almost made it to the door when someone grabbed her arm.

"Where do you think you're going?" Her mother's voice was strained and her familiar scent was tinged with the tang of fear.

"I have to find her," Ceren responded, yanking her arm free.

"Don't you dare—"

But Ceren had already grabbed the door and flung it open, bursting out into the hallway, where the chaos continued. She ignored her mother's pleas as she plunged into the surge of Draíolon rushing through the castle. To do what, she couldn't imagine. As she dashed toward the stairs that would take her up to Evelayn's room, the original shock of their loss of power seemed to be giving way to sheer anguish. The air was thick with the acrid tang of it.

It was a relief to fling open Evelayn's door and quickly shut it again, closing off the majority of sounds and smells. But the relief was short-lived when Ceren quickly searched the room and realized there was still no sign of Evelayn.

Loath to return to the chaos beyond the door, Ceren hurried over to the window to see if she could spot her friend outside.

Sunlight poured over the grounds, turning the grass emerald and reflecting off the other buildings of the castle. Bright and beautiful and completely at odds with the terror coursing through her veins. Ceren's gaze darted across the grounds, where Draíolon were in just as much of an uproar as those in the castle. But then she noticed a small circle of males and females who were completely still, looking at something on the ground.

Ceren squinted, her eyesight sharpening, and that's when she realized there was a girl on the ground, curled into a ball, a male hovering over her. She immediately recognized Evelayn's flaxen hair with the pale lavender streaks and Tanvir's bark-brown hair and the protective tightness to his body as he bent over her.

I'm coming, Ev. I'm coming.

Ceren turned and ran.

Some part of her knew that she needed to get up, that she needed to stop crying and act like the princess she was. Her people needed her; they needed comforting and guidance.

But Evelayn couldn't do it.

Sobs tore through her body, through the emptiness that gaped like a terrible wound. She was vaguely aware of Tanvir speaking to her, his voice low and concerned, but his words didn't penetrate the grief that throbbed through her head with the pounding of her blood.

She didn't know how much time had passed, only that she never wanted to move from that spot. Moving meant she had to stand up and face a world where her mother no longer lived, where she would never again see her violet eyes light up when Evelayn walked into a room, or feel the warmth of her embrace. Where she would never again hear her voice.

"Ev."

She shook her head, but Ceren reached out and gently brushed her fingers against the princess's cheek. Evelayn's tears came even harder.

"Ev, come with me. I'll help you to your room."

"I can't," Evelayn whispered. "She's gone. She's *gone* . . ."

"I know," Ceren whispered back, her voice thick with choked emotion. "But we need to get you somewhere private. Come on, Ev. I know you can do it."

She shook her head against the lawn, ignoring the murmurs of those gathered around them, no doubt cataloging every second of the spectacle of their princess losing control.

"Tanvir, help me," she heard Ceren mutter, and a split second later he had scooped her up, pulling her into his arms, against his chest. Though he had to be exhausted after everything that had happened that morning on top of their extra-long run, he still found the strength to sprint toward the castle as quickly as possible. Evelayn didn't speak, didn't open her eyes. She just let herself bounce against Tanvir's body, allowed him to carry her away from the probing eyes and whispers, as a door was opened and the daylight beyond her eyelids was replaced by the dimness of her home.

She was vaguely aware of being jostled, of Tanvir pushing his way through other Draíolon while Ceren shouted for them to move. But Evelayn tried to close it all out, to stay deep inside herself, where there was no sound, no judgment, no war, and no death. As he made his way to the stairs and carefully ascended, Tanvir's arms tightened around her body.

"Here, come this way."

It was quieter on this floor. Evelayn felt Tanvir nod at Ceren's hushed directions, his chin brushing the top of her head. Moments later they entered a room—her room, she realized as she inhaled the familiar scent—and the door shut behind them, blocking out all noise except that of their breathing.

"Should I lay her on the bed?"

Ceren must have nodded this time, because Tanvir strode across the room and gently laid her down on her feather-stuffed mattress, her bed still unmade from when Ceren had slept in it.

"Ev, look at me." Ceren's voice was close, coaxing—concerned. "Please open your eyes."

Evelayn shook her head again.

"I'm so sorry," Ceren whispered, her words turning into a half-strangled sob. She took Evelayn's hand in hers, gripping it tightly. "I can't believe it, either."

Tears leaked out from beneath Evelayn's eyelashes, even though she'd squeezed them shut as tightly as possible.

"I should go . . ." Tanvir's voice came from near the door, quiet and full of remorse.

Evelayn took a deep breath, inhaling through her nose to fill her lungs, trying somehow to stop the grief from consuming her.

And then she opened her eyes.

The curtains were still drawn, casting her room, Ceren, and Tanvir into shadow. Just as her entire world had been thrown into shadow. The darkness that relentlessly continued to spread from King Bain across Lachalonia, tearing families apart, and now this. Leaving Éadrolan without a queen.

And that's when it hit her. An icy realization that sharpened her grief into fear, hardened it to bitterness.

Evelayn's gaze shot to Ceren's, her eyes going wide.

When she finally spoke, her words were a hoarse whisper. "I'm the queen now."

FOURTEEN

THOUGH SHE HAD SPOKEN IN A NEAR WHISPER, EVELAYN'S words sounded through the room like the blast of a war-horn. Tanvir watched as she squeezed Ceren's hand once, and then let go to wipe her cheeks.

Her tears were suddenly gone, locked away as the sorrow that had turned her face even more pale than usual hardened into something else—something almost frightening. Her lavender-tinted hair was falling out of her braid, with pieces of grass and crushed leaves stuck in it. She was still in her running clothes, and her violet eyes were red-rimmed. The nearly overpowering scent of her grief still filled the room, but as Evelayn stood up, visibly composing herself, Tanvir watched her transform from a naïve princess into a cool, collected queen of Éadrolan.

"How many saw me?"

When she turned her gaze to him, Tanvir hesitated to answer. He knew she meant how many of her subjects had witnessed her collapse.

"Tell me." Her tone made it clear it wasn't a request.

"Perhaps twenty? More if those in the castle recognized you." Tanvir tried not to grimace, but Evelayn merely nodded.

"That's unfortunate. It won't happen again."

Ceren, who was still crouching beside Evelayn's bed, slowly stood up, shooting a baffled—and concerned—glance at Tanvir, before turning to Evelayn. He couldn't quite understand how Evelayn had controlled herself so quickly, so easily, after how distraught she'd been. At least, visibly. He could still scent her sorrow, but now there was more. Many emotions fought for control in his new queen.

"No one will fault you for it, Ev. You had just learned your mother was . . ." Ceren cringed as she trailed off.

Evelayn's jaw tightened, the only sign she still didn't have total control, but then she responded, "And yet, I refuse to show such weakness ever again. My subjects will be looking to me for strength. To somehow save them."

Tanvir's stomach twisted at the thought of her bearing up the weight of what was now coming to rest on her shoulders. But what else could he have done? At least he'd saved *her* this morning. *That* unexpected twist to King Bain's attack hadn't succeeded.

"Lord Tanvir, will you please send word to General Kelwyn to meet me in the throne room immediately? And please also send word that I am assembling a meeting with all the High Lords, priestesses, and advisors from my mother's council present at the castle."

Before he could respond, she turned to her only close friend and continued, "Ceren, will you find Tyne and ask her to have every available servant make sure refreshments are available in all the major rooms? And then if you could go help comfort those who seem most upset by this morning's turn of events, and assure them that I am handling it—that I will make Bain pay for what he has done—I would greatly appreciate it."

Ceren blinked and then nodded. "Of course, Ev. Whatever you need me to do."

Evelayn turned to Tanvir expectantly, and he, too, nodded. "Of course," he echoed Ceren.

"Do you want me to help you change first?" Ceren asked.

"No," Evelayn replied immediately. "My people don't need to see me in a dress to be comforted right now, they need to know that I am taking care of them—of Éadrolan. And I will. I *will*." The fierceness of her declaration was tinged with desperation, but Tanvir couldn't help the swell of pride within him.

Yet, grief, especially when buried, had a way of rearing its head at the worst of times, sometimes leading to terrible mistakes and decisions, as he well knew. He could only hope that she was truly as in control of herself as she seemed. For her sake—and for all of Éadrolan.

Exhaustion bore down on Evelayn, but she refused to give in to it. She'd tried to lie down to take a quick nap earlier, after hours and hours of meetings—mostly full of alarm and speculation, as no official word had reached them yet from the battlefront—but the moment she'd rested her head and closed her eyes, the loss of her mother had knifed through her again, fresh and agonizing once more. She didn't dare let herself cry, couldn't allow herself to mourn. She had to be strong. Her subjects were counting on it. And if she let herself break down, even in private, she was afraid the tenuous control she'd managed to wrestle into place earlier would crumble, leaving her a mess once again.

So she'd stood back up, dressed once more, and gone to the battlements to pace, watching with her sentries. High Priestess Teca had stayed long after everyone else to go over what Evelayn had to do to transfer the Light Power to her conduit stone. They only had three days from the time her mother was killed to reclaim it, or the power would return to the Immortal Tree deep inside the Sliabán Mountains from whence Draíolon power had supposedly originated before time began.

Evelayn knew how the first Light and Dark Draíolon had been gifted their powers to bring day and night, summer and winter, to the world—to work together to create a perfect harmony. And she also knew what happened when a queen of Éadrolan or a king of Dorjhalon died. The power remained dormant in their conduit stone for three days and the new queen or king had to complete a special ceremony to transfer the power to their own stone. If they were too late, the power returned to the Immortal Tree, and the monarch would have to travel to the sacred interior of the Sliabán Mountains, where the tree thrived without water or light, sustained by the power that flowed through it. But High Priestess Teca had explained it in much more detail, going over exactly what Evelayn had to do once her mother was returned to the castle.

It was yet another weight added to Evelayn's shoulders. If her mother's body wasn't brought back soon enough . . . if she failed to complete the ceremony . . .

There was an uncommon bite to the breeze that ruffled the cloak she'd hastily thrown on before leaving the silence of her room, a chill that made her wonder if their world was already changing because of her mother's death. It was summer—the height of Éadrolan's power. It should have been a balmy, mild night. Instead, she shivered as another gust sent a few strands of hair across her face. It was second nature to lift her hand, ready to summon light to warm herself. The chill sank much deeper than her skin when nothing happened and she had to let her arm drop to her side, the realization that her power was gone hitting her all over again.

Evelayn wrapped her arms around her waist, squeezing tight, trying to hold back the dread that threatened to crash over her now that she was alone, powerless. All day she'd done her best to act like she was strong—in control. To pretend she was the queen her people needed, that she *had* to be for them. But the truth was, she was scared. No, she was *terrified*. Bain had killed her mother. What hope did *she* have of defeating him?

Despite her best intentions, Evelayn's eyes began to burn. She blinked rapidly to force back the tears. And when that didn't work, she turned her face to the wind, letting it dry the moisture from her eyes.

"Your Highness—I mean, Majesty—"

Evelayn jumped and whirled around to see Lord Tanvir hesitating on the last step leading up to the turret where she stood.

"What are you doing up?" She hadn't meant it to sound so accusatory, and she grimaced when he flinched. He wore only a white linen shirt, loose breeches, and knee-high boots. His hair was hastily tied back, as though he'd done it himself, rather than called an attendant. He looked how he did when he met her early in the morning to go running, after he'd just rolled out of bed.

"I couldn't sleep," he said simply. "And I thought perhaps you, too, would find this to be a difficult night to rest."

"So you hunted me down."

Tanvir grimaced this time. "I wouldn't call it *hunting* you. But I was walking the hallways and did hear some sentries talking as they switched shifts. They seemed concerned that you were up here alone. I told them I would come check on you."

"My personal Light Sentries are standing guard at the base of the stairs. I'm not in any danger from attack." Which wasn't true, because if any Dark Draíolon made it to the castle before she succeeded in regaining her kingdom's power, they would all be slaughtered.

"I'm not sure that's what they were concerned about tonight."

Evelayn's eyes widened as she thought of how far from the ground she was where she stood on one of the many turrets that soared above the castle. "They think I would . . . that I could *possibly*—"

"No!" Tanvir burst out, cutting her off. "By the Light, *no*. I only meant that they wanted to make sure you weren't overcome by your grief, all alone up here. Your people care for you. They're worried."

"Oh."

"Though that does bring up a good point. You *are* very exposed out here. If Lorcan assumed his bird form he could kill you before you even knew what had happened."

Evelayn turned away, back to the wall that separated her from a fall that would spell certain death. He was right. But she couldn't bear to face her room yet.

"If you insist on staying up here, may I join you?"

Evelayn shrugged.

He was silent as he drew up beside her, leaning forward to rest his forearms on the top of the bricks. She glanced at him from the corner of her eye to see him staring down at his hands. Tension limned the lines of his body, making the muscles of his back and shoulders bunch.

"Why couldn't you sleep?" she finally asked.

He took a moment to respond, and when he did speak, his voice was soft. "Because I know what it's like."

Tanvir turned to look at her, a world of pain and grief darkening his amber eyes to burnt gold. She swallowed hard and tore her gaze from his to stare out into the darkness. She felt more than saw him straighten. When he took her shoulders in his hands and gently turned her to face him, she didn't resist, even though she was afraid of losing her hard-fought control. She clenched her jaw as her eyes met his in the darkness, her sharpened eyesight allowing her to see him perfectly. He stood close enough that she could feel the heat from his body.

"Your Majesty—"

"Are we back to titles, then?"

"Evelayn," he amended, his fingers tightening slightly on her shoulders, "you can't hold it in like this forever. This morning I watched you lock away the pain and do what you felt was necessary to help your people. And I admire your strength of will," he continued when she tried to cut in. "But you must know, it's all right to cry. It's all right to mourn."

She shook her head, even as her eyes began to burn again. "I *can't*," she whispered.

They were silent for a long moment, staring at each other. And then Tanvir hesitantly lifted one hand, slowly moving it toward her face, watching her the whole time to see if she protested. When she didn't, he tenderly tucked a strand of hair behind her ear, his fingers brushing against her cheek. Evelayn shivered again, but this time, it wasn't from the cold.

She didn't miss the way his gaze flickered down to her lips and then quickly back up to her eyes. Something deep inside her belly tightened as a wash of heat cascaded through her. What was wrong with her? How could she possibly be feeling *this* right now, when her mother's death was so raw, the pressure of what she had to accomplish to save her kingdom bearing down so heavily on her?

But the rebellious part of her—the part she worked hard to ignore, to push away, to run out of existence—wondered what *would* it be like to kiss him? Would she be able to lose herself in his touch, to bury her grief in something else, something she could barely understand other than as a need to step closer, to erase the space between them?

He wanted her. She understood that now—she finally recognized that scent for what it was. Which meant he knew she did, too. But did she dare?

His fingers still rested against her throat, just below her ear, but he hadn't moved, had barely even breathed as her thoughts tumbled recklessly through *should I* or *shouldn't I*. She swallowed and then took a small step forward, so that mere inches separated them. He was only a bit taller than she, so their eyes—and mouths—were almost on the same level. He searched her face, a muscle in his jaw ticking. He pushed his hand farther back, plunging his fingers into her hair, curling them around the back of her head. Her heart was a drum, thudding against her ribs. Her senses fired in every way possible—she was surrounded by him. Tanvir's scent, his touch, his gaze, the heat from his body. And suddenly, her grief felt far, far away.

Yes, I do *want this*, she thought, willing him to understand. *It's working.* It's working.

And still he hesitated.

They were so close, it barely took any movement to lift her hands to his hips, to clutch his tunic, pulling him closer and then flattening them against his muscled stomach. He groaned, a deep, low growl in his throat.

"Evelayn." Her name was a throaty plea. "I don't want to do anything you'll regret in the morning."

"I won't," she whispered. Evelayn could almost feel his lips brushing hers as they spoke. His breath was warm on her face.

"You don't know what you're doing right now. You've had a terrible shock."

"I'm not in shock." Which wasn't necessarily true, but it didn't matter. "By the Light, Tanvir, I'm a *queen* now. Not some youngling who doesn't know her own mind."

He closed his eyes and lifted his face to the sky, taking a deep breath. "I want to, Ev. You *know* I do."

"Then *do* it. It would be unbearably humiliating if I had to command you to give me my first kiss."

He made a noise almost like a laugh except it was a barren, hopeless sound, his gaze dropping to hers once more. "Your *first* kiss? Oh, Ev. It can't be like this. It can't be tied to losing your mother. You will regret it. I promise you would. Maybe not tonight, or tomorrow, but eventually you would resent me for allowing it to happen now. And I can't stand having anything else for you to hold against me."

Evelayn dropped her head and backed up, the blissful heat and desire ebbing out of her, leaving her cold and broken once more. Except for the warmth in her cheeks, where her embarrassment burned. "I don't understand what you're talking about. I don't hold anything against you—I wouldn't have held this against you, either."

"That's a relief to hear, especially after this morning. But I promise, there would come a day when you would have looked back and been angry that I kissed you the night your mother died."

Evelayn turned away from him, wrapping her arms around herself once more. "Stop assuming that you know me so well."

"Ev. Look at me."

She felt him come up behind her, but he didn't touch her.

"The last thing I wanted was to make things worse. You have to know that I care about you. That I . . . I . . ." He broke off, and she stiffened. "I don't know what's right anymore. I don't know what to do."

Tanvir sounded so forlorn, so upset, that Evelayn relented and turned to face him.

"If you truly cared for me, you would have known I needed you to be here for me tonight."

Tanvir looked miserable but he didn't argue with her. Instead he dropped his gaze to the ground that separated them.

They were silent for a few moments, the tension building and building until it seemed a wall stood between them that she didn't know how to break down. Finally, she said, "You should go."

His eyes met hers once more, pleading. "Please don't do this."

Though she still longed for his touch, Evelayn made herself stand up straighter, forced the mask she wore during the day into place. "I just need to be alone."

He studied her for a long moment, until her heart began to race once again, but he finally nodded. "If that's your wish, Your Majesty."

The use of her new title stung, yet she refused to let him see that.

He headed for the stairs, then paused. Evelayn stiffened, unaccountably nervous. What more was there to say?

Tanvir turned to gaze at her, his face full of unmasked grief. "I do care for you, Evelayn. I fear that I care for you far more deeply than is good for either of us. I hope that you will soon be grateful for my control this night. If I lose you, too, it would be unbearable. Your friendship has meant the world to me . . . in a world where I had little reason to feel anything other than remorse or pain. Regardless of the outcome of this night, I want to thank you for that. And tell you how very sorry I am."

Evelayn blinked, unsure if she'd truly seen a sheen of moisture in his eyes. But then he turned and was gone, leaving her chilled and alone, with nothing but the wind to keep her company.

FIFTEEN

E VEN THOUGH THEY WERE WHISPERED, EVELAYN STILL
heard the murmurs as she slowly moved down the aisle toward
the marble table where her mother's body lay, shrouded by a
white sheet. Hundreds of Light Draíolon had packed into the Great
Hall for the funeral—and, apparently, to see the new queen.

"She only turned eighteen a few weeks ago, how can she possibly
succeed when both of her parents failed?"

"She's too young and her power isn't controlled yet. King Bain will
rule both Dorjhalon and Éadrolan in weeks, mark my words."

Evelayn pretended not to hear them, determinedly staring ahead,
avoiding the white sheet. All there was to see was the outline of her
mother's body, not her face or the hole in her chest where King Bain
had managed to get past all her defenses and blast away her power and
her life. But Evelayn had seen both last night when they'd finally
rushed Queen Ilaria to the palace. It had taken two days. Two horrible,
long days in which Evelayn didn't sleep and could barely eat, pacing
the palace floors and turrets, waiting . . . and watching. And finally,

finally, they had come late the night before. The army had retreated before Bain could slaughter them all, hurrying as quickly as possible, without the aid of their power, shielded only by the Scíaths, back to the palace.

Evelayn stood so tall that her shoulder blades were nearly pinched together beneath the elaborate white-and-gray dress she had donned for the official funeral. Though her pulse pounded a staccato of fear and anguish against her throat, Evelayn refused to let it show on her face or in her posture. She'd vowed never to cry in front of her people again after that first terrible morning on the lawn, when she'd realized what had happened. Though she'd come close to losing it that night on the turret with Tanvir, so far she'd managed to keep her vow. Evelayn was now the only living monarch in Éadrolan—and her people were watching her closely.

But thinking of that night was a dangerous path as well, fraught with pain and humiliation, and she made herself cut the thoughts off.

Evelayn couldn't believe so many had gathered when the funeral had been thrown together so quickly. Because the army had barely made it back in time, she and the High Priestesses had only until this afternoon—the third day—to perform the ceremony that would transfer the Light Power to Evelayn's conduit stone. The previous night, High Priestess Teca had explained yet again what would happen, but Evelayn had had a hard time absorbing it. She still couldn't quite believe any of this was real and not some terrible nightmare from which she would awaken at any moment. Only the body lying at the front of the Great Hall testified to how very real the horrors of the last three days truly were.

When she reached the front, Evelayn paused for a moment, staring down at the white sheet. Then she slowly knelt down and let her head bow forward to rest lightly against the cool marble.

Tears burned frighteningly close to the surface, and though it was perfectly reasonable for her to cry at her mother's funeral, Evelayn refused to show even a small amount of weakness. Only Ceren, Tanvir, and the other Draíolon on the lawn that day had been witness to her breakdown. From that moment she'd remained stoic, resolute. Even when they'd carried Queen Ilaria's body into the palace. Even when she'd stared down at her mother's bloodless, discolored face and known in a horrible, gut-hollowing way that never again would she hear her mother's voice, never again would she see her smile. Evelayn had understood it in her mind, but at that moment, the reality finally reached her heart, turning her cold.

Evelayn inhaled slowly, breathing in the thick, musky scent of the flowers that encircled the marble table. They were layered in rows, a sea of colors and smells, to cover up the faint stench of decay that had already begun to cling to the remains of the former queen. Only once she had regained complete control did Evelayn stand and turn to face the assembled Light Draíolon.

High Priestess Teca waited off to her right, watching for Evelayn's signal to begin the ceremony to officially lay Queen Ilaria's body to rest eternally beside her husband, who had died ten years earlier—and to transfer the power to their daughter, the new queen of Éadrolan.

Evelayn looked out at the sea of faces, all staring at her expectantly, some with pity and sorrow creasing their foreheads or twisting their mouths into frowns, some sitting stiffly, eyebrows lifted and arms crossed. Finally, she found Ceren's familiar cornflower blue eyes, swimming with tears. Beside her was Lord Tanvir. He nodded slightly at Evelayn, an unspoken encouragement. She couldn't allow herself to feel anything as their eyes met, as the horrible night on the turret crept back into her mind.

Evelayn tore her gaze away and took a deep breath. She just had to get through this; every minute wasted was another minute closer to losing their power permanently.

"My people," she began, her voice echoing across the Great Hall, "we are gathered here to pay tribute to my mother, Queen Ilaria of Éadrolan. She led with wisdom and grace, and she died in valor, defending our people and our lands. Long may her name be spoken for good."

The crowd echoed, "Long may her name be spoken for good," and then High Priestess Teca stepped forward, ready to begin her part of the ceremony, while Evelayn walked to the chair in the front row that had remained empty for her, surrounded by the Light Sentries now assigned to be her constant guards. They couldn't do much until their power was restored, but they all bore Scíaths, presumably to surround her and deflect shadowflame or worse in the event of an attack. The large, silvery shields flashed in the sunlight, a vaguely comforting sight, but Evelayn wondered how long they would be able to hold off an attack if she didn't regain their power first. It seemed as though the Scíaths would just delay the inevitable.

She sat there for the next hour, barely hearing a word that was spoken, staring at the white shroud, willing herself to remain in control just a little bit longer. She could feel the presence of Ceren and Tanvir behind her, but she never once turned her head toward them.

And then, finally, High Priestess Teca gestured for Evelayn to stand again.

Evelayn slowly rose to her feet and waited as two lines of Light Sentries hurried forward and simultaneously lifted the poles on either side of Queen Ilaria, raising the mat and her body off the marble. Then they moved forward, careful to keep her body level as they marched down the aisle. Evelayn followed directly behind them, with High Priestess Teca and the rest of the priestesses after her. This was the hardest part, but at least it would also be done without the prying eyes of all those gathered. The crowd had to wait in the Great Hall while the ceremony was performed in the sacred coppice near the Dawn Temple where the previous monarchs had been buried.

It was a relief to walk out of the palace, away from the inquisitive gazes and the weight of her people's judgments. The sun was merciless as they crossed the manicured lawns, but soon the forest enveloped the procession in jade-tinted shade.

They moved quickly, knowing time was short, and within a few minutes the trees opened up into the clearing where a circle of white stones had been prepared next to the headstone marking her father's grave. The forest was abnormally quiet as the Light Sentries carefully laid the queen's body down in the center of the stones. One by one, they knelt around the circle and let their heads bow forward, paying one final tribute to Queen Ilaria. And then they stood and melted back into the forest, leaving only Evelayn and the priestesses.

"Are you ready?" High Priestess Teca looked to Evelayn.

No, her heart shouted, but Evelayn nodded.

"Do you remember what you must do?"

Evelayn took a deep breath and then nodded again. "Yes." The word was a mere whisper.

Fear threatened to consume her. Her lungs felt tight, as if she couldn't get enough air. The priestesses had to use their combined abilities to draw the power from Queen Ilaria's stone and join it back to Sliabán—to the Immortal Tree. Once the priestesses summoned the power back, they had to direct it to Evelayn's conduit stone as quickly as possible, before it overwhelmed and killed them all. And then it was her turn—the final act to reclaim the Light Power for Éadrolan. Evelayn had to call down the force of the sun to consume her mother's body. The kings of Éadrolan were buried, but the queens . . . they were taken back to the Light in totality, conduit stone and all. There had been no time for practicing, only a rushed explanation of what she must do.

Hands trembling, Evelayn moved so that she was at the head of the ring of white stones. The hush of the forest was almost unnerving, as if every living thing was holding a collective breath, waiting and watching her.

Slowly, she lifted her hands so that the gauzy sleeves of her dress fell back, exposing her forearms. *The power is connected to your thoughts, to your very will, just as it always has been,* Teca had told her. *You must concentrate. Think of nothing else but your desire to accomplish this task and force the power to bend to your control.*

Evelayn inhaled slowly through her nose, trying to control her building anxiety by filling her lungs and then, as she exhaled through her mouth, she nodded. There was no point delaying. They had to complete the ceremony quickly or the time would run out and she would have to journey to the Immortal Tree and try to reclaim the power by herself, without the aid of her priestesses.

If Bain didn't slaughter them all first.

High Priestess Teca and the other six priestesses chosen for the ceremony immediately took their places around the circle. The priestesses all joined hands and began to intone something in the old language, quietly at first, but gradually becoming louder and louder. Evelayn stared down at her mother's shrouded figure as their voices rose up to the sky, filled the still air, and plunged deep into the earth.

At first there was nothing but their words and the silent forest. When Evelayn reached for her power, there was only emptiness.

But then she felt it. Something growing, building around them—humming through the grass beneath their feet, flying toward them on the wind, rising from her mother's body beneath the white sheet. The priestesses' voices grew strained, and Evelayn looked up to see Teca staring at her, her normally petal-pink eyes almost completely white. The power was flowing back into them, filling the priestesses' bodies. They had to send it to her so it could be channeled through her conduit stone *now*. But rather than taking the next step, they were all frozen, staring at her, repeating the same phrase over and over.

Panic bubbled through Evelayn's body, a rush of terror that slicked her hands with sweat. Something was wrong. She was supposed to do something to transfer the power, but she couldn't remember what. Teca's eyes widened—she looked like she was in pain.

"What should I do? What's happening?" Evelayn stared in horror as a few of the priestesses began to tremble, their entire bodies shivering violently from the force of the power they had drawn upon. But, still, they didn't let go of each other.

Out of sheer desperation, Evelayn seized the hands of the two priestesses closest to her—one on each side. The surge of power was instantaneous—and excruciating. Her entire body hummed with it, burned with it, expanded until she felt as though she would explode from the fire in her veins, in her bones and muscles and skin.

The conduit stone, some voice of reason whispered beneath the agony. *Force it to the conduit stone.*

But how? There was nothing but pain and blinding, all-consuming power. With this amount of power she could do *anything*. The world was hers to command—except that there was no controlling it. Instead, she would die. They would *all* die . . .

Bend it to your control. Force it to the conduit stone.

Evelayn couldn't move, couldn't even blink. But she could still *think*—she still had a will of her own, even though the unblocked flow of Light Power was threatening to take that from her as well, to erase her beneath its unimaginable force.

No. She fought back, visualizing her conduit stone, the oval diamond she'd been born with, embedded in her breastbone. *Go,* she pleaded as the pain escalated yet again. *Go to the stone.* That was what was supposed to happen. Why wasn't it happening?

The two priestesses gripping her hands were shaking so hard they nearly threatened to toss her to the ground. If she couldn't succeed soon, the power would burn them all up from the inside out. And it *wasn't working.*

Terror raced through Evelayn's veins alongside the unadulterated power. The voices from the Great Hall came back, and she realized they were right. She was too young, too inexperienced. She was going to fail.

You weren't born to fail, my daughter. You were born to do what I couldn't: to restore peace to Éadrolan—and to all of Lachalonia.

Her mother's voice seemed to come from everywhere all at once. It was on the air, it echoed in her mind, it beat in her heart. It filled her, wrapping around Evelayn like the soft touch of morning sunshine, reaching her from beyond the separation of death, somehow, through the magic.

I know you can do this, Evie. I know it.

Only her mother had ever called her Evie. And just as she always had, Evelayn believed her. With every last ounce of strength and will she possessed, she concentrated on forcing the Light Power to the conduit stone. She managed to squeeze her eyes shut and clench her jaw against the irrepressible tide of power washing over and through her.

You are mine to command, and you will *go to the stone!* She spoke to the power as though it were a living thing, and suddenly, the stone in her breastbone burned white-hot against her skin as the power drained out of her body and began to flow through the conduit stone as it was supposed to.

With a cry that was half relief and half agony, Evelayn's eyes flew open and she stumbled back a step, breaking her hold on the two priestesses' hands. One crumpled to her knees on the ground, but the others remained standing, visibly shaken but still alive.

"You did it," Teca spoke, her voice trembling, though her eyes had returned to their normal rose pink.

Evelayn couldn't respond, letting her gaze drop to the white sheet on the ground instead. She still had one last task to complete to finalize the transfer of power to her stone. She had to call down the power of the sun to consume her mother's body. Had she truly heard her voice a moment ago, or had it all been in her mind—a desperate subconscious effort not to fail?

"Quickly now, Your Majesty. The time is nearly up to complete the ceremony," High Priestess Teca urged as she moved toward the priestess still on the ground, grabbing her elbow and assisting her back to her feet. They all backed away, leaving Evelayn plenty of space. "Remember, it will respond to your will, to your very thoughts, just as it always has. But now you have access to the entirety of the Light Power that exists in Lachalonia. You must be very careful not to draw too much or . . ."

Teca trailed off, but she didn't have to finish her thought. Evelayn knew the consequences if she called upon too much power—she had just experienced the incomprehensible amount of magic she had access to and had nearly died trying to harness it into her stone. But she needed enough to make sure she finished the ceremony correctly. Oh why hadn't they made her practice *this*, rather than shooting blasts of light at targets?

But then, she already knew the answer. Because only the queen of Éadrolan had access to *this* much power.

Evelayn closed her eyes and turned her face up to the sky, to the sunshine that warmed the earth and heated the breeze that ruffled her hair. She lifted her hands high above her head and took a deep breath.

Then she called down the sun.

There was a breathless pause when nothing happened . . . until, with a flash of heat, the power flowed out of the stone, up her raised arms, and out into the sky. There was *so much*. With a sound like the crack of thunder, a thick beam of blinding, scorching light exploded toward the earth, completely filling the circle of stones, taking her mother's shrouded body from view.

Evelayn's arms began to tremble from the force of holding the beam there without letting any more power come through the stone. But she didn't want to let it go—not yet. Tears filled her eyes as she stared at the glowing white stones. The heat was almost unbearable. Evelayn could feel her hair singeing, and the wetness on her cheeks dried almost instantaneously.

"Your Highness, that's enough!" She could vaguely hear Teca's shout through the roaring of her blood in her ears and the thundering of the beam of sunshine she controlled. Evelayn wanted to ignore her, didn't want to face what came after this, but she knew the High Priestess was right.

"Good-bye, Mama." Evelayn whispered, even as her entire body began to shake from the effort of simultaneously holding on to the magic and holding it at bay. And then she released the power.

The beam immediately disappeared, revealing charred grass and nothing else. It was done. The Light Power had been reclaimed and was now entirely under Evelayn's control.

And Queen Ilaria—her mother—was gone.

SIXTEEN

ANOTHER GOBLET SHATTERED AGAINST THE STONES around the massive fireplace of the manor Bain had commandeered near the border of Éadrolan, but Lorcan didn't so much as flinch. Blood-red wine dripped down to the floor, pooling where ashes of previous fires remained.

"How did this happen?" Bain roared.

A trio of servants huddled nervously in the corner of the room. Lorcan could scent their terror like fetid meat. Abarrane and Lothar were seated beside Lorcan at the table, where only a few pieces of their cutlery and one goblet remained. The rest of the dishes, along with their meal, were scattered around the room, broken into pieces.

They'd been midluncheon when they'd felt it. The flare of heat and the diminished force of their magic—Evelayn had apparently succeeded in reclaiming her power.

"It's not *possible*." His father spun and faced them, his stone flashing crimson in his forehead.

The blast of shadowflame came so suddenly that Lorcan barely managed to throw up a shield in time to deflect it, jumping out of his chair to face his father.

"Bain!" his mother shrieked, also jumping to her feet.

"*You* failed me." Bain bared his teeth, his lip curling in a sneer.

"I did exactly as you instructed. You succeeded in killing Queen Ilaria. The plan succeeded." Lorcan's fingers twitched, his muscles tight in anticipation of his father's next attack.

"*She reclaimed her power!* That is *not* success!" Another blast of shadowflame, but this time it exploded into the table, blasting it apart. Lorcan threw up another shield to protect himself from the debris.

The far door flung open, and Bain's council hurried in, responding to the summons he'd immediately sent out. General Rednon, Maedre's replacement, was first, followed by the others, General Caedmon entering last. Bain immediately went still, his fury masked— for the moment. But Lorcan saw Rednon's eyes widen as he took in the destruction in the room.

"Do you feel that?" Bain asked, his voice deceptively calm. When no one answered, he barked, "General Rednon, I asked if you feel that!"

The general startled, his fire-orange eyes flying up to meet his king's.

Run, Lorcan wanted to warn him. But there was no point. Running wouldn't save him—it would just prolong what was coming. So instead, he watched silently as Rednon took a hesitant step forward.

"I'm not sure if I—"

"It got hotter a minute ago, wouldn't you agree? And yet, there is no fire in the room. Why, exactly, do you think the temperature just rose . . . and my power waned?"

Rednon blanched.

"You said you would *take care* of her. You were supposed to keep this from happening." Bain's voice was a mere whisper, but it cut through the room like a sword.

Faster than the blink of an eye, the king shot writhing black cords of shadow to encircle Rednon's body.

"Sire, I—"

The bindings tightened to cut off his words—and his air—so that his mouth merely opened and closed but no further sound came out.

"You *failed* me," Bain snarled.

Lorcan watched with everyone else as Rednon turned red and then purple as he silently suffocated in front of them. The food Lorcan had managed to eat before the king's outburst curdled in his stomach, but he stood stoically as his father murdered yet another Draíolon.

Finally, Bain released the cords and Rednon crumpled to the ground with a dull thud.

"And now what?" The king looked past the dead general to the rest of his council. "Éadrolan has regained their power. The wards will be back up within the hour."

There was only silence for a long moment, but then General Caedmon stepped forward. Lorcan barely hid his surprise. Caedmon had seemed smart enough to stay out of the focus as much as possible up until that point.

"Sire, if I may. I have an idea."

Bain lifted his cold gaze to Caedmon's disconcertingly pale eyes. "Indeed. Well, let's hear it. And hope that you don't join poor Rednon in his fate after failing me."

ॐ

Tanvir stood by the window until his legs cramped and his back ached, waiting and watching. The priestesses had returned and those gathered to mourn had already finished the feast prepared for them and begun to leave the castle to return to their homes in Solas or elsewhere. And still Evelayn had not returned.

He heard Lady Ceren approaching, but didn't turn to acknowledge her.

"She still hasn't come back?" Her question was quiet, hesitant.

"No."

He hazarded a glance to see her watching him, her light blue eyes red-rimmed. This was Evelayn's closest friend, her confidante, and really all that was left that could constitute family. "She's been through a lot. Give her time."

Tanvir's eyebrows lifted. Did she know what had happened on the battlements? Of course she did; if there was anyone Evelayn would talk to, it would be Ceren.

"For what it's worth, I think you did the right thing. I'm sure it wasn't easy to try to protect her that way, even if she can't see that yet."

"Thank you," Tanvir murmured as his gut twisted with guilt.

Ceren drew up beside him and turned to face the window, and he resumed his vigil. They were silent for a long time, watching the Draíolon come and go. But still no sign of the queen.

"I knew she could do it," he finally spoke. "I knew she was strong enough to reclaim the power."

"I believed in her, too," Ceren agreed.

Tanvir's gaze traveled over the thinning stream of Draíolon. Most who didn't live at the castle had left, hurrying to beat the charcoal clouds that had formed on the horizon and now tumbled toward them from the west, heavy with rain. "I think her people were sad she didn't come back to celebrate regaining their power with them."

"Would you have felt like celebrating today—even if you had brought back power to your kingdom?" Ceren glanced up at him again.

"No."

"If I had to guess, I would say she's probably at the Lake of Swans. That's where she usually goes when she wants to be alone or when she's upset."

"She'll be soaked if she stays out in this storm. It's not safe."

Ceren turned toward him and waited until he looked down at her once more. "She'll come to us when she's ready." She placed one hand on his arm, a gentle touch to let him know she understood. And then, with a final glance out the window, Ceren curtsied to him. "Good evening, Lord Tanvir. And remember, be patient."

He bowed and watched her go before turning back to the window, just as the first few droplets of rain splattered against the glass, running down the pane like tears.

SEVENTEEN

CEREN ABSENTLY CUT UP THE MANGO SLICES ON HER plate, but the majority of her focus was on Evelayn, sitting at the head of the table, her dinner untouched. Ceren still wasn't used to seeing her closest friend's white-blonde hair intricately woven around the diamond-studded diadem Queen Ilaria had always worn. Her mourning dress was gauzy, silver and white, symbolizing the deceased's entrance into eternal rest in the world beyond this, a place of light and beauty. Evelayn was stunning—even pale and grieving, with dark bruises beneath her violet eyes. In fact, every time Ceren glanced across the table at Lord Tanvir, his gaze was on the new queen, his expression a mix of longing, regret, and concern. But Evelayn was oblivious, staring down at her plate, pushing the fruit and delicate pastries around her plate with her fork, never taking a bite.

"What is she going to do?" the Draíolon with mulberry-colored hair seated next to Ceren whispered to her, pulling Ceren's attention away from Tanvir and Evelayn. "King Bain won't wait much longer to launch a full-scale attack against us—mark my words."

"He wouldn't dare—his army sustained heavy losses before Queen Ilaria was killed *and* it's the middle of summer. He knows that even with a new monarch, we are in the height of our power right now. She completed the ceremony, didn't she? We got our magic back. Maybe she'll surprise us," the man argued, his voice similarly hushed.

But Ceren could hear them perfectly from her seat, and she was sure others could as well. Evelayn was too far away, but Ceren knew the new queen was aware of the murmurs, the fears and concerns swirling around the Light court. It had only been a handful of days since Evelayn had completed the ceremony, but already her people were restless, wanting to know what was next. Wanting reassurance that their new queen was going to be able to defend them from the threat to the north.

"You've barely touched your food, Lady Ceren."

Ceren started and turned to look at the Draíolon on her left side. He had pale blond hair—not quite as white as Evelayn's, but close— and eyes the emerald green of grass in the full lushness of summer. "Have we met?" Why did he know her name? If she'd seen him before, she could have sworn she'd remember.

"I'm afraid not. I've been on the front lines of the war for five years."

"I'm sorry to hear that."

He shrugged. "It was my duty. I'm just grateful to have made it back home, especially when I find myself in such lovely company."

Ceren hoped he didn't notice the rising color in her cheeks, even though she thrilled at his compliment. How old was he, anyway? He had no lines on his face yet, so he was definitely still in his early prime— most likely under a hundred. But his eyes were haunted, not those of a youngling, either. Whoever he was, as soon as he realized she had only reached maturity six months ago, he would probably bid her a quick farewell and never seek out her conversation again. So she might as well enjoy it now, she reasoned. "Do you have a name? Or do you wish me to guess it?"

"Though it might prove entertaining indeed to have you try and guess, I apologize for not introducing myself earlier. I am Quinlen, of the House of Teslar. Perhaps you have heard of my father, Lord Teslar?"

Ceren tried not to choke on the sip of wine she'd just taken. "Yes, perhaps I have."

Everyone knew Lord Teslar—one of the top generals in the army, and the High Lord of the House of Teslar. She racked her brain trying to remember how many children he had and if she'd ever heard of Quinlen before. Was he the oldest? He couldn't be that old if he'd only been fighting on the front lines for five years—

A door at the end of the dining hall suddenly flew open, and two Light Sentries entered, dragging another Draíolon behind them. There was a collective gasp around the table, and a few of those gathered jumped to their feet. Ceren immediately looked to Evelayn, who watched while keeping her face an emotionless mask.

"What is the meaning of this?" The queen pushed back her chair and stood up. The other Light Sentries who had been hovering in the background rushed forward, but Evelayn lifted a hand and they paused before getting too close.

The Draíolon they brought in had skin the color of snow with a silvery sheen to it, and pale blue hair. His eyes, when he looked up at Evelayn, were completely white except for his dark pupils. Ceren's hands turned to ice when she caught his scent—he smelled of winter, of blizzards. He was a Dark Draíolon from Dorjhalon.

"He claims to bring a warning," one of the Light Sentries sneered, yanking the male's arm back even harder. The Dark Draíolon flinched but didn't fight back. "He wants us to believe he's here to *help*."

Fear pumped through Ceren's veins as she glanced between the captive Draíolon and Evelayn. Silence as heavy as the moment between a lightning strike and the subsequent roar of thunder hung over the room as the queen's eyes narrowed, and then she slowly moved toward the Dark Draíolon.

Her guards closed in, following right behind her. They halted when she paused only a few feet away from the two Light Sentries and the supposed informant from Dorjhalon.

Palpable tension radiated off Quinlen, who was one of the Draíolon who had jumped to his feet at the intrusion. He obviously didn't trust the man, and Ceren couldn't help but wonder if it was some sort of trap. *Get away from him*, she thought, wishing she dared speak out loud.

Queen Evelayn stared down at the Dark Draíolon for a long time while everyone waited in tense anticipation. The male held her gaze silently. Finally, she nodded.

"I will hear what he has to say."

She brushed past them and swept out of the room as the Light Sentries scrambled to turn and drag the Dark Draíolon out the door, following their queen, leaving the rest of the room in stunned silence.

At first no one moved, and then Lord Tanvir shoved his chair away from the table and rushed after her. Ceren wished to do the same, but fear planted her feet to the ground. What if it *was* some sort of trap?

"One Dark Draíolon won't be able to do anything to her, especially here. She'll be fine." Quinlen touched her elbow hesitantly, disconcerting Ceren with his ease in reading her emotions.

"I hope you're right," Ceren finally responded, staring at the door with her heart in her throat.

The door to the throne room was already shut when Tanvir sprinted around the corner, moving so fast the castle became a blur. He didn't care if she was mad at him, he *had* to be in that room with her—he didn't dare leave Evelayn alone with a Dark Draíolon. Two Light Sentries guarded the entrance, but he didn't even pause to acknowledge them before throwing open the door and rushing into the throne room. Let them try and stop him, if they wanted to. The new queen needed him by her side.

When he burst into the room, all eyes turned to him. Evelayn's eyebrows lifted slightly, but other than that she showed no sign of surprise at his entrance. She sat stiffly on her throne as the Light Sentries forced the Dark Draíolon to his knees on the ground in front of her. They had him bound with cords of light, even though he'd shown no signs of struggle nor attempted to escape.

Good, Tanvir thought as he strode to the front of the room, stopping at the bottom of the dais where the throne sat. Queen Evelayn's council was gathering along the other side of the room in their customary seats. A few of them didn't bother hiding their irritation at his arrival.

"What is the meaning of this intrusion, my lord?" Queen Evelayn's violet eyes met his, and for a moment that existed only in the space between one breath and the next, everything else faded away and there was only her and the sudden spike in his pulse. But then he blinked and clarity returned.

"I wish to claim a position on the council, to be by your side, to offer my aid in any way possible, my queen."

She studied him for a moment. He'd heard that a monarch's direct connection to the magic gave him or her the ability to extend their senses out through that line of power to their subjects—in essence, to feel what their subjects were feeling. It had been less than a week . . . he hoped she was still too inexperienced to be able to control her power that way. It was enough that she could probably scent him and ascertain some of what he was feeling. He didn't want her to realize how quickly his heart was beating or sense the emotions he was working to suppress. At least, not right now.

Finally, she nodded. "As you are now the High Lord of the Delsachts, your request is granted. You may stay."

There was a murmur from the right side of the room, where the council members were all now seated. Tanvir exhaled and flashed her a quick, grateful smile. She didn't return it, but he noticed the fingers of her right hand curl around the diaphanous material of the skirt of her dress. Perhaps there was hope that she would forgive him after all. She had continued to avoid him as much as possible after completing the ceremony to reclaim their power. He'd tried to do as Ceren suggested and give her time and space. However, when she couldn't avoid him, she'd ignored him instead, hiding behind her cool, reserved demeanor, leaving him uncertain and wondering if he'd destroyed any hopes of ever getting close to her again.

But she'd let him stay. That had to mean *something*.

Queen Evelayn finally stood, suddenly looking far older than her eighteen years, and stared down at the Dark Draíolon, her gaze imperious. A thrill of apprehension ran through Tanvir's veins. Though she'd been successful at completing the ceremony to retake control of the Light Power, this was the first time he'd felt that power surround her in such a tangible way. Even her scent had changed subtly—there was now an underlying hint of something sharp beneath the usual violet and sunshine that was so intoxicating, almost like the acrid smell of lightning. She was young, it was true, but she was *magnificent*. A hard knot tightened Tanvir's stomach as he thought about what the future might hold for her.

Don't think about that, he told himself. Dwelling on fear never led to anything good, as well he knew. His whole life had been composed of different levels of fear. He'd been raised during war, had lost both of his parents to that war, and most recently, his sister had become its victim. He'd made terrible decisions because of fear, as had many others.

"What is your name?" Evelayn spoke, jarring Tanvir from his morbid thoughts and drawing his attention back to the Dark Draíolon.

"Caedmon, Your Majesty," the man responded immediately.

"And what message do you have for me, Caedmon, that is worth risking your life to come in our midst to deliver? Choose your words wisely, for they may well be your last."

The Light Sentries tightened the cords around him at her words, but she lifted her hand to stop them.

"Let him speak."

Tanvir watched Caedmon silently, waiting with everyone else.

"Your Majesty, I don't come to deliver a message, but a warning. I'm tired of this war. Our people are tired of it. We wish for the same thing as you—for peace. You are young, Queen Evelayn, but I am not. Though it was a decade ago, I remember peace. I remember the time when our two kingdoms lived in harmony—in balance."

Tanvir glanced between Caedmon and Evelayn. The queen's eyes were narrowed, though her expression remained impassive as she listened.

"Our world is suffering because that balance has been upset. And the longer this war continues, the worse it gets. If King Bain succeeds in killing you and trying to take your power for himself, I fear the results would cause irreparable harm to Lachalonia. And many others agree with me. This island has existed since before recorded time, Light and Dark working together to create the harmony that breeds life of all kinds. That balance of Light and Dark affects not only our world, but the world beyond ours as well, outside of Lachalonia."

"I know all of this," Queen Evelayn interrupted. "State your purpose in coming before I tire of your presumption that I am not only young—as you so blithely pointed out—but also naïve and uninformed."

"Many apologies, Your Majesty." Caedmon bent his head in supplication. "That was not my intent at all. I merely wished for you to understand my views so you will believe my purpose in coming. I wish to tell you of King Bain's plans so that you might be prepared for the trap he intends to lay for you, and help you beat him at his own game. I wish to help you defeat my king."

EIGHTEEN

CAEDMON'S WORDS HUNG IN THE STUNNED SILENCE that followed his declaration. Evelayn's breath caught somewhere between her heart and her throat, right beneath the conduit stone that warmed her skin day and night since she'd completed the ceremony. Did she dare believe that he was telling the truth? She knew she had to tread lightly and be very, *very* careful. But she couldn't keep the tiny seed of hope from burgeoning out of the dazed stupor of grief she'd been caught in for the last few days.

"How are we to know that you aren't here to lead us into the very trap you claim to be informing us of?" she finally asked, keeping her voice cold, refusing to allow even a hint of softness into her expression— not yet. "Your claim is interesting, I grant you that. But I find it hard to believe that after a decade, your desire for peace is suddenly strong enough to seek me out, when you never attempted to do so with the former queen."

Caedmon looked up at her again, and she could see no guile in his strange white eyes. She scented no dishonesty, though she wasn't entirely sure yet *what* it would even smell like. But there was nothing besides the frosty scent of ice and the bitterness of sorrow.

He met her gaze squarely when he responded. "I was not yet in a position to be privy to his most secret plans until recently, and there was never an opportunity like this where I believed it possible. King Bain has been very careful to always protect himself to the utmost. Though he judged your mother to be weaker than the former queen—which is why he started this war—he knew Ilaria was still a powerful queen in her own right, that she wouldn't hesitate to kill him to stop the war.

"But he thinks *you* to be the very things you accused me of believing—though I am not fool enough to actually believe it. Especially after you completed the ceremony. Something he didn't think you capable of, by the by." The Dark Draíolon smiled at her in an almost fatherly kind of way. As if he was *proud* of her.

"What is your point?" Evelayn cut in icily, refusing to let him soften her with compliments.

Caedmon's expression turned grim. "You ruined his plans by reclaiming your power. But because he believes you to be too young and naïve to rule effectively, he thinks that this is still his chance to press his advantage and plan a different attack while you are weak with grief and your magic isn't under complete control."

"I'm listening," Evelayn allowed, gesturing for him to continue. She glanced briefly at Tanvir to see him watching her closely. His amber eyes were too distracting, and she quickly looked back at Caedmon. She couldn't risk allowing herself to lose focus and miss any hint of deception on the Dark Draíolon's part. If he were her subject— and if she'd already mastered the ability, which would take years according to High Priestess Teca and General Kelwyn—she could have stretched out her awareness to try to ascertain his emotional and physical state. But he wasn't her subject, and she had no access to the power he wielded, and therefore no access to him.

She had to rely completely upon her own senses and feelings, and hope they didn't lead her astray.

"He is planning on sending the majority of his army to march on the city of Ristra, coming from the northwest, to draw out your army. He is bringing almost all of his priests to create a concentrated attack that will bring down the wards in that one location. He knows that your generals will encourage you to stay as far back from the front line of fighting as possible, especially because you are young and your mother was just killed. That is how *he* has fought this war, hiding behind thousands of Dark Draíolon, surrounded by his most powerful priests and warriors."

Evelayn barely kept herself from nodding. She knew this from the lessons she'd had with High Priestess Teca and Kel, and from talking with her mother. It was why her parents had never been able to reach him, or any of his family. When any of the Dorjhalon royals joined the fight at the front lines, all four of them—King Bain, Queen Abarrane, and the two princes, Lorcan and Lothar—were constantly protected by concentric rings of Dark Draíolon, each ring growing smaller the closer one got to the royal family, but also more powerful, until the closest ring of all, made up entirely of the High Priests of Dorjhalon.

Queen Ilaria hadn't wanted to risk her priestesses' lives the way Bain did his priests'. She'd insisted that all those not at the front lines holding up the wards stay at the palace, to train the growing generation and to protect her people there from attack.

That tactic had ended with both Evelayn's father and now her mother being killed by Bain. Perhaps Bain was the wiser one, after all.

"He is planning on setting up a decoy. He'll keep the formation the same as always, but rather than staying in the security of the rings of protection that he's formed—and that your army will expect to see—he will take a small group with him and come from behind. He plans to ambush and kill you."

"How exactly does he plan on coming from behind?"

Caedmon looked slightly confused. "Through the Undead Forest."

Evelayn remained motionless, swallowing the incredulous laughter that threatened to burst out. "The Undead Forest," she finally repeated. "I see."

Caedmon's eyebrows were still drawn down as if her reaction was . . . unexpected. Which was confusing to *her*. To hide her uncertainty, she quickly continued, "This supposed plan is completely unlike him—it holds far too much risk. He defeated my mother without putting himself in so much jeopardy, why try this now on me?"

Something flickered across Caedmon's face—but it wasn't confusion, or even guilt or fear. It was sadness . . . it was *pity*.

"My dear Queen Evelayn, did no one tell you how your mother was killed?"

Something simultaneously bitterly cold and scalding hot flashed through Evelayn's body. "What do you mean?" Her voice was as frigid and hard as the mountains of ice said to be at the northernmost reaches of the world, far beyond the shores of Lachalonia. "What is he talking about?" She looked up to her council, seated to her right, including High Priestess Teca and Kel, listening to the entire proceedings.

"Your Majesty, I don't believe now is the best ti—"

"If there is *anything* that has been kept from me that holds any bearing on what this male is telling me," Evelayn cut the High Priestess off, "then it is imperative that you tell me immediately. Punishments for withholding vital information from the ruling queen of Éadrolan will be decided later." Evelayn had to consciously keep her hands from forming fists at her sides, she was so furious.

Teca inclined her head. "As you wish, Your Majesty." She flicked her hand at a Draíolon sitting two seats down from her—General Olena, the head general of all Éadrolan's armies. Olena stood, her jaw tight. Olena was nearly three hundred, and was showing her age, with streaks of white standing out against the dark plum of the severe braid she wore down her back and the first signs of lines at the corners of her eyes and mouth. Her mahogany skin hid any hint of a flush if she was blushing at all, but Evelayn didn't miss the meaningful glance between her and Kel before she faced the queen fully.

"We intended to tell you very soon, Your Majesty, after you had some time to mourn—"

Evelayn lifted her hand, and Olena immediately fell quiet. "Just *tell me*." She allowed a hint of the fury she felt to seep into her voice, just as she'd seen her mother do many times when she was displeased.

"It was a trap, my queen." When Olena spoke again, her voice was much quieter, almost ashamed. "He purposely allowed our army to break through his front lines, to kill many of his Draíolon, to make us think we were finally gaining the upper hand. He played it just right—the way they fought back let us think we could win as we came into the height of our power, as summer solstice draws near. They even began to retreat. It was a huge risk on his part; his army is greatly weakened because he allowed so many to die for his farce. Queen Ilaria didn't want to miss the chance to press our advantage and ordered us to push forward.

"And then he used Lorcan as a decoy. The prince led a battalion against us, drawing the queen into a fight, distracting her. Our scouts had repeatedly informed us that the ring was still in place, protecting King Bain—or so we thought. Your mother knew she could defeat Lorcan. She thought to hold him captive and force Bain to agree to end the war in return for his son and heir."

The general paused for a moment, as if she didn't want to continue. Evelayn hardly dared breathe as she pictured her mother falling perfectly into his trap—riding forward to her death rather than the victory she thought was within her grasp.

"But King Bain wasn't with his priests," High Priestess Teca prompted quietly.

"No. He sent Lothar with another force to distract me and my battalion. Then Bain attacked Queen Ilaria from behind while she fought with Lorcan. He took her completely unaware. She never even had a chance to defend herself. In ten years he'd never left the protection of his priests before. None of us expected it."

There was no possible way he'd made it past the wards though, unless . . . "He came through the Undead Forest to avoid the wards." Evelayn's words fell like stones from her lips. *No one* went through the Undead Forest that spanned the easternmost reaches of Lachalonia, where the Spirit Harbinger dwelled—and more.

Caedmon nodded grimly.

Evelayn stood like a statue in front of the throne, the crown on her head pressing into her skull. She didn't dare move, afraid she would break into pieces in front of everyone again.

"And now he believes if it worked once, it will work again." Tanvir spoke up, his voice tight with thinly veiled anger.

"Yes," Caedmon agreed. "That is his belief. But this time *you* will be prepared. If you listen to me."

"Why would he do it again? We know he was willing to do it once, why wouldn't we guard ourselves against it happening a second time?" General Olena questioned Caedmon now as Evelayn tried to force the all-consuming grief and pain back down, *away*. "Especially here? He thinks to sneak his way through Éadrolan undetected to attack us from behind? It's ludicrous."

"He is blinded by greed and drunk with victory. He thinks Queen Evelayn is too young and untrained to be a true threat—and he is counting on the fact that you won't expect him to try it twice, and would think it is too much of a risk for him to travel through your kingdom during the height of summertime. Prince Lorcan also believes it will work again and is pushing his father to try it against you. I, too, have been pushing him to follow through on this plan, because I saw a chance to put into play a plan of my own. Lothar is the only one against it."

"How do you know all this? Why should we trust anything you're saying?" Evelayn finally spoke up again, her conduit stone pulsing hot against her breastbone. The magic itched for release, she could feel it building in her. Or was it her own rage and grief, calling to the magic, pulling it to her? She took a slow breath through her nose, trying to calm herself.

"Because I am second-in-command to his top general and privy to all of his war councils—including the secret ones."

Kel jumped up from his seat, his expression dark with anger. "You are that high up in his army and expect us to believe that you wish for this war to end with your king defeated? That *anything* you've told us is the truth—and not an attempt to trick the new queen into making a mistake as fatal as her mother's?"

Caedmon turned his head to look at Kel. "Yes. If anything, it should prove the truth of my statements. I was sent as a scout to find the best route for King Bain to take with Lorcan and those he is bringing with him to set the trap—including me. If they knew I was here, telling you this, my life would be forfeit. I'm risking everything on the hope that you will see the truth in my eyes and hear it in my voice." He looked back up at Evelayn.

"And how did *you* get past our wards?"

"The same way as my king. Through the forest." Caedmon shuddered.

"Why would he send the second-in-command of his entire army as a scout?" Tanvir piped up now, before Evelayn could ask the same question.

"Because there are only a handful who know his true plans. There are many Dark Draíolon who wish for this war to end—who long for peace. King Bain can feel the unrest growing in his people and he's nervous that they may soon rebel. He suspects that Lothar is against the war and may even be trying to enact a plot so he can inherit the kingdom and power and end the war. King Bain knows he must move fast and that as few people as possible can know the truth of his plans, or else risk their discovery."

Several Draíolon began speaking at once, but Evelayn lifted her hands, silencing them all as she stared at Caedmon.

"Lothar wishes for peace," she repeated.

"That is the rumor. I haven't spoken with him about it, because I dare not reveal myself when I have worked so hard to get into a position of trust with the king—hoping for a moment like this, when I could help the Light Kingdom defeat him and somehow find a way to restore the balance and bring peace back to our land."

"You can't possibly believe—"

"Enough!" Evelayn cut off General Olena's protest. She studied Caedmon, letting the silence build, drawing out into minutes of tense waiting. He never flinched, not even when she slowly began to descend the stairs toward him, the long, full skirts of her dress swishing across the marble.

When she stopped in front of him, Caedmon had to tilt his head back to look up at her from where he still knelt on the hard ground. She lifted a hand and sent a coil of light around his neck, wrapping it tight enough to begin limiting his ability to breathe.

"Swear to me," she snarled. "Swear to me on the Immortal Tree—by forfeit of your life—that what you say is true."

Caedmon nodded, his silvery skin mottling. "I swear," he choked out. "I swear!"

Evelayn released the band of light slightly and he repeated himself, his voice rasping against his raw throat. "I swear on my life by virtue of the Immortal Tree. If what I say is false, let me die now."

Evelayn stared into his disconcertingly pale eyes, searching for any hint of artifice. Something deep inside told her that he was telling the truth. Was it an instinct worth following, or only a desperate hope? A chance to end the war . . . to restore peace. It was too good to be true. But maybe, just maybe—

"He will think I am leading him straight to victory, but instead, I will be leading him to his death. I swear it, Your Majesty." Caedmon's expression turned pleading, his eyes shining with what looked like withheld tears. "The Draíolon I was Bound to was one he 'sacrificed' to draw out your mother. She died along with hundreds of others. He allowed an entire battalion of our people to be slaughtered, just to make it look authentic. He will stop at nothing, and I finally have a chance to do something about it. Please, *please* believe me," Caedmon begged. "But you must decide quickly. My time is short before he grows suspicious. I must return as quickly as possible so he will believe me to still be true to him."

Evelayn glanced at her council—at the horror on General Olena's face, and the contemplation on Kel's. High Priestess Teca looked torn, as did the others. And then she turned to Tanvir. He inclined his head slightly, in what looked like a very subtle nod.

Finally, she turned back to Caedmon. "Release him."

Caedmon's head bowed forward as he audibly sighed with relief, but Evelayn had already turned away to stride up the stairs. "Assemble the entire war council immediately," she announced, spinning to address the room again from the top of the dais. "Today we will finally make a plan to defeat King Bain and restore peace to Lachalonia."

NINETEEN

THE FIRE HAD LONG SINCE BURNED DOWN TO EMBERS and Ceren was unwillingly dozing off, her neck bent at an odd angle, when the door finally opened and Evelayn walked in. Without turning, Evelayn said, "Somehow I knew you'd be here waiting for me."

"I have hot tea ready for you, and your favorite scone. Well . . . it was hot a few hours ago. Now I guess it's tepid tea. Yum?" Ceren held up the cup she'd prepared long ago.

Evelayn didn't laugh. Her shoulders sagged forward and the circles under her eyes were even more pronounced as she crossed the room and took the cup from Ceren.

The new queen slumped into a chair, took a sip of the cold chamomile-and-lavender tea—usually her favorite drink before bed— and made a face.

"I did try to heat it up again once or twice. But I gave up when the fire died for the second time. It's too blazing hot to keep a fire burning tonight."

Evelayn nodded in agreement and bravely took another sip before setting the cup down. "I'm sorry," she said. "I thought we'd never finish."

"More meetings?" Ceren asked carefully, not wanting to pry, though she was near to perishing from curiosity. She hadn't seen Evelayn since she'd marched out of the dining room earlier to question the Dark Draíolon. Rumors were racing around the castle.

Evelayn nodded again and reached up to pinch the bridge of her nose.

"Do you wish me to call for Tyne to bring you something for your head?"

"No, don't bother her. Let her get some sleep." Evelayn stood up and moved over to her window, staring out into the dark night.

"I could put this tea to good use and pour it on a cloth—then you could lay it over your eyes. Maybe that would help?" Ceren offered, standing as well.

Evelayn flashed her a grateful smile. "That sounds lovely actually."

"Turn around. I'll help you undress, then you can go lie down and I'll get it ready."

Evelayn's lips trembled and she sounded near to crying when she whispered, "What did I ever do to deserve you?"

"Oh, stop," Ceren protested, though she warmed at the sentiment. "Let me undo these ties. They must be cutting off your oxygen to make you talk like that."

She pulled Evelayn in for a quick hug, then spun her around before she could protest and began to pull at the strings that Tyne had done up that morning. As she worked, Evelayn began to talk, the whole story tumbling out in a rush. How she'd questioned Caedmon, what he'd told her, how her mother had died—and what King Bain was planning.

"So what are you going to do?" Ceren asked, her mind whirling as Evelayn finally stepped out of the dress and went to lie down in only her shift. It was too hot for a nightgown. Ceren began to pick up the dress to hang but Evelayn waved her hand.

"Leave it. I don't ever want to wear that dress again."

Ceren paused and then slung the beautiful gown over the back of a chair instead. Tyne could take it away in the morning and reuse the fabric or give it away. Though she tried to hide it, some of the dismay she felt must have shown on her face, because Evelayn hurried to add, "I found out so many horrible things today. That dress will only serve to remind me of them. You may have it, if you wish."

They were almost the same size, though Evelayn was taller, so Ceren would have to have it tailored, but she was secretly thrilled. Though she was from the nobility, her family was nowhere near as wealthy as the queen of Éadrolan. It was rarely a point of conflict between them, as Evelayn shared everything she had with Ceren willingly. "Thank you, perhaps I will have it remade into something so it won't remind you of today when *I* wear it."

Evelayn nodded and closed her eyes, reaching up to pinch the bridge of her nose again. Ceren quickly got to work preparing the makeshift tincture for her friend. The other reason Ceren had never truly begrudged Evelayn her wealth and position was she knew full well it came with more pressures, more worries, and more death than Ceren would ever wish upon anyone—not even Julian, the Light Draíolon who had teased her ruthlessly for years when they were younglings.

Ceren gently laid the cool, moist cloth across Evelayn's eyes, and her friend sighed in relief, blindly reaching out to grab Ceren's hand.

"I don't know how I'm going to defeat him," Evelayn finally whispered, her voice broken. "Even if we plan everything perfectly, it still falls to me to do it. I'm the only one with enough power to kill another royal."

Ceren squeezed her hand tightly. "You can do it, Ev. I know you can. You reclaimed our magic, didn't you? You harnessed the power of the sun! Surely this can't be harder than that."

Evelayn suddenly shot straight up, the cloth falling to her lap. "The power of the sun," she repeated. "That's it!"

"It is?"

"Oh, Ceren, you're a genius!"

"I am? I mean, yes, I am. But just for the sake of argument, why, exactly, am I a genius?"

But Evelayn had jumped to her feet and rushed over to her wardrobe. "Hurry, help me put on a dressing gown or something. I have an idea."

"I thought you had a headache . . ."

"There's no time for headaches. I must reconvene the war council."

"Now?"

"Yes, *now.*"

Ceren shook her head, but hurried over to help Evelayn get dressed once again.

TWENTY

THE DIMMING LIGHT OF DUSK CREPT THROUGH THE west windows of the council room. It had been a week since Evelayn had come up with her idea to defeat King Bain, but they were no closer to figuring out exactly *how* to pull off her plan than they had been seven days earlier.

"He'd never fall for that. Bain would scent the other Draíolon and recognize the trap." General Kel was arguing with Olena—again. Every time someone presented a new idea for how to ensnare King Bain long enough for Evelayn to follow through with her part, someone would inevitably point out why it was flawed or wouldn't work at all.

Evelayn's headache had become a nightly nuisance. And daily, too, if she was being totally honest with herself.

Caedmon had told them he had a falconry and would send one of his personal falcons as soon as he knew any more details of King Bain's plan. Since his birds weren't magical, they were capable of crossing the barrier the priestesses were upholding at the border of the two king-doms, to deliver messages back and forth. There was still a risk of it being intercepted, so Caedmon and Evelayn had agreed on a code to use in their communications before he left.

But now she lived in fear of receiving his message and learning their time was running short. How soon would Bain orchestrate his attack? In a week? Two? Or perhaps months from now? She had no way of knowing. Not until Caedmon told her—*if* he told her. There were still those who thought she had made a grave mistake placing her trust in him.

"Perhaps we should end early tonight," someone suddenly cut in to the ongoing argument.

Evelayn looked up to see Lord Teslar watching her shrewdly.

"I believe we're all exhausted and could use a good night's rest," he continued. "Maybe then we can come at this problem with fresh perspective tomorrow?"

"I agree," Evelayn immediately upheld the suggestion before anyone could dissent. They'd been up so late every night, after meeting throughout the day as well, that she hadn't had the energy or time to run since before her mother's death. She desperately needed the chance to clear her head and exercise away some of the worry and stress that hovered over her, tightening the hold on her lungs and stomach until she nearly always felt short of breath and her appetite was mostly gone.

There was a murmur of agreement from the long, rectangular table where all the top generals, lords, and High Priestesses who had been invited to the meetings sat. Only those she trusted the most—or whom her mother had trusted, as was the case with Lord Teslar.

How had he known that she'd needed a break? There was no mistaking the timing of his suggestion, coinciding with the exact moment she'd squeezed her eyes shut against the onslaught of another skull-splitting headache. But she thought she'd been subtle about it. His son Quinlen, who shared his father's shrewd green-eyed gaze, and Ceren had been spending quite a bit of time together recently, if what Ceren told her at night when Evelayn collapsed into bed was true. Perhaps her friend had confided her worries to Quinlen, who had then told his father?

Regardless, she was grateful for the respite as they all stood up and went their separate ways.

Evelayn had included Lord Tanvir despite her conflicted feelings about him—General Kelwyn had chosen him to help train her for a reason, he was the High Lord of the Delsachts, and she did trust him to look out for her well-being, if nothing else. He was nearly to the door when she called out, "Lord Tanvir, if you would, I'd have a word with you before you go."

He immediately froze and turned, bending into a deep bow. "As you wish, Your Majesty."

Oh, how she *hated* when he used her title. Especially *that* one. But then again, they were not in private and he was nothing to her—wasn't he? So what else was to be expected?

High Priestess Teca shot her a glance, but Evelayn stood tall. She didn't need to offer an excuse to speak to one of the council members alone.

Once everyone had left and the door shut, Tanvir took a hesitant step toward her and then stopped again. She was getting better and better at recognizing and deciphering scents, especially for Draíolon whom she knew well. And she knew him as well as she knew most, other than Ceren, now that her parents were both gone. That, combined with her growing mastery of the Light Power, which allowed her to sense her subjects' emotions—at least a little bit—made her fairly certain he was nervous. Even anxious.

Perhaps he did care for her, after all.

"I'm sure you're wondering why I asked to speak to you, my lord," she began, "especially after our, um, last conversation." Her neck warmed at the reminder of the terrible night on the turret when he'd rejected her. He opened his mouth, so she quickly barreled on before he could say anything. "Seeing that I am apparently going to be able to retire at a normal time tonight, and assuming that I am actually able to sleep, I wish to run in the morning. Regardless of the uncertain nature of our association with each other at this point, I would still rather run with you than be trailed by my sentries. Are you still willing to go with me?"

Tanvir's eyes had grown wider throughout her little speech, but he immediately said, "Yes, of course," and the freshness of relief immediately replaced the sharp anxiety that had discolored his scent. "Are you sure having just me will be enough assurance of your safety, now that you are the queen?"

"If it was enough for the princess, I don't see why it should be any different for the queen. We haven't heard from Caedmon, so we know King Bain isn't going to attack tomorrow. It should be fine."

"As long as we can trust him," Tanvir pointed out.

"I don't have any other choice. If I can't trust him, then we have no hope of ever defeating Bain."

Tanvir was quiet for a moment. "For what it's worth, I think you made the right choice. I believe he will come through for us."

There was a loud knock at the door and then Aunt Rylese burst into the room, looking faintly scandalized. "My dear Evelayn, there you are. When everyone else from the council meeting showed up to dinner except for you and Lord Tanvir, I knew it would be best to come in search to make sure everything is quite all right." She shot Tanvir a disapproving glare.

Evelayn managed to hold back her sigh of frustration—barely. By the Light, she was the *queen* now. At what point would Rylese quit her hovering and worrying? Though it had no doubt offended her aunt sorely, there was a reason Evelayn hadn't included her in the council meetings.

"Thank you, Aunt. We were just finishing discussing a specific point of preparation I've asked Lord Tanvir to oversee. He will join you at dinner shortly, I'm sure."

"And you?" Aunt Rylese pressed.

"I will dine in my room tonight. I'm afraid I have a rather violent headache."

"But—everyone is hoping to see you!"

"And I am deeply sorry, but I must take advantage of the meeting ending at this hour and go rest. Please send my apologies to all those gathered and assure them that we are working toward a way to guarantee peace for our kingdom again." Guilt over not making an appearance to help calm her subjects only worsened the pounding in her head.

Aunt Rylese was apparently quite appalled at her lack of fortitude as well, for she harrumphed loudly and spun on her heel to storm out of the room, pausing only to flick her wrist at Tanvir.

"Come along then, my lord. We'll let Her *Majesty* get her rest."

When the door had shut behind them, Evelayn plunked down into the nearest chair and let her head drop forward onto her crossed arms on the table. She would wait just a moment to let them get ahead of her and then she would sneak up to her room before anyone else could waylay her.

A loud crash of thunder startled Evelayn and she jumped, only to half fall out of the chair she still sat in. Her neck and back were stiff and her right arm was entirely asleep, her hand numb. The council room was darkened, with the occasional flash of lightning illuminating the abandoned table and chairs. She was completely disoriented.

Why hadn't anyone come looking for her, or woken her up? How long had she been asleep in the council room, with her head on the table?

Evelayn stood up, her body protesting the movement, but froze when lightning struck yet again—a blinding flash of light. The outline of the windows was burned onto her retinas, along with what had looked like a dark bird, careening wildly through the gusting wind and rains of the cloudburst. But when she blinked and squinted into the darkness, there was no sign of a bird. Had she imagined it? Or had Caedmon come through with a message after all?

It could just be a bird from the forest, she chided herself. Though it would mean that her time to figure out a plan was short, she longed to have a message arrive—to prove she hadn't misplaced her trust.

Evelayn waited for the next flash, but when it came, there was nothing there but an empty, rain-drenched courtyard and the swaying trees beyond.

With a shake of her head, Evelayn turned and exited the room, passed the Light Sentries who waited on either side of the door, to hurry to her room, and nearly ran directly into High Priestess Teca.

"Your Majesty." Teca seemed far less surprised to see Evelayn than Evelayn was to see her, which led her to believe the High Priestess had been standing in the hallway the entire night waiting for her to emerge. "If we might have a private word?"

Evelayn wanted nothing more than to climb into her bed and try to rest as much as possible before meeting Lord Tanvir in the morning for their run, but instead she sighed. "Of course."

They went back into the darkened room, shutting the Light Sentries out.

"I am sure you wish to retire to your quarters, as do I, so I will make this brief and to the point," Teca began. "You are now the queen of Éadrolan, and the only royal left with the ability to act as the conduit for the Light Power."

"Yes . . ."

"Normally you would be considered far too young to broach such things, but bearing in mind the direness of our situation, there's no avoiding the issue."

Another flash of lightning illuminated the stern downturn of Teca's mouth.

"I'm afraid I don't understand." Evelayn tried not to let her irritation bleed into her tone, but she was too drained to summon her usual mask of geniality. "What are you saying?"

"You need to be Bound and produce an heir. And quickly."

Evelayn's irritation flared into anger in the blink of an eye but she bit it back through sheer force of will. "Excuse me, but I don't think it is your place—"

"It *is* my place, because you are the queen," Teca cut her off. "If something happens to you before you have a daughter, there will be no one left who could reclaim our power. None of us knows what would happen to Éadrolan, Lachalonia, and even the world beyond ours if that happened."

A sudden clap of thunder accentuated Teca's words, rattling the windowpanes with its ferocity.

"Even if I were to be Bound *tomorrow* and impregnated immediately following the ceremony, I wouldn't be able to give birth to an heir before facing Bain." Evelayn's voice was practically strangled from the effort of holding her anger in check.

"That may be true, but—"

"So I will ask you to allow me to focus on the problems immediately at hand," Evelayn continued over Teca's protest, "and refrain from adding unnecessary pressure to the situation." Even as the words came out, she knew they made her sound like a youngling.

"You are the *queen* now, Evelayn. 'Pressure' is guaranteed to be your constant companion. You'd best find a way to deal with it, no matter how great it becomes."

"That is quite *enough*." Evelayn held one hand up, palm flattened toward Teca. "There is nothing I can do about being Bound at this moment, or about providing an heir. Our only hope is for me to focus on surviving Bain's attack and somehow defeating him. Then I can worry about that."

"If you don't succeed, there won't be anything *to* worry about."

Evelayn turned on her heel and flung the door open. "Good night, High Priestess."

Teca stiffened at the dismissal but then strode toward the Light Sentries who still stood guard in the hallway. "This discussion is not over, Your Highness."

Evelayn waited for the older Draíolon to disappear around the corner before allowing her shoulders to sag slightly. She understood Teca's fear, but it was too late now. Even if there were time, who would she possibly hope to be Bound to? The memory of the near-kiss on the turret with Tanvir flashed through her mind, but she quickly forced it away.

No, she told herself firmly as she finally made her way to her quarters and her bed. *Do as you told Teca. Focus on the problems at hand. Focus on surviving.* Because if she didn't, Teca was right. There was no one else to reclaim the power, not even an infant who could one day grow up and travel to the Immortal Tree.

If she failed, the Light Draíolon were doomed.

TWENTY-ONE

EVELAYN SLEPT UNEASILY, WAKING EVERY HOUR OR SO, vacillating between nightmares and thinking she heard phantom knocks signaling that she had received a message from Caedmon. But no one came to summon her, and she reluctantly rose at dawn to put on her loose running pants and leather shoes. After quickly braiding her hair, Evelayn hurried out into the humid, gray morning. Her Light Sentries silently followed her down the stairs and into the courtyard where Lord Tanvir already waited in the mist, swinging his arms to loosen up. With Teca's words from the night before still ringing in her mind, Evelayn had to quell sudden nerves that sprang up when Tanvir glanced over and their eyes met.

"There's no need to accompany me." She turned to the sentries, trying to compose herself. "Lord Tanvir will run with me this morning."

"Your Majesty, our orders are to guard you at all times. We could lose our positions," one of them spoke up.

"I am your queen, and I say that I shall be quite safe with Lord Tanvir's protection. We won't go far. We'll merely circle the castle a few times."

The sentry looked uneasy, but gave her a little bow. "If you insist, Your Highness."

"I do." Evelayn smiled to ease the severity of her tone and then turned to where Tanvir stood.

"Shall we?"

"After you." He gestured for her to lead and she took off toward the trees.

The breeze was still brisk from the storm the night before, the sky dark with clouds and the air thick with mist and fog. The soggy ground sucked at their soft boots and soon they were both mud-spattered and damp, but as their feet pounded in synchronization, Evelayn finally felt as though she could breathe fully for the first time in days . . . maybe even longer. She hadn't felt this calm since before the last time she'd gone running, that sun-drenched morning when her power had surged out of her body and she'd understood what had happened to her mother.

They silently dashed through the forest, a bit slower than normal because of the weather and mud, but still, she was running. Evelayn's muscles burned from disuse and she gloried in the pain. It was a pain she could control and conquer. Unlike the jagged wound that was her mother's death, or the pressing burden of needing to somehow defeat Bain, save her kingdom, and not leave it without an heir.

Ahead of them a dark bird swooped between two trees, reminding her of the one she thought she'd seen in the flash of lightning. Its cry echoed through the fog, taunting Evelayn. "Sneaky bugger," she muttered. It had been silly to get her hopes up last night. Caedmon had only left a week ago. Who knew if he'd even made it back to King Bain's castle yet.

"What did you say?" Tanvir asked from where he kept stride just behind her.

"Nothing," Evelayn said more loudly.

"Do you mind if we rest a moment? I need a drink of water."

Evelayn slowed down and then stopped. They had circled the castle a couple of times already, making a wide loop through the surrounding forest, staying close to the trees and avoiding Solas, to the northwest of the castle, as well. It was difficult to tell exactly where they were with the thick fog obscuring their vision in all directions, and Evelayn shivered involuntarily, her mind going back to the last time they'd run—and been attacked. With everything that had come afterward, she'd completely forgotten about the three Dark Draíolon who had found them and tried to assassinate them both. Had they come through the Undead Forest, too? Had they been part of King Bain's plan—but failed?

"Are you cold?" Tanvir asked, holding out his flagon to her, when she shivered again.

"No." She took a quick drink of water and handed it back. "The fog just made me nervous, considering what happened last time we went running. Maybe it was a mistake not to bring my sentries, after all."

"We protected ourselves then, and we could do it again. But now you have a battalion patrolling the edge of the Undead Forest—no Draíolon should get through without our knowledge."

"True," Evelayn agreed, rolling her shoulders to relax slightly. She was overtired and overwrought—her nerves were always on edge.

"Your Maj—um, Evelayn." He quickly changed when she shot him a look. "Do you still wish me to call you by your given name when we're in private?"

"Of course."

"All right." He took a deep breath. "Evelayn, I had an idea this morning as I was getting ready to go running. It would be . . . risky. But I think it could work."

Evelayn's pulse leapt. She wasn't sure what she'd been expecting him to say, but that wasn't it. "How risky?"

"Very."

Evelayn pursed her lips. She didn't like the sound of *very risky*. But if it would work . . .

"Tell me."

"They'll never agree to this," Evelayn said with a shake of her head.

"You said it yourself, if we have no other choice, they'll have to agree to it."

They were quiet for a long moment as she studied the ground intently, not daring to meet his gaze. Finally, she spoke: "It will have to be me."

"*No.*" His response was immediate. "Absolutely not." Tanvir stepped in front of her, filling her vision. "I never intended it to be *you* who went. I'll go if you wish, but you must stay here where it's safe."

"Until Bain is defeated, safety is only an illusion that we comfort ourselves with to sleep at night." Evelayn wrapped her arms around herself. "She's an Ancient. If the legends are true, she has more power than any Draíolon other than a royal, and she hates to be disturbed. If I send someone in my stead, they could be tortured or killed for daring to enter her lair. It has to be me. I can't be the cause of any more death. Not when I could have prevented it."

She stared forward unseeingly and nearly jumped when Tanvir softly touched her chin, tilting her face to his.

"This was not what I intended when I decided to tell you my idea. I never would have brought it up if I thought you would take it upon yourself to do it."

"Then I'm glad you didn't think it through completely, because it *will* work. And so far, it's our only hope."

They stood so close together that she could feel his warm breath on her cheeks. But it was desperation that lurked in Tanvir's amber eyes, not desire, and his jaw tightened at her vehemence. "I'm sorry, Evelayn."

She pulled her face free from his grip. "Don't apologize again. I can't take it."

Tanvir reached out to cup her cheek, forcing her to turn back to him. Their gazes met and held. When he brushed his thumb across her lip, Evelayn's mouth parted involuntarily. She could barely draw breath into her lungs.

"That's not what I meant." His voice was even rougher than his skin. "By the Light, Ev, I've never felt *anything* like what I feel when I'm with you. I want you so much, it terrifies me. I want to make you happy . . . but I can't. As much as I wish I could, I know—"

"*Stop,*" Evelayn spoke against his thumb, which still lingered at the corner of her mouth. "Stop telling me that you know better than I do what would make me happy or not. My whole life, everyone has always told me what I can or can't do—what will make me happy or not. Or rather, what will make my people happy or not. Can't I just have *this*? This one thing, with you, that's just for *me*?"

"Evelayn," her name was a low growl deep in his throat, a husky sound that sent a corresponding reverberation through her body. He closed his eyes briefly, his fingers stroking down her cheek. Waves of longing spread down her neck to the rest of her body. "Forgive me," he whispered. "Forgive me."

"For wha—"

Evelayn's question was cut short when Tanvir's mouth closed over her own. She froze in shock—hardly able to believe he'd truly done it—and he immediately pulled back.

"Was I wrong to—I thought—"

"Yes! I mean, no. I mean . . . Just kiss me again."

Tanvir lifted his other hand so that he cradled her face in both hands, and this time slowly leaned in until his lips barely brushed hers, a tender, hesitant kiss that stole her breath and made her ache for more. She grabbed his hips to steady herself. He kissed her again, longer this time, his mouth moving over hers. His hands dropped to wrap around her, pulling her closer, so their bodies melded together. Evelayn gripped his tunic as his hands roamed over her back and hips, pressing her into his chest, his stomach. A strange power—different from her Light Power—grew within Evelayn; a heated, grasping need that urged her to get closer to Tanvir, even though they were already clutching each other, their kissing turning fevered in the misty morning.

The cry of a bird nearby startled Evelayn back to reality, and with a gasp she broke from Tanvir's embrace. She turned away, breathing more heavily than if they'd been running the entire time. Her lips felt swollen when she lifted her fingers and pressed them against her mouth, still slightly stunned.

"Ev . . . was I wrong to . . ."

She shook her head, still trying to regain control of herself. It wasn't an everyday occurrence that she was the one barely able to catch her breath. Finally, she faced Tanvir again. His eyebrows were pulled down in concern and she couldn't resist teasing him—at least a little.

"I forgive you, by the by."

Tanvir's eyes widened. "For which part?"

"For not kissing me on the turret. You were right. I wanted a distraction, but it wasn't the right time."

"Oh. Well, um, thank you?"

Evelayn smiled at him and then laughed—the first time she'd laughed in over a week. "Thank *you*. Despite what you may think, you make me *very* happy, Lord Tanvir."

His answering smile was rather shaky. "You make me happy, too, little though I may deserve it."

Evelayn took his hand in hers, lacing her fingers through his, reveling in the satisfaction that came from feeling free to do so—at least in private. "Goodness, my lord, if you keep sounding so grim, I'm going to start to think the worst of you."

"Perhaps you should," he muttered. "I've seen things . . . done things . . . that I'm not proud of, Evelayn. War is a cruel master and it can make beasts of us all."

Evelayn's smile slipped. She stepped closer to Tanvir and imitated what he'd done earlier—cupping his chin in her hand and forcing him to look at her. "I know you had to fight in some terrible battles. You actually saw the people you love die in front of you. It was a mercy that I wasn't there when my parents were killed, I know that. I don't hold any of it against you, Tanvir. You've done what you had to do to survive—to lead your battalion. I understand that."

A muscle jumped beneath her hand where his teeth clenched. He didn't speak, just shook his head slightly. She peered at him, almost certain it looked like his eyes glistened with suppressed tears. But then he bent forward and pressed his lips to hers again. This time his kiss felt almost desperate, as if he were suffocating and she was his only air. She clung to him, holding him tightly, wishing she could absorb his pain and grief, to take it away from him and allow him his happiness.

He pulled away first this time. Before she could say anything else, he glanced up at the sky. "We should get back. They'll never let me run with you again if we're late for the meeting."

Evelayn sighed. "Are you certain we can't just stay here the rest of the day? I rather prefer *this* kind of meeting."

Tanvir laughed softly.

"No, I know, don't say it. You're right. Let's go." Evelayn gestured for him to lead this time. She followed Tanvir back to the castle, her lips still burning with the memory of his kiss.

TWENTY-TWO

THE GARDENS WERE STILL DAMP, THE JEWEL-COLORED flowers dappled with drops of dew and their perfume heavy on the humid air as Ceren ambled down the path. Beside her, Quinlen was quieter than usual. They'd been meeting to go for walks in the morning for the past few days. She wasn't fool enough to go dashing through the forest at breakneck speeds like Evelayn. She much preferred walking—and speaking—to her companions.

"I waited for Evelayn last night as long as possible," Ceren had told him when he'd asked how the young queen was after a good night's rest. "But she never came up to her room, and my mother is getting irritated with me being out so late with her. I had to retire to my quarters. I'm not sure where she was."

"I'll ask around quietly. I hope she was able to get the sleep she needed," Quinlen had responded.

"She must have, if she got up to run this morning."

He'd nodded, but they'd fallen silent and hadn't spoken again since.

"Is it very difficult?" Ceren finally asked, when they'd begun their second loop of the gardens, unable to stand the silence any longer.

"What?"

"Being here? Instead of at the warfront. Or do you prefer the peace of the castle to the fighting?"

Quinlen was quiet for a long moment, contemplating. He had a habit of thinking over his answers, responding thoughtfully—carefully. He was so different from Ceren, but she was fascinated by it . . . by *him*, if she was truly honest with herself. She'd never known someone who was so methodical and calm.

"I much prefer peace, although I do sometimes feel less . . . useful here than I did on the warfront. And there's no comfort in knowing that the peace here is not permanent—that I must soon prepare myself to face the battlefield once more."

Ceren nodded. "I think I understand what you mean." The stones were slippery from the mist and rain, and as her attention was fixated on him, Ceren didn't notice the uneven edge until it was too late. She tripped, twisting her ankle just enough to send her careening forward.

Quinlen grabbed her elbow and yanked her back; she crashed into his chest, his arms going around her to steady her, so she didn't tumble to the ground.

Ceren's face burned hot as she regained her balance. Quinlen released her, except for one hand still on her elbow when she stepped back.

"Well, that was nicely done." She tried to laugh off her humiliation.

"Perhaps it would help if you take my arm?" He let go of her to offer his elbow, and she gratefully tucked her hand into it.

"Well, maybe it was nicely done, after all." This time her laugh was genuine, and Quinlen joined her.

"You didn't have to go to such drastic measures to get me to offer you my arm."

"I'll bear that in mind next time." Ceren shook her head at herself and was about to ask him if he planned on attending any of the meals in the dining hall that day, when Evelayn and Tanvir burst out of the trees across the courtyard from them, sprinting to the castle.

Quinlen and Ceren stopped short, watching them dart across the lawn. They were both so intent on their goal, neither noticed the couple in the garden watching them race past.

"Well, she seems to be in better spirits," Quinlen commented.

"Yes, she does," Ceren agreed, watching Evelayn with narrowed eyes. She looked better than she had in . . . well, since before her mother's death. There was color in her cheeks, her eyes were bright, and she'd been smiling.

"Do you wish to continue on, or head in to break our fast?"

Ceren forced herself to turn back to Quinlen. "Let's walk a little bit more. Then we can go in. I'm not sure I want to face my mother just yet."

He laughed with her again as they resumed their walk, but Ceren couldn't get the look on Evelayn's face as she'd run by out of her mind. If she didn't know better, Ceren would have thought she looked . . . happy.

She didn't care how mad it made her mother, tonight she was waiting until Evelayn showed up.

"Absolutely not! It's out of the question."

General Olena's outburst wasn't unexpected, and she wasn't the only one who had reacted badly to Tanvir's idea—even though Evelayn was the one to present it.

"Your plan is to petition *Máthair Damhán*? It would be a suicide mission. We only have one Royal left. If we agree to try this plan, there is no way the queen will be the one to go," Lord Teslar agreed.

High Priestess Teca shot a pointed look at Evelayn.

"The queen is sitting right here, and she is perfectly capable of hearing you," Evelayn bit out, her patience growing thin. "Listen, all of you." She raised her voice to a near shout over her council, until they fell silent and turned to her. "I know that it would be incredibly dangerous. But I am the only one who can do it. A queen or king is the only one with enough power to pose a threat to her—I'm the only one who could hope to walk into her lair and not be killed immediately."

"No, not immediately. Perhaps she'd let you *think* you'd survive," General Olena griped.

Evelayn was getting very irritated with the woman her mother had placed in charge of the armies when she'd forced Kel to stay at the castle. She took a deep breath to calm her rising temper. "What possible purpose could she have for killing me? If she did, there would be no successor to the Light Throne, and the power would be uneven indefinitely. Surely an Ancient knows and understands the need for balance."

General Kelwyn spoke up next. "This bears more thought and

careful consideration. I, too, am deeply concerned at the prospect of sending our queen to do this. But if she succeeded . . . the silk from Máthair Damhán *would* be the perfect trap. If we used it correctly, Bain wouldn't be able to scent or see it. If we could somehow ensnare him using the silk, Queen Evelayn would have the opportunity she needed."

"I just need to bring her something worth bargaining for—something she'd want desperately," Evelayn supplied.

"What could an Ancient possibly need from us?" Lord Teslar piped up again.

"I don't know—yet," Evelayn added quickly. "But we'll figure something out. The priestesses at the Dawn Temple can search all the texts they have on the Ancients to see if they can discover something useful."

"And you plan on getting to her . . . how?" General Olena pressed. "Her lair is on the northern side of the Sliabán Mountains. In *Dorjhalon*."

Lord Tanvir spoke up for the first time. "We'd have to sneak into Dorjhalon and travel to her lair."

"Oh, is that all? Just sneak into Dorjhalon?" Lord Teslar scoffed simultaneously to General Olena bursting out, "*We?* Does that mean you intend to accompany her on this ill-fated mission?"

Evelayn held up her hand to prevent General Olena from saying anything else. "Nothing has been decided yet, including who would accompany me if I went. I want you all to think on this today and we will reconvene tomorrow morning to discuss it further. But give it an objective, thoughtful analysis. We have to destroy Bain somehow to restore peace. We all know that in a fight he would kill me. He's too experienced, too powerful. My only hope is setting our own trap for him, something that gives me the upper hand. I can harness the power of the sun and call it down to consume him—but I need him to be immobilized first, at least momentarily. This is the only solution any of us has come up with that could work. There is nothing lighter or stronger than Máthair Damhán's silk. If I somehow got Bain to chase me right into it, he would be trapped for at least a few moments before he could free himself. That's all I need."

Evelayn made herself sound much more confident than she felt. She didn't dare look at High Priestess Teca, who could have called her bluff. It had taken her longer than a few moments to harness and call down the beam of sunlight that had taken her mother away. But she could practice. She had a *little* time . . . she hoped.

"Until tomorrow then?" She rose before anyone else could voice any other negative opinions, and everyone grudgingly followed suit. Evelayn's gaze strayed to Tanvir, who nodded encouragingly at her, even though she knew he didn't want her to go any more than anyone else in that room did. But her duty was to do everything in her power to protect her people—and for the first time, she at least had *hope* of succeeding. And if she failed, well, it wouldn't be any worse than not having tried. Bain would get to her eventually, and as she'd admitted, she had no hope of surviving a direct confrontation with him.

She could do this. She *had* to do this.

There was no other option.

TWENTY-THREE

THE SUN HAD LONG SINCE BURNED OFF THE MIST AND fog of the morning, and the air had turned humid and hot as Evelayn made her way through the forest to the grove where her father was buried and the ring of stones stood in memory of her mother. Her ever-present sentries kept a respectful distance, allowing her to enter the clearing alone.

Every monarch picked where they wanted their final resting place to be; her parents had picked this grove because it was where they'd met and where her father had eventually asked Ilaria to be Bound to him. As Evelayn silently moved toward the stones, she tried to imagine them when they were young and falling in love.

She knelt down at the head of the ring of stones where her mother's body had been laid out—the same place where she'd stood to call down the power of the sun.

Did you mean what you said that day—if that was truly you? she asked in her mind, not even daring to whisper in case the sentries had better hearing than most. *You said I was born to do what you couldn't, to bring peace to Lachalonia. But I don't know if I can do this. I'm scared, Mama.*

Evelayn tilted her head up to the sunshine that washed over her from above, trying to convince herself that the warmth and comfort it gave her was her mother's way of holding her close from where she was, high above her daughter in the Final Light.

Please help me. Help me protect our people. Help me succeed.

Evelayn knelt there silently for a long time, letting the sunshine press her in its golden embrace, but when the tears felt perilously close to rising to the surface, she finally stood and turned away, back toward the forest, her sentries, and the castle.

She still had no answers, but she felt a little bit better. At the very least, seeing the still-blackened stones had been a reminder that she was capable of calling down the sun.

Evelayn slowly meandered toward the castle, in no hurry to rush back to the concerns and scrutiny of her court. Perhaps she could quickly go visit the swans. She hadn't been to her lake since the night of her birthday, nor had she tried to shift, with all else that she'd had to deal with.

Evelayn changed course, heading to the lake, and was nearly there when she heard someone approaching from behind. Nerves ever on edge, she whirled, only to see Ceren walking toward her.

"Thank the Light, it's you."

"Who did you expect?" Ceren laughed as she got closer. "Certainly not Tanvir, based on the petrified look on your face. Pretty sure *that's* not the response he would elicit."

"I was *not* petrified. And regardless, I'm not sure I know what you mean," Evelayn hedged, hurrying toward her swans and away from Ceren's knowing grin.

"I'm not sure I do either, since I haven't had a chance to ask you what happened in the forest this morning with a certain handsome lord who is so besotted with you, he continues to be willing to torture himself by chasing you at all hours of the day and night."

"Nothing happened." Evelayn sat down heavily on her log, not even sure why she was trying to hide the kiss from Ceren. Perhaps because it was still so new and she hadn't even had time to process it herself yet?

"You know I can scent your guilt, right? Tell me the truth." Ceren sat down next to her.

"I liked it better when we were younglings. At least then you couldn't smell when I lied to you."

"Is lying to me such a common problem?"

Evelayn laughed in spite of herself. "No. But it's rather inconvenient currently."

They were quiet for a moment and then Ceren said, "You don't have to tell me, if you don't want to. I honestly didn't mean to make you feel uncomfortable."

"You didn't! It's not that." Evelayn shifted on the log, watching the flock of swans glide through the center of the lake, surprisingly not frightened of all the noise they were making. She kept her eyes on the birds as she admitted, "He kissed me."

Ceren squealed and the swans shuffled their wings nervously. "I knew it had to be something good! I've never seen you glowing like that before."

"Glowing like *what*? When?" Evelayn finally turned to Ceren.

"I saw you two running back to the castle. You were so wrapped up in each other, you didn't even notice me and Quinlen in the gardens. Or anyone else, for that matter."

Evelayn groaned. "Well, that's lovely. So everyone knows?"

"Goodness no. I'm the only one who knows you well enough to have noticed exactly how happy you were. I'm sure everyone else thought it was merely from getting out to run again," Ceren assured her. "Even Quinlen only commented that you seemed to be in better spirits."

"Which brings up the question—why were you in the gardens with Quinlen?" Evelayn deflected the focus of the conversation.

"Oh, we just walk together in the mornings sometimes. Nothing exciting like you."

"But you do care for him. I can tell." Evelayn pressed Ceren with a smile.

Ceren shrugged but she couldn't keep from smiling, too. "Well, yes. I do. But I'm not sure if he's actually interested or only looking for easy companionship. Or perhaps he thinks I'm a way to you."

"I guarantee that's not it at all. He's never even tried to speak to me, other than brief formalities. He's interested in you. And I promise to watch for you next time, so I can see for myself."

"I appreciate that," Ceren reached out and patted Evelayn's hand, "but you're not getting out of telling me exactly what happened this morning. You don't have to be the queen when you're with me, you know. You can just be a young Draíolon who's falling in love and needs to talk to her closest friend about it."

"Who said anything about love? I never said that," Evelayn protested. But of course as soon as Ceren brought it up, it was all she could think about. Was *that* what she felt for Tanvir?

"I know you, Ev. You won't even let a male Draíolon kiss your hand unless you truly care for him, let alone anywhere on your *face*."

Evelayn was quiet. It was true, she guarded herself against every-one, especially any male who showed interest in her. But with Tanvir, it was different. She *wanted* him to touch her, she wanted to be close to him. She wanted to talk to him, and see him, and kiss him. But she didn't dare call it love—not yet. Maybe not ever. Love meant forever. It meant Binding herself to someone—if she was lucky and if he loved her back. Love was what her parents had shared.

Ceren watched her, waiting patiently for her to gather her thoughts.

"I'm not really sure why I feel differently with him . . . but I do." Evelayn couldn't look at her friend as she haltingly began to tell her some of what had happened that morning. Not even Ceren needed to know *every* detail.

She'd just reached the point when they kissed the second time, when her sharp hearing caught the soft footfalls of someone hurrying toward them.

"Your Majesty." A messenger burst through the trees just as Evelayn stood and turned to face whoever was coming. "A note arrived for you. At the castle."

Evelayn's pulse skipped a beat.

"General Kelwyn told me to fetch you, that it was urgent."

Evelayn glanced apologetically at Ceren, who still sat on the log.

"Go," Ceren said with a rueful smile. "Now you must return to being the queen."

"We'll talk more later?" Evelayn asked and Ceren nodded.

She could only think of one message that would be so urgent—it had to be from Caedmon.

TWENTY-FOUR

Lorcan's mother had just left the room a couple of minutes earlier when there was another knock. The door opened, without waiting for his approval, to reveal Lothar in her stead.

Lorcan resumed polishing the sword he'd been working on, not acknowledging his brother. They hadn't spoken much since their father's plan had proven successful and he'd killed Queen Ilaria.

Well, the first part of his plan, rather. Nothing had gone right after that, and they'd all suffered the brunt of the king's wrath since.

Just a little bit longer, he reminded himself.

The door shut with a dull click, and Lothar moved to sit down in the chair across from him. All Lorcan's weapons were laid out on the table. He didn't need them in a fight very often—if ever—but for some reason it had always been calming to him to hold real steel in his hands, to sharpen the blades, to polish them until they gleamed. The solid weight and the repetitive motions helped clear his mind.

"You could tell me," Lothar finally spoke, but Lorcan continued to ignore him. "You could try actually *trusting* me."

Lorcan set down the sword and picked up a dagger—one of a matched pair—and began to work on it. There was nothing to say to his brother. A part of him hated what all this was doing to them, but it didn't matter. Everything had already been set into motion and soon, *soon*, it would finally be done.

"Look at me!" Lothar suddenly bellowed, slamming his fist on the table. Lorcan flinched at the unexpected outburst but kept his eyes trained on the dagger. The edge was sharp enough to slice through flesh with the barest amount of pressure. If he wasn't careful, he could cut his finger off.

The draw of magic was so sudden and fast, he barely had a chance to glance up before the blast of shadow struck him square in the chest, knocking him and the chair over backward. His head cracked against the floor, softened partially by the dark gray fur rug. He lay there for a moment stunned, staring at the dark ceiling. Had *Lothar* truly just done that? His flesh burned and he glanced down to see a bloody hole in his tunic right over his sternum.

Lothar shoved his chair back and stormed over to tower above him, the blood-red conduit stone in his forehead catching Lorcan's attention. It was often easy to forget that his brother also had the ability to become the king and conduit for the Dark Power. That he could become very dangerous if he ever chose to make an effort.

Lorcan could have jumped to his feet, or shifted and attacked back. But instead he just stared at his brother, waiting for his body to begin to heal.

"I know you are planning something," Lothar spoke quietly, his voice cold. "But you don't have to do this. Together, we could . . ."

"Together we could . . . *what*?" When Lothar trailed off Lorcan finally sat up, his tone mocking. "What is it you think *we* could do? Are you suggesting treason—or worse?"

Lothar's neck flushed red but he didn't back down. "Father is just using you. He manipulates you into doing what—"

"You think I don't know that?" Lorcan hissed, glancing meaningfully toward the door, a subtle reminder to keep their voices down. He slowly stood up, taking his time until he was practically nose to nose with his younger—and slightly smaller—brother, glowering down at him. "*I* am not planning anything."

"I'm not as naïve as you all assume I am. Nor am I as weak as you treat me."

Lorcan had to give Lothar credit—his brother had taken him by surprise, something that was difficult to do. And he still wasn't backing down. But Lothar had no idea what was truly at work, what had already been set into motion.

"What is it you want, Lothar? Peace? To overthrow our father and go to the new queen and beg her forgiveness for killing her parents? Then we can all join hands and dance merrily all together, just in time for Summer Solstice, drunk with relief, right?" The words were scornful, spat at Lothar in a furious whisper. "Go back to your books and your worthless dreams and let me handle reality."

Lothar stared at him for a long moment, until the anger in his eyes cooled into something worse—pity. "You don't have to do it, Lorc. Whatever it is they're trying to get you to do. You don't have to be their pawn."

"I am *no one's* pawn," Lorcan growled. "Now go, before I decide not to be so forgiving and pay you back for this." He gestured at the partially healed wound on his chest. "You ruined one of my favorite shirts."

Lothar's lips tightened into a thin line, but he finally nodded and strode past his brother. Lorcan heard the twist of the handle, but Lothar paused before opening the door.

"If you ever change your mind, I will always be here for you. Just like I always have been."

Only after the door shut and the sound and scent of his brother had gone did Lorcan relax his grip on the dagger he still held and let the anger he'd summoned seep out, leaving him cold and deflated.

He shucked off his shirt and tossed it onto the ashes in the hearth.

Though Lorcan had denied it, Lothar was closer to the truth than he realized. *A pawn.* A piece in an ever-changing game, moved and utilized at everyone's will but his own.

Not forever, he promised himself as he sat down and went back to polishing the dagger. Some of his blood had spattered on the blade.

Just one more scar among many.

Evelayn paced the council room, waiting for everyone to gather, a note clutched in her right hand. It had to be from Caedmon if it warranted reconvening the council when she hadn't planned on meeting again until the next morning. Though that's where Tanvir's focus *should* have been, the note and everything it meant was far from his thoughts. He watched her silently, trying to keep his emotions in check. Whenever he was near her his feelings were always in a tumult—but after that morning, it was worse than ever. The memory of kissing her was equal parts unimaginable joy and heartrending pain.

She was breathtakingly beautiful at first sight, but the more he got to know her—her strength, her humor and wit, her tenacity and grace—the more stunning she became, until she was nearly always on his mind, filling his thoughts during the day and his dreams at night. It was a cruel fate that had put her in his life *now*.

When High Priestess Teca came in and took her seat, the doors were shut and Evelayn turned to face them.

"I've received word from Caedmon," she began without preamble. Her expression was drawn but determined. "He made it back to Bain and confirmed the king's plans. He has decided to go through with it just as we were told, and intends to attack the week of summer solstice."

A few of the council members immediately began to murmur in disbelief, and even Tanvir felt gut-punched.

"That's so soon!"

"Impossible! He can't be *that* big a fool!"

But she wasn't done.

"He feels that is when we would be caught most unaware," Evelayn continued loudly, her voice cutting over the others. "He believes we'd never expect him to launch an attack during the week of our highest power." She paused, glancing down at the parchment she clutched. "I see no reason or benefit for Caedmon to deceive us in this. I trust him. And I move that we put our plan into action immediately. I can be ready to leave at first light."

There was an outburst of sound all around Tanvir, but he just sat in his chair stunned. Three weeks? He'd known this was coming—it was inevitable—but to only have three weeks to prepare?

She'll succeed, he assured himself. *That's the plan and it* will *work*.

"I volunteer to go with you," General Kelwyn stood from his spot beside Evelayn, and General Olena immediately jumped to her feet also.

"I offer my services as well."

"We still haven't agreed that *anyone* should go on this accursed mission, let alone the queen!" Lord Teslar burst out, also jumping to his feet.

"Enough!" Evelayn cried, but it was like a pebble dropping into a lake. The shouting and arguing continued, growing ever louder. Tanvir was on the edge of his seat, prepared to try and get everyone's attention for her when she shot a burst of light out of her hand to explode against the far wall with a loud boom.

"I said that's *enough*," she repeated coldly into the sudden silence.

All eyes were fixed on the queen, and one by one the council members all resumed their seats, some looking abashed and others—like General Olena—visibly irritated.

"I appreciate all your opinions and concerns. However, *I* am the queen of Éadrolan and I have made my decision. It is final."

Tanvir's heart beat faster in his chest as she stood tall at the head of the table, the sharp scent of her power still lingering around her.

"The silk is our only hope of defeating Bain, especially if we only have three weeks until he attacks. I will leave at dawn with General Kelwyn and Lord Tanvir, because they are both knowledgeable in this war and can keep up with me. General Olena and High Priestess, I leave it to you both to see to the preparations for the rest of the plan, so that when I return, we are prepared for Bain. Lord Teslar, I need you to take a message to the priestesses at the warfront and to all of the generals still stationed at the border. Everyone else assist those three as you best see fit." Evelayn looked around the table. "That is all. You are dismissed."

She turned on her heel and marched out of the room, leaving everyone at the table sitting in stunned silence.

Tanvir almost felt like applauding, but instead he merely stood up, bowed slightly to everyone else, and followed Queen Evelayn from the room.

General Kelwyn was already waiting for Evelayn the next morning when she reached the appointed spot in the courtyard, her pack strapped to her back and a full flagon of water at her side, but Tanvir wasn't there yet. She'd been hoping to see him alone first, as there had been no time to speak to him in private the night before; she'd been too busy preparing everything for her trip, including a plausible excuse to give the court for why their queen would be gone for a week.

In the end, Ceren had saved the day. She'd come up with an idea to claim that Evelayn needed a week to rest and mourn the loss of her mother in private, and would be accompanying Ceren to her family's holdings in Diasla—a city partway between Solas and the castle, and the Sliabán Mountains.

"Are you sure you're willing to leave the castle—and Quinlen— for an entire week?" Evelayn had questioned but Ceren had been immovable.

"This is far more important than a few walks around a garden or a shared meal or two. Of course I'm sure. Just as long as you promise not to get killed and to come back as quickly as possible." Ceren had waved her hand in the air, trying to sound blasé, but failing miserably when her eyes filled with tears.

Evelayn had hugged her then, trying to keep her own fears at bay. "Of course I promise. This week will be over before you know it, and then you can go back to arguing with your mother and flirting with a certain handsome Draíolon in the gardens each morning."

Ceren had responded with a watery laugh. "Sounds heavenly."

"It will be. Soon this will all be over and you will have a lifetime of walks in the garden to look forward to. No more attacks, no more war."

"Now *that* really does sound heavenly."

They'd hugged again and then Ceren had left to prepare her part of the plan.

"Where is Tanvir?" General Kelwyn's deep rumbling voice broke through Evelayn's thoughts and brought her back to the reality that if things went badly that very well may have been the last time she'd ever see Ceren.

No, she told herself viciously. *Don't even think that. This will work. It has to.*

She'd secured the offering from the priestesses in her pack; something as valuable as Máthair Damhán's silk.

"I'm sure he'll be here any moment." Evelayn turned to the castle, watching for his familiar frame to emerge. The sun had crept a bit higher in the sky when she began to feel uneasy. He was never late for their runs—why this morning?

Just when she was about to suggest they go looking for him, he rounded the corner, striding toward them in the burgeoning dawn, looking harried.

"I apologize most profusely," he began before he'd even reached them. "I had to finish taking care of a few pieces of business before I could go."

"What business could have been more important than this?"

Tanvir turned to Kel. "A few pressing matters with my family's holdings. Again, I apologize."

"It's fine. Let's go." Evelayn started to walk toward the forest north of the castle. "General Kelwyn has spent the night studying what route we should take, so he will take the lead for now. We must make up time this morning. When we stop to eat, he can fill us in on where to go, and thereafter we can take turns leading. The only way we are going to make it there and back in time is if we run as fast as we are able from sunup until sundown." She paused at the outskirts of the castle grounds and turned to Kel and Tanvir. "I know I've asked a lot of you both and I don't pretend that this is going to be easy."

"It's my pleasure to serve you, my queen." General Kelwyn pressed his fist to his chest and bowed to her.

"And mine, *Your Majesty*." Tanvir winked at her, so quickly she almost didn't catch it, before also bowing. With General Kel there, she realized he probably wouldn't dare use her given name.

That would make for an even longer week than she'd anticipated.

"Thank you, both. General, after you."

Kel straightened and then took off at a sprint, Evelayn at his heels and Tanvir taking up the back. They had three days to reach the border and cross into the southeastern tip of Dorjhalon near the Sliabán Mountains, one day to bargain, and three to return to the palace. It would only be possible with a grueling pace that most Draíolon couldn't maintain for one morning, let alone six out of seven days. But Tanvir and Kel weren't just any Draíolon. As the forest blurred around them, and the hours passed, Evelayn was more certain than ever that she'd made the right choice.

This will work. This will work. She chanted it to herself all morning and again during the afternoon, after they paused to quickly eat around midday, the sweat dripping down her face and spine as she sat on a fallen log.

By the time they finally stopped to set up camp for the night, shortly after the sun set and the forest had fallen into shadow, even Evelayn was gasping for air, her tunic soaked through. Tanvir had bent over to grasp his knees, trying to catch his breath while General Kel sat down to stretch on the mossy patch of ground they'd found in a small clearing where they could sleep.

When Evelayn had recovered slightly she began to search for kindling to start a fire.

"Your Majesty, please, let us do that," General Kelwyn protested, quickly rising to his feet.

"Kel, stop. I'm not going to sit here and watch you two wait on me hand and foot after running as hard as we did all day. I'm not your queen right now. We are a team and I will do my part."

He looked like he was about to argue, but when she glared at him, he shut his mouth and merely nodded.

"As you wish, Your Majesty."

"And no more of that while we're out here, either. My name is Evelayn."

"If you say so, Your Majesty."

She shook her head at the stubborn general and went back to collecting firewood, wandering between the trees a few lengths away from the clearing.

"Let me help you, *Your Majesty*," Tanvir's voice came from behind, soft and teasing. "Unless you wish for us to sit back and watch *you* wait on *us*. I could find a way in my heart to be satisfied with that arrangement."

Evelayn turned to face him, one eyebrow lifted. "Just for that, I will *let* you carry this load for me, *my lord*." She tossed him the armful of sticks and branches she'd collected, which he barely caught in time to avoid dropping them all over the forest floor.

"As you wish." He echoed what Kel had said earlier.

They fell quiet as she scoured the ground for more firewood and piled the viable options into his arms.

When they were some distance from Kel and the camp, Tanvir spoke again. "I still can't believe this is happening—that you're doing this. I never wanted to risk you this way."

"It was a good idea. *And* it was my choice to make. I have to do what I can. If this is the only chance of saving my kingdom . . . well, then . . ." She shrugged, even though her heart beat faster as she thought about the looming challenges ahead.

"Why do you have to do that?"

Evelayn paused, glancing over her shoulder at him. "Excuse me?"

Tanvir's expression hovered somewhere between exasperation and appreciation. "I don't even know how to describe it. You're stubborn and headstrong, but you're also so determined . . . so brave. I want to throttle you *and* kiss you—all at once."

He took a step toward her, a tendon in his jaw tightening.

"I'm not keen on the idea of being throttled." Evelayn stood frozen to the same spot, the soft earth compressing beneath her feet as he took another step closer. His familiar citrus and spice scent mingled with the musk of the damp soil and the fragrance of the flowers and plants surrounding her.

"Then stop being so frustrating."

Evelayn's heart thumped against her rib cage. "I'm not sure I know how."

Tanvir laughed softly, "Now *that* I believe."

He finally stopped when the load of wood he held was the only thing separating them. "If my arms weren't full of branches right now, I think I would be tempted to find a different use for them."

Evelayn's neck warmed and her belly tightened, but she tried to keep her expression placid. "I believe I already expressed my feelings about being throttled."

"And I believe that you are purposely trying to frustrate me now."

"I'm not sure that would be wise," Evelayn said lightly, belying the tumult inside her, but he must have scented her true feelings, because he growled softly, an almost animalistic sound. Her heart skipped up into her throat at the sudden fierceness of his expression, all the teasing wiped away.

"You really have no idea what you're doing to me, do you?" he rasped.

Evelayn swallowed, feeling somehow immobilized by his amber gaze, his eyes still shining brightly in the falling darkness. She took a deep breath to calm her trembling hands and caught a different but still familiar scent. Tanvir must have noticed at the same time she did, because he quickly took two steps back and turned away, just as Kel strode into the clearing.

His sharp gaze traveled between them, and Evelayn forced herself to adopt the composed mien she wore at the castle whenever she was in public, willing herself to be calm, to not give their still uncertain feelings away.

"That armful looks more than sufficient for one night," was all Kel finally said to Tanvir.

"I agree." Evelayn nodded at Kel and then began walking back to the camp. "We'd better hurry and get some rest. We should begin again at first light tomorrow."

She didn't glance back to see if the two males followed her or not.

TWENTY-FIVE

E VEN THOUGH THEY PUSHED THEMSELVES TO RUN AS
fast as possible, a building exhaustion slowly began to diminish
their pace so that they didn't reach the border until the end of
the third day. Evelayn had hoped to be at Máthair Damhán's lair by
then, and they were still a good day's travel from where the Ancient
lived in a cave in the Sliabán Mountains. The teasing of that first night
seemed a distant memory as tension coiled tighter and tighter around
the trio, a relentless and increasing pressure as every day brought them
closer to the summer solstice and Bain's attack.

Each day also brought an earlier dawn and a later sunset, so that
they were running the majority of the time, with only a few hours of
rest under the cover of night. By the time they reached the border, the
wear of the grueling task she'd set them had increased to the point that
the moment she finally halted at the edge of their kingdom, Evelayn's
muscles cramped in painful protest.

"Hopefully the message reached the priestesses in time," Tanvir commented, the first time he'd spoken in hours, as he pulled one foot back and stretched with a grimace.

"The wards are to prevent Draíolon from coming *in* to Éadrolan. Not to keep them from going out," Kel reminded them.

"That's what I'm worried about."

"It'll be fine," Evelayn finally cut in. "I can get us back in if the wards are still up when we return."

Tanvir and Kel both turned to her with eyebrows lifted. She smiled confidently at them though inside she was a mess of fear and uncertainty. The truth was that she didn't have a clue how to get past the wards. She could only hope the priestesses got the message in time—and that she and her companions made it to the lair and back in time to come through the gap that would only be opened for the brief window she had calculated they would need. And they were already taking longer than she'd anticipated.

They would have to make up time somehow.

There was a marked difference between the two kingdoms—making the border easy to recognize. Éadrolan was a riot of color: jeweled flowers and bursts of sunlight, emerald grasses and jade trees. Dorjhalon was just as lush, but it was shadowed, even in summer. The trees grew close, evergreen needles weaving together into a nearly impenetrable wall at times, blocking much of the brightness of the sun. Even the bushes crowded in on one another. There were flowers, but they were muted compared to those in Éadrolan. Palest of pinks and deep, rich purple. Dusky whites that bordered on gray. And Evelayn's favorite—the wild black roses that grew in clumps throughout the Dorjhalon forests, with the crimson corollas at the center of the petals that looked like pricks of blood on velvet. Her father used to bring her bouquets of them as a child when he would visit Dorjhalon. Back when there had been peace and free travel between the two kingdoms.

Evelayn stared into the shadows of King Bain's kingdom and took a deep breath. They didn't have time to waste on apprehension. Her only option was to press forward. She closed her eyes as she stepped across the border into Dorjhalon, bracing for—she wasn't sure what. A shock? A wave of debilitating pain?

But nothing came. When she opened her eyes, she stood on Dorjhalon soil for the first time in her life.

Kel and Tanvir quickly followed. She turned to them and gestured. They nodded in unspoken agreement, and the trio took off running toward the east. It seemed dangerous to speak now, to risk alerting any Dark Draíolon to their presence.

They had to travel quickly. And silently.

The sun had set, throwing the forest into even darker shadow, when Kel finally spoke from behind Evelayn.

"We should stop. It'll be too dark to see soon."

But she ignored him—and the burn of her muscles—and kept going.

"Your Majesty," Kel's voice was strained. "Please."

But Evelayn pressed on. If they ran through the night, they could reach the lair by dawn. They could still negotiate for the silk and possibly get back to the border in time before the priestesses closed the gap.

Darkness fell faster in Dorjhalon, and it felt all-encompassing. Evelayn almost had to squint, sharpening her vision as much as possible, to keep from getting hit by wayward branches or tripping over roots. She'd heard that Dark Draíolon could see better at night than Light Draíolon could, which she supposed made sense, since it was the power of the darkness they wielded. Just as the brightness of the sun didn't bother her at all, but irritated the Dark Draíolon's eyes.

She felt someone closing in on her from behind and she kicked her heels up, pushing herself even faster. But whoever it was didn't give up. He grabbed her elbow and yanked them both to an abrupt halt.

Evelayn whirled to face Tanvir, who still gripped her arm.

A wave of anger rose, drawing with it a surge of power, making her stone burn hot in her sternum.

"We have to stop before someone gets hurt." Tanvir spoke quietly but urgently. "Or worse." He gestured behind them and Evelayn looked past his sweat-streaked face to see Kel quite a distance away, leaning against a tree.

Her heart sank. If she'd pushed him too hard—

She shook off Tanvir's hand and sprinted back the way she'd come, skidding to a halt beside the general who had come to mean so much to her after her father's death, and hesitantly reached out to touch his shoulder.

He didn't react, not so much as a flinch or a glance in her direction. He merely kept his forehead pressed into the arm he had lifted against the bark of the trunk, breathing in and out. In and out. A sound that was much more labored than it should have been.

"I'm sorry, Kel," Evelayn whispered.

He finally turned to look at her, his face flushed. She'd barely ever seen him break a sweat before. "No, my queen. It is *I* who am sorry. For failing you. For not being up to the task."

Evelayn shook her head, a strangling sense of despair choking back a response.

She felt more than heard Tanvir drawing closer to them.

"I'll start setting up camp," he offered softly.

They were silent for a long moment, the only sounds that of Tanvir preparing a place to sleep and Kel's still-harsh breathing. Finally, she managed to say, "You haven't failed me. It was foolish of me to think I could do this at *all*, let alone so quickly. I've pushed us too hard and we still won't make it back in time." She paused and her shoulders sagged in defeat. "I don't know how to get through the wards. Even if I am somehow successful at bargaining for the silk, we may very well be stuck in Dorjhalon. Rather than helping my people, I may have just served myself on a platter to Bain."

At that Kel looked directly at her. "Don't you *dare* give up. I followed you here because I could see the determination in your eyes, I could feel your certainty that this would work. True, we aren't going to make it back to the border in time, but you are the queen. You have access to all the Light Power in Éadrolan—including that which the priestesses wield. You have passed every test thrown at you so far, and I know you will get us through this one, as well." Kel straightened, pushing away from the tree to stand at his full height—a good three or four inches taller than Evelayn. "I apologize for my moment of weakness. It won't happen again, Your Majesty. Perhaps if we sleep for just a few hours, we can begin again before the sun rises?"

Evelayn merely nodded, too overcome to speak. Kel bowed to her and turned to help Tanvir prepare a meager dinner from what was left of the supplies they'd brought.

They didn't dare light a fire, so it was dried fruits and hard cheese to help stave off the hunger that gnawed at their bellies and sapped their strength. They ate in silence.

The distant cry of a hawk sent a shudder down Evelayn's spine as they finished their small meal. She knew hawks were more plentiful in Dorjhalon, but it was an unfamiliar sound to her. The haunting call set her nerves on edge.

"You two go to sleep. I'll keep watch," Tanvir said quietly.

"But you need to sleep, too," Evelayn pointed out.

"I'll switch with him," Kel offered. "That way we can both get some rest."

"But you need—"

"*You* need your strength the most, Your Majesty. For what lies ahead tomorrow."

Evelayn fell silent once more at the reminder of what she had to do in the morning—and who she had to face.

"I'll be fine," Kel added. "I just needed a little rest. We don't have far to go now."

Evelayn finally gave up arguing and lay down on the bedroll she'd already spread out. Besides being gloomier, it was also colder at night in Dorjhalon than in Éadrolan, even in summer, and she couldn't help but shiver as the blanket of darkness wiped the last smudge of light from the sky above them.

"Here," Tanvir murmured and gently laid his bedroll on top of her, blocking out some of the chill.

"Thank you," she whispered, but he didn't respond.

Even though she had been the one pressing to keep going, a bone-deep exhaustion washed over her, quickly pulling her down into the oblivion of sleep.

She dreamt of being caught in a massive web, of spiders crawling all over her skin—in her hair, her ears, even beneath her clothes. She screamed and thrashed but only grew more entangled, trapped in the nearly unbreakable threads of the spider's silk. When she reached for her power to blast her way free, there was nothing there. She was completely empty. And that's when she realized her chest was cold, so very, very cold. Something was wrong. Terribly, horribly wrong.

"She knows the queen is coming." A deep, unfamiliar voice came from somewhere near the web, a whisper that felt like a shout. "All is prepared."

What? What is prepared? Evelayn tried to speak, but no words came out of her mouth.

"And you guarantee she will succeed." Another voice, from the other side of the web. This one strangely familiar, but as was often the case in dreams, the name escaped her.

One of you help me!

Again the words remained stuck in her throat. And the spiders kept multiplying, covering her body, covering her face.

"She will succeed," the first voice promised, but it sounded farther away than before.

No! Come back! Help me!

But somehow she knew he was gone. Evelayn redoubled her efforts to escape. And finally—finally—the threads snapped. She fell out of the web, the spiders sluicing off her skin like water, as the wind whipped past her . . . but she never hit the ground. Instead she just continued to plummet, falling through an endless pit of darkness, the only sound the echo of her screams—

Evelayn jerked awake to see Tanvir still sitting beside her, staring out into the dark forest, Kel lying on his side, snoring softly.

Shaking off the lingering terror of the nightmare, Evelayn rolled over beneath the warmth of Tanvir's bedroll and closed her eyes once more.

TWENTY-SIX

EVELAYN GLANCED BELOW, BUT SHE COULD BARELY SEE Tanvir or Kel a ways down the treacherous, narrow path. They'd followed her along the first half, but after that she'd forced them to let her go alone. She wasn't sure at what point they could be in danger from Máthair Damhán, and she didn't dare risk it. However, the farther away they got and the closer she was to reaching the cave of the Ancient's lair, the more she wished they were still by her side. Her blood pounded a beat of fear at the base of her throat.

Stop it, she scolded herself, turning back to the rocky, slippery trail that snaked up the albino mountainside. *You are a queen. Act like one.*

The lair was partway up the north face of the White Peak, the largest of the Sliabán Mountains. The entire mountain was white—hence its name—and barren of any vegetation other than the Immortal Tree, which lived deep within its bowels. Evelayn had never been to the Tree before, but she felt the well of power beneath her feet. It pulsed through the very ground, flickered in the air all around her. It was sacred ground she trod upon, ground that Máthair Damhán supposedly helped protect.

The Sliabán Mountains stretched across both Éadrolan and Dorjhalon, creating a point where both kingdoms met—as well as the Undead Forest that constituted the eastern border of the Draíolon kingdoms. The White Peak was near the center of both Éadrolan and Dorjhalon, and it was considered neutral ground, the seat of power for both Light and Dark Draíolon. But the fastest way to reach the Ancient's lair was through Dorjhalon. Evelayn couldn't quell the sense of apprehension that coiled in her belly and sent a trickle of sweat slipping down her spine.

Her steps slowed as she neared the ledge that marked the opening to Máthair Damhán's cave. She'd heard stories and read accounts of the Ancient—what she looked like and what she did to her prey. But no one had ever been to see Máthair Damhán and lived to tell of it, at least not in Evelayn's lifetime, or her mother's before her.

Evelayn's hands were slick with sweat when she grabbed the ledge and hoisted herself up onto the large rocky expanse smoothed into a flat sheet by thousands of years of rain and snow. The mouth of the cave gaped before her, a giant, dark maw that threatened to swallow her up and never again let her see the light of day.

Evelayn clenched her teeth against the terror that threatened to overwhelm her, and took off her knapsack to pull out the offering. She glanced down at Tanvir and Kel one last time and then turned to the cave and walked out of the sunlight into the darkness.

The temperature immediately dropped at least ten degrees. Evelayn shivered but cautiously continued forward. At first the cave looked and smelled like she expected a normal cave would—craggy stone walls, a musty quality to the air, rich with the scent of dirt and rock. But as she slowly moved forward, the walls grew smoother, almost glistening in the darkness.

Evelayn decided to risk summoning a small handful of Light. The instant the thought entered her mind, the conduit stone in her breastbone flared hot and the cavern exploded with light, nearly blinding her. She swallowed her scream and pulled back the power as quickly as possible, until she held just enough to see the space directly around herself more clearly. In the brief instant when the entire cave had been illuminated she'd glimpsed walls coated in slime and webbing, entrapping dozens of carcasses and even some skeletons. Not Máthair Damhán's spider silk, which Evelayn had come to bargain for, but the webs of her kin. The small insects that lived throughout their world. Although, based on the size of some of the carcasses and skeletons trapped in the webs, the spiders who lived *here* were not small at all.

Evelayn shuddered but forced herself to continue forward, to the tunnel she'd noticed at the back of the cavern. All around her she sensed the same pulsing power that flowed through the mountain, which she'd detected before; but now it was even stronger. Being this close to the source of her magic obviously strengthened her, based on what had happened with the Light Power moments earlier. She could barely even feel the constant ebb and flow of the draw from her people; the sense of the Immortal Tree being so close was all-consuming. But still, Evelayn could scarcely keep her hands from trembling as she cupped the Light with her left and clutched the offering with her right.

She'd nearly reached the tunnel when some instinct, born of fear or deep-rooted, visceral knowledge, urged her to stop. The light she wielded flickered, and she wondered if she should douse it altogether.

But the thought of standing at the mouth of the tunnel in utter blackness was too terrifying.

Long moments passed, and Evelayn began to wonder if it had been nothing more than her own silly fears that had urged her to stop before descending into the tunnel. But then her heightened hearing caught the barest hint of sound—of soft legs scraping against stone. Many legs.

"To what do I owe this singular honor?" A voice came from deep within the tunnel. It sounded female—to a degree. But the words were strangely clipped and accompanied by a faint clicking. "A queen of Éadrolan, come to see *me*."

Evelayn straightened her spine, standing as tall as possible as she faced the black tunnel. There was a peculiar scent wafting from the opening and growing stronger every moment. A scent that spoke of darkness and perseverance and avarice and of enduring years beyond measure. "I mean you no harm."

There was a hissing laugh. "Of course not, because harming me would make it rather difficult to obtain what you seek, would it not?"

The scent was stronger than ever, but still Evelayn couldn't see anything in the thick, inky darkness of the tunnel.

"I offer you what no Draíolon has ever offered before in exchange for your revered silk, Máthair Damhán. I beseech you to help me—to help all of Lachalonia." Evelayn extended her right hand forward—the one that clutched the Solascás. The crystal vial flickered in the darkness with the glowing contents it held.

"I have lived since before recollection, before the First King and Queen and will live beyond the last. What need have I for your worthless trinkets?"

And Máthair Damhán finally appeared, not on the ground heading toward her as Evelayn had assumed, but scuttling toward her on the ceiling. Evelayn smothered a yelp of alarm and involuntarily jumped back a step. The Ancient paused, all six of her eyes trained on the young queen.

To cover her increasing terror, Evelayn pressed, "The Solascás isn't worthless. It is one of the vessels that contain the pure essence of Light Power, captured by the First Queen when she claimed her power, and kept for eons in our temple. There are only two left in existence."

"And yet, you only thought to offer me one." Máthair Damhán suddenly dropped from the ceiling, flipping in midair to land on her eight legs.

Evelayn flinched but held her ground, now standing only ten strides from the Ancient.

She was grotesquely beautiful. The lower half of her face was almost that of a woman, a slender nose and jaw, full lips the color of ink, with elongated canines that curved into pincers peeking out. Her main eyes were nearly the same as Evelayn's except larger, and entirely black. But above that her head became completely insectoid, with two other, smaller sets of eyes and thick, coiling ropes of black hair growing out of the ridges on the top of her skull. She had arms and hands, but instead of nails, she had long black talons, and her body was the bulbous torso of a spider, with all eight legs—each one longer than Evelayn—holding the Ancient up so that her head soared above her.

"What is it that you want, Evelayn, Queen of Éadrolan?"

Evelayn tried to hide her shock that Máthair Damhán not only knew who she was but also her name. "A skein of your silk."

"No, youngling. I'm well aware of why you came here. But what is it that you *want*?"

Evelayn searched her mind for an answer to satisfy the Ancient's question. And then it dawned on her. "Balance. I want to stop King Bain and restore peace to Lachalonia."

"Ah, balance. A tricky thing. Even when attained, it can so easily be upset again." Máthair Damhán struck out so quickly, slicing into Evelayn's palm with a talon, that the Ancient knocked the Solascás from her hands before she could react. It crashed to the stone floor and shattered. A blast of light knocked Evelayn off her feet to land with a thud on the ground a dozen paces away, her head cracking against the rock. "One wrong move, and it is gone."

Evelayn moaned and rolled over onto her knees, ignoring the sharp pain and the warmth of blood oozing down her neck to lift her head and stare at the shattered crystal on the ground. Her one bargaining chip was gone. Dismay threatened to overwhelm her, but she fought it back, refusing to have come all this way for nothing.

She slowly, deliberately climbed back to her feet and met Máthair Damhán's inhuman stare with a cold glare. "You say that you have lived since before time began, and will live past the last of our world? I wouldn't be so sure. You have rejected our offering of goodwill—a priceless emblem of power—and have threatened to upset the balance of our world further. You are right. Balance is hard to obtain and possibly even harder to maintain." Evelayn summoned her sun-sword and it flared into existence faster than a blink of an eye, brighter and more powerful than it had ever been before, aided by the power that flowed through the White Peak into her conduit stone—into *her*. "But it is worth fighting for, and fight I will. Even if it means fighting *you*. You know the power I have access to as the Queen of Éadrolan, standing on the ground upon which the Immortal Tree lives. You may be Ancient, but the power I wield is infinite and you will not triumph."

Máthair Damhán's lips curled into a feral smile, exposing all her pointed fangs. "You are so very young. Brave, it is true. But also foolish. If I had wanted you dead, Queen of Éadrolan, you would already have joined your parents in the Final Light. That is not my wish. And I have no need for your offering. But I *will* give you the skein of silk you request."

Evelayn's sword dropped an inch as she watched in stunned silence as the Mother of Spiders, the Ancient tasked with protecting the Immortal Tree, reached up with two of her enormous legs and began to spool a strand of iridescent silk from her spinneret.

In a matter of moments she had finished, lifting the gleaming skein to her hands and holding it up.

"You speak of balance, young queen, but I wonder if you know where the true imbalance began?"

Evelayn couldn't take her eyes off the silk. "I . . . I'm not sure what you mean."

"Do you think the power you wield was always yours to conquer— to disperse through the stone that burns in your breast?"

Evelayn finally looked away from the silk to meet Máthair Damhán's chilling gaze. "What—what are you talking about?"

"Once the power was only Ours. Until it was taken by the First, claimed and chained to your bodies through those stones. I have no need for your gift because I can still access your power for brief moments. No more than what that vial would have given me, but it is something. However, I can't keep it. And so, if it is balance you truly wish for, the silk is yours. But only if you grant me a favor."

"What favor?" Evelayn repeated, her terror returning along with a pulsating sense of dread.

"Ah, that is the crucial question, isn't it?" Máthair Damhán inched toward her, lowering the silk until it was almost within her reach. "You must promise me this favor without knowing what it is, believing only that I, too, long for balance. I will aid you in your quest today to stop the Dorjhalon King, but in return, *you* will aid *me* when it is time."

Evelayn's heart pumped uncertainly in her chest, her hands clammy once more. An unknown favor given to an Ancient by a queen of Éadrolan? What could Máthair Damhán possibly need from her? The stone in her breast burned hot, almost as if it was trying to warn her.

But what choice did she have? Without the silk she was certain to fail. With it, she had the chance to stop Bain. She'd told her council that surely an Ancient would wish to maintain peace and balance in their world—and it seemed that Máthair Damhán did indeed want balance. But what frightened Evelayn was that she had never heard a story of power being stolen for the Draíolon from the Ancients. What exactly *was* Máthair Damhán's definition of balance?

Everything inside her felt cold, except for the burning stone, when Evelayn finally said, "One favor."

The Mother of Spiders presented the skein to her with another curl of her black lips. It was lighter than Evelayn could have ever imagined; it felt as though she were cradling a cloud in her hands. Smoother than water, but strong enough to entrap even a Draíolon as powerful as the King of Dorjhalon. There was nothing in all of Lachalonia that was its equal. "Thank you," she murmured and then turned to the mouth of the cave. She'd begun to walk away but paused when the Ancient spoke again.

"Use it well, little queen," Máthair Damhán said, a note of warning in her voice, "for you may find it came at a higher price than you had anticipated."

Evelayn whirled to look at the Ancient again, but when she faced the tunnel there was nothing but shadow and the faint remnant of Máthair Damhán's scent.

TWENTY-SEVEN

ONCE SHE WAS OUTSIDE IN THE LIGHT, EVELAYN tucked the precious silk into her knapsack and tried to ignore the nagging sense that she had made a terrible mistake. But if she hadn't made the deal, she would have returned empty-handed. It would only have been a matter of time before King Bain succeeded in killing her, and her people would lose their power—possibly forever. She'd never heard of any Draíolon other than a direct descendant of a royal being born with a conduit stone. Which was what had spurred High Priestess Teca's lecture about being Bound and producing an heir, she knew.

But Máthair Damhán's claim that the power had once only belonged to the Ancients had shaken her. Where *had* the conduit stones come from—and why did they only pass from royals to their children?

The hike back to Tanvir and Kel was a blur. She was vaguely aware of a throbbing pain in her head and the heat of the sun on her neck and face. Her gaze was trained on the treacherous path, so she didn't see the concern on the two males' faces until she was nearly to them and finally looked up.

Kel watched her in that direct, disconcerting way of his, not betraying any sort of reaction. Tanvir, however, took a half step toward her. When their gazes met, a shadow of dismay darkened his expression.

"You weren't successful?"

"I have the silk."

A look of confusion crossed Tanvir's face before he broke into an exultant smile. "You did it? You have it?"

"Yes."

He cocked his head to the side, his eyebrows pulled down slightly. "I'm not sure I understand . . . Why aren't you celebrating?"

"I . . . I am just in shock, I think." Evelayn stumbled through her response. She didn't want to tell him or Kel what she'd done—what she'd promised. A favor to Máthair Damhán. *You may find it came at a higher price than you had anticipated* . . . the Ancient's warning burrowed beneath her skin, a painful burr that kept her from smiling.

"If we hurry, perhaps we can still make it back before the gap closes, Your Majesty," Kel finally spoke up, thankfully not commenting on her lack of excitement at achieving her goal.

Evelayn squinted up at the sky. The sun was past its zenith, but not by far. The negotiation had been quicker than anticipated. Perhaps . . . if they sprinted the entire way back to the border . . .

"I'll take the lead." Evelayn took off at a dead run and didn't glance back at the White Peak—or the black tear halfway up the pale stone where Máthair Damhán waited for the day she would call in her favor.

Evelayn ran harder than she ever had before, until the sweat poured over her eyes and down her neck, soaking through her clothes. She didn't turn to see if Kel and Tanvir were keeping up or not. She didn't watch for Dark Draíolon waiting to attack. She just *ran*.

The forest had begun to fall into shadow once more when they burst out of the trees, the border in sight. The priestesses had been instructed to leave a gap in the wards until sundown of the fourth day. The sun was already sinking below the western horizon. Evelayn's breath came out in harsh gasps as she kicked up her heels and extended her stride even more.

Almost there, almost there.

She just hoped sundown meant after the sun had completely set to the priestesses, not as soon as it reached the horizon.

Evelayn was only a few feet away from the border when she slowed, hesitating slightly. She wasn't sure what would happen to her if the wards were back in place . . .

"Your Majesty!"

Evelayn barely heard the shout over the roar of her blood in her ears and the harsh gasps of her breathing. *There's no time for fear.*

"Evelayn!"

She sprinted right past the border into Éadrolan.

With a cry of triumph—and relief—Evelayn whirled to face Dorjhalon. Kel and Tanvir emerged from the forest, but Kel's arm was around Tanvir's shoulders and they were moving in a strange half limp, half jog toward her, with Tanvir doing most of the work and Kel doing most of the limping.

Tanvir glanced up and a grin broke across his face, even though he was sweating and straining with the effort of dragging Kel toward her. "You made it!" He called out.

"What happened?" Evelayn shouted back, stepping closer to the border once more.

"No! Stay there!" Kel was the one who yelled this time.

She glanced at the western horizon and her heart sank in dismay. The sun had nearly set, the last curve of its fiery girth was barely visible above the tree line. *Hurry, hurry!*

They were only a few steps away when there was a draw of power through her stone; at the same time she felt a surge of power in front of her.

"Wait!"

But they were already dashing across the border—or *into* it, rather. Tanvir and Kel were both blasted backward, landing with two dull thuds on the barren ground in Dorjhalon.

"Tanvir!" Evelayn lurched forward, but made herself stop, realizing if she crossed through the same thing would happen to her.

Kel was slow to get back up; Tanvir had to help him to his feet. Evelayn couldn't see any visible injuries, but his usual verbena and mint was laced with something sharp and lingering—a scent that made her think of pain and suffering.

"What happened?"

Tanvir glanced up and followed her gaze to Kel, whom he still supported, even though they were both standing.

"He fell and snapped a bone in his leg. We didn't have time to properly set it and have any hope of reaching the border in time, so he insisted we keep going. It's healing wrong."

Kel wouldn't meet her eyes, staring at the ground the entire time Tanvir spoke. Guilt mingled with the pain, creating a thick, fetid musk.

There was a long silence and then Tanvir said, "You have to keep going."

"And leave you in Dorjhalon?" Though she couldn't see the wall that now separated them, she could sense it—could feel the draw of power through her stone. Evelayn wished to beat her hands against it, to tear it down.

"You don't have a choice. Summer solstice is nearly here, and Bain *will* attack."

Kel finally lifted his head, his eyes dark with pain. "Listen to Lord Tanvir, Your Majesty," he urged, clinging to formalities even now.

"No. I'm *not* leaving you there. You'll be captured or killed. Or you'll have to journey through the Undead Forest . . ." She trailed off with a shudder, not needing to say any more about the risks of a journey through the sacred—but terrifying—woods on the eastern shore of Lachalonia, where it was rumored more than one Ancient lived, including the Spirit Harbinger. She refused to let them suffer any of those fates.

"Step back," she ordered.

Alarm flashed across Tanvir's face. "What are you going to do?"

"Just get back," she repeated pointing toward the trees from which they had emerged a few minutes prior. "I'm going to try and break down the wards, but I don't know what will happen when I do."

Tanvir helped Kel limp back toward the forest while Evelayn took a deep breath and closed her eyes.

She could sense the magic of the wards—the power being drawn through her stone by the priestesses. But she'd never tried to unravel it before, to figure out how the priestesses did it—or how to tear it down. When she reached for the power it was there, a massive well waiting to be tapped, and it surged up at her call almost effortlessly.

Evelayn opened her eyes and glanced up at the nearly dark sky. The sun was completely gone, so calling a beam of sunlight to burn a hole in the wards, which had been her only idea, was not an option. Her stone burned hot in her breastbone, waiting for her.

What do I do?

Evelayn took a step closer, so that she stood on the edge of the border, but she couldn't feel the invisible wall made by the priestesses far away in Ristra, where the largest battles had been fought. She knew there were some priestesses who traveled up and down the line of the border, making sure the wards held all across the two kingdoms, from the ocean to the west to the Sliabán Mountains that marked the eastern edge of the borderlands before the Undead Forest. But they couldn't wait for one of them to show up and help them—that could take days or weeks.

She lifted her hands, palms out, trying to *touch* the wards. There was *something* there, but it felt like an elusive dream, a slippery, hazy half-remembered thing that she couldn't quite hold on to. Evelayn closed her eyes again, trying to shut out everything else. She slowed her breathing. There was only her and the power for which she was a conduit.

She *had* to be able to figure it out.

And finally, *there*, beneath the slight breeze that brought the scent of juniper from Dorjhalon into Éadrolan, was an intricate web of Light Power. Evelayn exhaled softly. The subtle complexity of the exquisitely crafted tapestry was . . . stunning. No wonder it took decades for the novices to study and learn before becoming full priestesses.

But Evelayn was no ordinary Draíolon, and she didn't have time to be subtle.

She let the tiniest bit of power trickle out of her fingertips into the wards, testing their makeup. Instead of releasing from her body, the power wove itself into the wards, connecting her to them. She could feel the strands stretching to the mountains on her right and back to Ristra, a day's running away on her left, and beyond. There were two unbelievably thin layers—one on the Dorjhalon side and one on the Éadrolan side—a subtle but important difference between the two. That difference had to be the key, she realized, because the wards allowed Draíolon to leave Éadrolan, but kept them from returning.

If she could somehow push the layer closest to Éadrolan through the second layer . . . perhaps it would create a hole that Tanvir and Kel could come through.

Evelayn sent more power out of her hands into the invisible wards, her eyes still closed, trying to feel her way through. Her power coiled around the delicately woven strands of the first layer. The only thing she could think to do was to send it out, toward Dorjhalon, much as she'd done when she had trained with Kelwyn, trying to hit targets. She swallowed once, hard, sending up a silent prayer—*please let this work*—and then pushed the threads away from her, toward King Bain's kingdom. There was a blink of time, the space between one heartbeat and the next, when nothing happened. And then the first layer exploded through the second in a collision of power that blasted Evelayn off her feet, throwing her backward through the air to land flat on her back, staring up at the velvet sky, unable to breathe.

TWENTY-EIGHT

E VELAYN!"

She heard someone shout her name as if through a tunnel, echoing distantly. Her head ached. Her whole *body* ached. And then someone was there, hovering over her.

"Ev, are you all right?"

She blinked and Tanvir's face came into focus as he knelt beside her, lifting a hand to brush her hair back from her forehead.

"I . . . I think so—"

And then it dawned on her.

"It worked!" Evelayn slowly sat up, still a bit dizzy, but exultant.

Tanvir grinned at her just as Kel limped up to them. "I knew you could do it," he said.

Kel sat down heavily next to her on the ground, allowing Evelayn to look at his leg more closely for the first time. It was definitely crooked.

He noticed her gaze and waved her off. "You two go ahead without me. I'll be safe now that we're in Éadrolan. I can find a healer to help me when I make it back to the castle."

"No," Evelayn immediately responded. "I got you in this mess and I'm not leaving you behind." She'd already mostly recovered from tearing the hole in the wards; only a lingering shakiness in her hands remained. She knelt beside the general and gently probed at his leg. There was a large lump where he'd snapped the long thighbone, and when she pressed she could feel that it had started to fuse back together off-center.

"What can we do?" She glanced up at Tanvir, who knelt beside her.

"We're going to have to re-break the bone and set it so it heals correctly," he replied darkly.

Kel grimaced but didn't argue. "Do what you must."

"How do we do that?" Evelayn glanced up at the inky sky above them. The first few stars were already blinking in the black expanse, and there was a slight chill to the air wafting toward them from Dorjhalon.

"If you hold him, I will do it. I've had to do it before on the battlefield."

Evelayn nodded and moved to Kel's torso, trying not to think about why he'd had to do this before—or on whom.

"Hold his arms down, don't let him thrash."

"My leg is broken, not my ears, Lord Tanvir. And I'm perfectly capable of holding still on my own," Kel finally spoke up, but his voice was strained and the air was rank with the scent of his pain and fear.

"How about if I just hold your hands," Evelayn offered, "and you can squeeze them if it hurts too much."

"If you insist." Kel sighed, but she caught the flash of relief across his face. She moved so that he could rest his head in her lap and lifted his arms so she could grip his hands.

"Ready when you are." She nodded to Tanvir, who had been busy cutting off the leg of Kel's pants and tearing the fabric into strips.

"I just need to find something to set it for the night, and we can get this over with." He hurried over to the tree line and quickly returned with two long branches and set them beside Kel. "All right. This is going to hurt. Are you ready?"

Kel nodded, his hands flexing in Evelayn's.

"Here we go," Tanvir muttered under his breath. Then he grabbed Kel's leg with both hands and yanked.

There was an audible snap. Kel's back arched, and he squeezed Evelayn's hands so tightly she was afraid he was going to break *her* bones. But he didn't make a single noise, not even a groan. His forehead beaded with sweat as Tanvir worked, quiet and efficient. Evelayn kept her eyes on Kel's face, rather than watching.

There was another snap and this time Kel's head thrashed, his teeth baring, as though it was all he could do not to bellow in agony.

"Almost done," Tanvir assured them.

Evelayn glanced up to see him placing the pieces of wood and quickly binding them with the strips of fabric to Kel's now-straight leg.

"All finished," Tanvir finally announced, rocking back on his haunches to survey his handiwork.

Kel sighed in relief, and his grip relaxed on Evelayn's aching hands.

"We'd better rest here tonight. He shouldn't move that leg until morning, when the bone has had a chance to fuse back together." Tanvir stood up and brushed the dirt off his knees. "I'll prepare camp."

"I can help," Evelayn offered, but he waved her off.

"Stay with him and rest. It will only take a moment. And I'll take first watch."

He turned and strode over to where they'd dropped their packs without another word, and Evelayn didn't protest. Now that Kel's leg was fixed and on its way to healing correctly, exhaustion washed over her once more—as well as the memory of all that she'd done. The silk, the promise, and tearing the hole in the wards.

Evelayn glanced across the border, contemplating what to do about the gap she'd created in their defenses, when she saw a flicker of movement in the depths of the forest. Fatigue gone in an instant, she narrowed her eyes, straining to see through the darkness. For a long moment, nothing moved. Evelayn hardly dared breathe. And then, with a mournful call, a bird took flight from the spot where she'd first noticed something.

Spooked, Evelayn slowly stood and stepped closer to the border. If that *had* been a Dark Draíolon, he or she could have walked right in to Éadrolan and then gone back to alert the king as to the hole in the wards. She couldn't leave her kingdom vulnerable like this—somehow, she had to fix what she'd done.

But she had the sinking feeling that fixing the hole was going to be much more difficult than making it.

"Eve—er, Your Majesty? Is everything all right?"

"I thought I saw something," Evelayn responded to Tanvir without turning around. "It ended up being a bird, but what if it had been a Dark Draíolon? I can't leave the hole like this. I have to try and repair what I did."

"Do you know how?"

She simply said no, and then closed her eyes and stretched her hands out, once more searching for the infinitesimal layers of magic she'd felt before blasting through them. Tanvir didn't speak again, and

Evelayn tried to ignore the fact that he was probably watching her, waiting for something to happen, wondering how she was going to accomplish this when she'd admitted to not knowing how.

Long minutes passed while she concentrated, searching for the layers, but there was only the cool night air and a faint, pulsing ebb of power from the hole she'd torn in the wards. A cold finger of fear scraped down her spine. How big *was* the gap she'd created? What if she'd destroyed the wards completely?

Panic threatened to swoop in, but Evelayn forced herself to breathe through it, to try and hold it at bay and *think*. Perhaps, if she walked a little bit closer to Ristra where the priestesses created the wards, she would find the severed threads? Evelayn began to slowly tread the line of the border, with one hand still extended, reaching for something . . . *anything*.

"Evelayn, where are you—"

Tanvir's question was silenced by Kel shushing him, but Evelayn ignored them both, suddenly freezing in place.

There. A flicker . . . no, a thread!

A wave of relief crashed over her when she took another couple of steps and the threads multiplied and grew until it felt exactly as the invisible wall had before she'd destroyed a section of it. The double layer was intact; she could feel the connection all the way back to Ristra.

"Oh, thank the Light," she murmured. At least it wasn't as bad as she'd feared for a few agonizing minutes. But she still didn't know how to duplicate it and fill in the chasm. If only she'd had time to train with the priestesses, like all other royals did when they came into their full power. *There's no sense wishing for what can't be,* she scolded herself. *Focus. You can do this. You* have *to do this.*

Evelayn lifted her hands to the magical wall, and shut her eyes once more. And again, she was awed by the complexity of the threads that made up the two layers. They were strands of Light, so unbelievably thin as to be invisible, woven together to create the different sides of the wards. Could she create that? As Kel had said, she *should* be able to . . . But when Evelayn tried, calling to her power, trying to coax it out a tiny bit at a time, the light that burst out of her hands was still far too big—and too visible—to be right.

She had the uncomfortable sense that she was being watched, but Evelayn didn't turn to face Kel and Tanvir. They didn't need to see the frustration and fear of defeat on her face. Instead, she decided to try something else. If she couldn't figure out how to *create* the wards, perhaps she could stretch them somehow? She was the conduit for *all* their power, including that which made up the wards. They should bend to her will, allow her to manipulate and pull them.

A cold draft from Dorjhalon blew Evelayn's hair away from her face, biting through her tunic, but she ignored the chill and called to the Light, willing the threads to come to her. Almost immediately the strands leapt forward, toward her outstretched hands. Triumphant, Evelayn repeated the process, taking a few steps closer to Kel and Tanvir, and then calling the wards to her. And every time, the power responded, stretching, growing, filling in the void. Until finally, *finally*, after continuing a good twenty paces past where Tanvir stood watching her with his arms crossed, she found the eastern edge of the wards where the gap ended. When she urged the two to join, they did so seamlessly, merging into one great whole.

The wards were complete once more.

Evelayn exhaled slowly, tension seeping out of her as she turned to face Tanvir. She was thrilled but completely drained now that she'd succeeded, and her fear slowly began to ebb away.

"Did it work?" He asked, taking a step toward the border.

She held up a hand to signal him to stop. "Yes. So don't you dare go through to the other side, because I'm not doing all of that again."

Tanvir laughed lightly. "Never fear, I fully intend to stay on this side of the border."

Evelayn made her way back over to where Kel still lay on the ground, visibly pale, even in the darkness, but smiling at her despite the pain he was undoubtedly experiencing. "I knew you could do it."

"Well, that makes one of us." She dropped unceremoniously to the ground beside him. "But at least I figured it out."

"I'll find us something to eat," Tanvir offered, and she nodded, too exhausted to even try to help.

"Despite everyone's fears and doubts, you did it, Your Highness. You have the silk and the wards are back in place. I think your mother would be impressed."

Evelayn smiled gratefully at Kel's praise. Yes, she'd done it, but she couldn't forget that it had all come with a price. *Think about that later,* she told herself.

For now, they had to focus on getting back to the castle and putting her plan into action.

It was time to defeat Bain.

TWENTY-NINE

THE SKY WAS STILL NAVY BLUE, ONLY THE FIRST FEW blushing streaks of light snaking across the expanse, when Tanvir startled awake. It was the same nightmare again, as it was nearly every night. Nervous that he'd cried out in his sleep, he glanced over to where Evelayn sat near Kel; she'd been there since taking over watch a few hours prior, but she continued to stare out into the forest, unaware that he had woken. Her hair was falling out of its braid, and a streak of dirt smudged across the alabaster skin of her cheek. She was grimy and unkempt. And she was stunning.

As he watched, her head listed forward for a moment but then snapped back up with a jerk. That tiny indication of weakness—of exhaustion—made something inside him ache for her. Other than the morning on the lawn when she'd realized her mother had died, she'd never been anything but resolute in her purpose. She was so strong, so indomitably determined . . . it was easy to forget that she had only reached her maturity a brief time ago. Her power block had been removed for less than a season. And she had already been forced to become a queen, to shoulder the burden of a war, to learn to wield her power all at once, to face an Ancient, and now to return home to finalize her plan to stop King Bain—something neither of her parents had been successful at achieving.

And yet she never seemed to waver, never faltered in the face of doing what she must to save her people.

Evelayn turned to look at him, as if sensing his gaze, and when their eyes met, it felt as though time itself paused momentarily. Everything grew very still; even his heart stopped beating for the space of a breath. In the early morning light her violet eyes were vivid, so vibrant . . . and they entrapped him completely.

The force of what he felt for her hit him so strongly in that moment that he could no longer deny it. He was in love with the queen of Éadrolan.

"What are you thinking?" she whispered.

"You don't want to know," he whispered back.

"Try me."

But Tanvir shook his head. He was afraid of what loving her meant . . . afraid of where it would lead him. Instead of speaking, he silently crawled over to where she sat, and then sat back on his heels, reaching up to stroke a finger down her cheek, wiping away the streak of dirt from her soft skin.

She looked at him steadily, no hesitation on her face. He could scent her growing desire, see it in her eyes, which darkened to the color of plums. Evelayn wanted him, he knew. But did she feel what he did? And if so . . . what did that mean for them?

"What are you thinking?" she repeated, her voice low and throaty.

Tanvir reached up with his other hand to cup her face on both sides. The first ray of sunlight broke to the east, painting her skin golden. Her lips parted slightly, and it was more than he could resist. Tanvir bent forward to kiss her, a soft, hesitant brush of his mouth against hers.

What are you doing? You can't have this. You can't have her, he chastised himself, but then she kissed him back, pressing in closer so that she could wind her arms around his neck and he was lost. She gripped his shirt, meeting his passion and desperation with her own.

I love you. The words were right there, ready to be spoken, as her mouth parted beneath his, as his hands roamed over her back and plunged into her hair, slanting her head beneath his.

I love you. He suddenly broke away, breathing heavily, staring into her flushed face, her questioning eyes.

"I love you, Evelayn." The words slipped out before he could stop them, a hushed admission that made everything inside him stop and cringe, waiting for her response.

She seemed stunned for a moment but then she smiled—such an achingly beautiful, hopeful smile that it stole his breath. "I'm afraid I love you, too, Lord Tanvir."

"*Afraid* is an interesting word choice." Tanvir smiled back at her. "But accurate," he continued before she could say anything else. "I'm afraid, too. You have no idea."

She leaned forward to kiss him again, a soft press of her lips against his, making his heart thunder beneath his ribs. "So what now?" she asked against his mouth.

"I'm not sure."

Kel groaned from behind them and Evelayn jumped back.

"I see one of your fears is getting caught," Tanvir teased, even though he felt hot and cold all at once, his blood pounded through his veins like a warning. *Do you know what you're doing?* That little voice in his head nagged at him. The answer was no, he had no clue what he was doing. But he knew he loved her. And if she loved him . . . perhaps . . . just maybe there was a way to be together. Somehow. Even though she was who she was. And he was who he was. Could they make it work? Despite everything?

"I think he's waking up. I hope his leg healed enough to run today." Evelayn watched Kel while Tanvir watched her.

"I'll get us something to eat and then we should get started," Tanvir suggested, standing and glancing toward the eastern horizon, where the sun was nearly risen. It was no time to worry about whether they could be together or not—first they had to finish what had been started. They had to defeat Bain. Only then could they begin to hope for a future.

Together or not.

Shifting was like breathing to Lorcan. He dove out of the darkened sky toward the tower but had returned to his Draíolon form before his feet even touched the stones.

His mother waited for him in the shadows, her cloak pulled up against the wind that buffeted the turret. Lorcan bent to kiss her cheek, and he felt it crease into a smile.

"I take it the trip was successful?"

"Indeed." He straightened and glanced around to make sure they were truly alone.

"There's no one here besides us. Do you think me that careless?"

Abarrane pulled her cloak more tightly around her body. "But we must return soon or your father will begin to wonder."

"Of course." Lorcan held out his arm, but she didn't take it.

"All the pieces are falling into place, my son."

He nodded, even though he couldn't quite quell the jump in his pulse that belied the fears born of a lifetime of being ruled by his father's bloody fists.

"And what of Lothar?"

Abarrane's nose wrinkled at the mention of her second son. "He will have his part to play, just as we all do."

"But does *he* know that?"

She was silent for a long moment. "We'd best return. Dinner will begin soon and you know how much Bain hates it when we enter a meal late."

His mother wound her fingers around his bicep, making it seem as though he were guiding her, when in reality her nails had dug into his skin, propelling him forward, toward the door that would take them down a long winding staircase, back into the depths of the palace.

They walked into the dining hall side by side, but luckily no one had sat down to eat yet, so their entrance didn't cause any undue attention.

His mother let go of his arm to take her place beside the king. Lorcan saw Lothar standing by himself a few strides away, watching those gathered silently. He made his way to his brother's side and nodded a hello.

"How was the flight?"

Lorcan successfully hid his surprise that Lothar knew he'd been gone in his hawk form and ignored the question. "Father seems to be in a celebratory mood."

"You know he's always happiest right before murdering hundreds of Draíolon."

"Careful, Loth, or you might be accused of treason and join those hundreds." Lorcan's voice was mocking, but the warning was sincere.

"You might be careful yourself, *Lorc*, or you might be accused of becoming just like him." Lothar's disgust left a rank smell lingering in his wake as he stormed away.

Lorcan grabbed a goblet of mulberry wine from a passing server bearing trays of the drink and downed half of it in one long gulp. The liquid warmed his throat and belly, but not enough. Once, Lothar had looked at him with hero worship in his eyes. Once, they had been so close, they didn't even know the meaning of the word *secrets*.

That had been a long time ago.

The bell rang to signal the start of supper, and Lorcan sighed. He finished the rest of the wine and placed the empty goblet down on a side table before sauntering over to the large dinner table.

"My son—my heir! Here, sit at my side." His father gestured to the seat on his left.

"Of course, Father." Lorcan smiled through gritted teeth and did as the king bade, all too aware of Lothar's cold stare from farther down the table.

When everyone had been seated, King Bain signaled for the servants to pour wine in everyone's goblets and then he stood, holding the gleaming crystal aloft so that it flashed in the firelight.

"Many, many years have led us to this moment. Only one obstacle remains, but not for long!"

Lorcan's gaze flickered to his mother. She smiled brightly up at her husband, ever the dutiful wife and supportive queen.

"And so tonight, raise your glasses with me!"

All the other Draíolon did as he commanded, lifting their glasses toward their king. Lorcan reached for his as well, his fingers so tight on the flute he had to consciously remind himself to relax before he snapped it in half.

"To the ultimate victory!" King Bain roared.

"To the ultimate victory," Lorcan echoed darkly with everyone else's enthusiastic cries, and then drained his entire goblet of blood-red wine.

THIRTY

THEY ARRIVED AT CEREN'S FAMILY HOME JUST BEFORE sunset the next day, their progress hampered by Kel's only partially healed leg. There were no servants or grounds-people to be seen, just as Evelayn had instructed. Only one window in the large manor glowed from the light of a fire within as the sky dark-ened to a bruised navy purple above them.

Even though Tanvir had offered to help support Kel, he'd refused, choosing to limp in silent pain all day through the forest toward the rendezvous point. Evelayn was relieved to see signs that Ceren was still waiting for them as they hurried as quickly as they were able, despite their being much later than planned.

It was all part of the ruse; none of her subjects had seen her leave with Ceren, they'd only been told that's where the queen had disap-peared to. But they would *all* see her coming back with her dearest friend, her two trusted advisors and guards in attendance—if things went as planned.

They were halfway across the overgrown gardens when the side door banged open and Ceren burst out with a relieved, "Oh, thank the Light, I'd thought you'd all died!"

Even though she was being perfectly sincere, for some reason her exclamation made Evelayn burst out laughing. And once she started, she couldn't stop. Ceren's eyes widened in surprise, but when Evelayn doubled over, clutching her stomach, she heard Ceren ask, "Is she . . . all right?"

"I'm not sure," was Tanvir's baffled response.

It wasn't funny, not in the least bit. None of them had died, and she *had* secured the silk, but it had come at an unknown cost—even beyond Kel's leg. Perhaps she was finally snapping under the strain of all she'd suffered and tried to accomplish in such a short time. And there was still so much to do—so much at stake. With that sobering thought, Evelayn finally straightened and managed to subdue her inexplicable hysteria. "I'm sorry." An uncommon heat suffused her neck and cheeks. "I don't know what's wrong with me."

"It's been a . . . rough few days," Tanvir said, eyeing her with concern.

"You must be exhausted. Come in and I'll find you something to eat and then you can rest. It's too late to leave tonight." Ceren took Evelayn's arm, weaving her own through it, and guided Evelayn back to her home.

They ate a quick dinner of sliced fruits and sweet breads that Ceren had prepared for them—just in case—and then Evelayn quickly excused herself to go find a bed and attempt to get some sleep.

The next morning, after a night of tossing and turning, and waking up sweat-drenched from nightmares, Evelayn quickly washed and dressed in the gown Ceren had brought specifically for their return, to make it look like she truly had been convalescing at her friend's home to mourn her mother's death. As she pulled the periwinkle-blue, tissue-thin sleeves up her arms, Evelayn caught sight of her reflection in the mirror and winced. Dark bruises rimmed her eyes, and her skin looked ashen. She was visibly exhausted and worn down. Not a very convincing look for someone who had supposedly been resting for as many days as she'd been gone.

If only she truly *had* come here to rest and mourn. By the Light, she certainly needed that time, that chance to heal. But there was no such luxury available to her—not until she defeated Bain and somehow restored peace to Lachalonia.

A knock at the door startled her, but she quickly called out, "Who is it?"

"Ceren, silly. Were you expecting someone else?" The door opened as she spoke and Ceren came in, shooting her a pointed look.

"Of course not. I'm glad you came—could you help me? It would seem I have yet to master the ability to twist my arms in such a way as to lace up my own gown."

Ceren laughed as she walked over to her. "They make your dresses impossible on purpose, so that you must be reliant upon a lady's maid to help you—and keep an eye on you." Her friend winked at her in the mirror as she pulled the ribbon tight so that the dress no longer gaped in front.

"You're probably right."

"I'm *always* right," Ceren corrected her. "Which is why you're not going to lie to me when I ask you what's wrong. Because I know something is bothering you."

Evelayn's empty belly clenched, and she struggled to keep her expression neutral. Of course Ceren would guess something was wrong; she knew Evelayn far too well. But she couldn't burden her friend with the worry that pressed in on her, the fear that she had made a terrible mistake giving Máthair Damhán an unknown favor.

"Tanvir told me he loved me," she blurted out, when Ceren lifted an eyebrow, her eyes narrowing.

"*What*? Oh my—that's wonderful news. Why would you be upset about that?" Ceren's mouth formed an O and then she rushed on. "Oh dear, do you not feel the same? I thought you were forming some very strong feelings for him, but maybe I was—"

"No," Evelayn cut her off. "That's not it. I do . . . I love him. And I even told him that I did. But . . ."

"But . . ." Ceren prompted her.

"He didn't seem happy about it when he told me. If anything, *he* seemed upset." Evelayn turned to face her friend.

"That is . . . unusual. Did he say anything else that might help you understand why?"

Evelayn shook her head. "I'm not sure. This is going to sound terribly conceited, but sometimes it seems as though he doesn't think himself . . . worthy of my affections."

"That's not conceited, it's stating facts. You are the queen, Ev. And I'm sure that intimidates him. At least you know he's not pursuing you *because* you are the queen. Otherwise, he would have no such qualms about professing his feelings."

"That's true . . ."

"You will just have to show him that he is worthy of you—and that you wish for him to be Bound to you!"

Evelayn choked on a shocked laugh. "Ceren! I never said *that*."

"When was the last time you told a male that you loved him—besides your father?"

Evelayn winced. "Well . . . never, but—"

"He's the one for you, Ev. I can see it in the way you look at each other." Ceren suddenly embraced her. "Oh, I'm so happy for you."

"Me too," Evelayn echoed, though her mind was only half on Ceren. Did she wish to be Bound to Tanvir? Was he truly "the one" as Ceren insisted?

"All right," she finally said, disentangling herself. "Enough of that. We don't have time to worry about love and being Bound right now. We have to make our grand return to the castle, and then I have to put an end to this war. If we survive that, *then* I'll let myself think about . . . everything else."

"Always so practical," Ceren grumbled, and Evelayn shook her head as she bent to put on her slippers. "I'll go make sure the carriages are prepared. I sent out notes over an hour ago, so they should be here by now."

"Thank you," Evelayn called out as Ceren opened the door. She waved her hand in acknowledgment and then Evelayn was alone once more.

King Tanvir. If they were Bound, that's what he would become.

Evelayn glared at her reflection in the mirror. "Stay focused," she scolded herself. And then she turned and gathered up her belongings, including the spider silk hidden beneath the clothes she'd worn during their trek through Dorjhalon.

It was time to return home, to whatever fate lay ahead.

THIRTY-ONE

W E SHOULD PROBABLY RETURN TO THE CASTLE SOON."

"Just one more time before the sun sets," Evelayn called back.

Ceren sighed and resumed pacing outside the copse of trees, waiting for the blistering heat after Evelayn called a beam of sunlight down into the small clearing again. Ever since they'd returned to the castle, Evelayn had grown increasingly agitated, and spent nearly all her waking hours attempting to shift or practicing using her power. Ceren understood what was at stake and that the brunt of it fell on Evelayn's shoulders, but she worried about how hard her friend was driving herself. Today she'd been at it for hours while Ceren kept watch, wondering how Evelayn hadn't completely drained herself from the effort of drawing upon such powerful magic over and over again.

The now-familiar roar and scorching heat of sunlight crashing into the earth filled the air once more. It lasted for a few moments and then in the blink of an eye was gone again, leaving behind only the acrid scent of ozone and burned earth.

A minute later, Evelayn finally emerged from the copse of trees and Ceren gasped.

"Ev! What did you do to yourself?"

"I'm fine." She waved Ceren off, but then stumbled and nearly fell. Her face was soot-stained, her skin pale and sweaty, but when Ceren grabbed her arm, she was as cold as ice.

"You're not fine. We need to get you inside and call a healer." Ceren whistled, a signal to the sentries who waited even farther off to come to her aid if necessary.

"I said I'm *fine*," Evelayn repeated, yanking her arm out of Ceren's grasp. She stumbled again, but this time Ceren stood frozen, Evelayn's anger still stinging in her ears.

"I was only trying to help," she said softly.

"Well stop. You can't help. Are you going to face Bain with me? Are you going to hold my hand if I fail, and watch as he cuts me down and takes our power for good?" Two bright spots of color burned in Evelayn's otherwise alabaster cheeks.

Ceren shook her head. "I'm sorry, Ev. I'm sorry this has fallen to you."

Evelayn stared at her for a long moment, her eyes glistening in the amber light of dusk. Then she shook away the emotion and stalked forward toward the castle grounds and her sentries who stood in a row a few lengths away.

Ceren waited until they'd gone before slowly following, picking her way through the graveled walkways that wound through the gardens. The evening air was heavy with the perfume of hundreds and hundreds of beautiful flowers in full bloom. Summer solstice was only a week away—only seven days until Bain attacked.

"Pardon the interruption, Lady Ceren. But would you mind very much having some company?"

She turned to see Lord Quinlen standing a little way off, watching her. "I'd like that," she finally responded, even though there was a part of her that actually longed to be alone.

He stepped forward and offered his arm. They walked silently for a few minutes, the only sound that of the crunch of gravel beneath his boots, watching the sky turn from blue to fire to molten gold and then slowly drift into darkness.

"I'm sorry," Ceren said at last. "I'm afraid I'm not very good company tonight."

"You are the best of company no matter your mood," Quinlen responded. "If you wish to talk about whatever is weighing so heavily on you, I am here for you. But if you prefer to keep it private, I am not averse to silence."

Ceren half laughed, half sighed. She couldn't tell him everything—*she* shouldn't even know everything, but Evelayn had confided in her. The dangerous plan their queen had concocted was only known to a select few, and though Quinlen's father was one of them, Ceren didn't dare risk talking freely about it with Quinlen unless he gave her definitive proof that he already knew what Evelayn was going to attempt to do next week.

"Silence it is, then." Quinlen glanced up at the castle, where the windows glowed with candlelight, and the shapes of those moving within became distorted shadows undulating across the castle grounds.

"I wish I could speak freely," Ceren said quietly. "But I *can* tell you this much. The queen hasn't been herself since . . ."

"Her visit to your country home?" he supplied when she trailed off. She thought she detected a note of irony and wondered if he *did* know the truth of what Evelayn had been doing during that week when the court had been told she'd retired to the country with Ceren. His father *was* on Evelayn's council . . .

"Yes, exactly," was all she said though, still afraid to reveal more. "She's been . . . on edge. Pushing herself too hard. Testy, even." Ceren cringed even as the words came out. It hurt her feelings that Evelayn had been so short with her earlier that evening, but she couldn't blame her—and Ceren was appalled to find herself complaining about her dearest friend to her only other friend at court.

"She's under an enormous amount of pressure and doesn't dare reveal any sign of weakness to her court," Quinlen said slowly, in that careful way of his. "You are her closest friend and though it stings, perhaps the very fact that she has been testy with you is a testament to her trust and affection. She only dares show a glimpse of what she's truly experiencing to *you* and none else."

Ceren was silent for a long moment, digesting what he'd said. Then she came to an abrupt halt. "You're right. Thank you, Quinlen." And before she could second-guess herself, she rose up on her toes to press a quick kiss to his cheek. "Please excuse me! I must go find her!" Then she turned and rushed back to the castle.

She glanced over her shoulder to see him bowing, a smile on his lips and three fingertips pressed to the cheek where she'd kissed him.

Evelayn was lying on her bed, still fully clothed, trying to ignore the incessant pounding behind her skull, when there was a soft knock at the door. She recognized Ceren's scent even before she cracked it open and meekly asked, "Can I come in?"

"Of course." Even those two words made the headache worse, and she squeezed her eyes shut.

"Oh, Ev. Why didn't you tell me it was this bad?"

She just shook her head and then winced when the pain escalated again.

"Let me call for Tyne, she can—"

"No," Evelayn burst out, despite how much it hurt. She lowered her voice to a whisper. "You were right. Everyone is watching me. I can't risk her telling anyone that I . . . That I am . . ."

"You are not weak, so don't you dare say it," Ceren cut her off. "But I understand. I won't call for her."

"I just need to sleep for a little bit. It'll go away."

"Can I get you a cool cloth or anything to help?"

"No." Evelayn opened her eyes to see Ceren hovering nearby, her forehead creased with concern. "But thank you."

Ceren nodded, and Evelayn shut her eyes again. Even the smallest bit of light made it worse—to the point she thought she might vomit.

"I know you're under so much pressure, and I want you to know that I'm always here for you. You don't have to hide what you're going through from me."

Evelayn nodded, not daring to speak. Her throat tightened as tears threatened to surface. Even after how cruel Evelayn had been when she'd snapped at her earlier, Ceren was nothing but kind to her. Kindness she was pretty certain she didn't deserve.

"I *know* you can do this, Ev. You don't have to push yourself quite so hard."

Evelayn swallowed a sob and blindly reached out until Ceren grabbed her hand and squeezed it tightly. "I wish I had a choice. I truly wish I did."

"You always have a choice. Even if it feels like you don't."

Maybe for any other Draíolon except the queen, Evelayn thought. But rather than speaking again, she just held on to Ceren's hand and nodded.

"You *must* learn to shift. How else will you be able to avoid becoming entrapped in the spider silk yourself?"

Evelayn sat silently at the head of the table, pale and drawn. Dark bruises turned the delicate skin beneath her eyes a deep purple. Tanvir had barely been able to speak with her since they'd returned to the castle, let alone steal a moment or two alone. Watching her now sent a spike of fear through him. He knew the strength that ran through her, he knew the determination that drove her . . . but she looked so fragile as High Priestess Teca lectured her yet again.

"I assure you that I *am* trying. I spend hours every day attempting to shift. It's not as simple as you seem to think." Evelayn's gaze flickered to his but quickly dodged away again to the others at the table.

"You have mastered calling down the beam of sun. From now on you must spend all of your waking hours learning how to shift. I don't know how else you will be able to lead him into the trap without ensnaring yourself in the process." The High Priestess spoke in such a severe tone, Tanvir expected Evelayn to snap back at her, but instead the queen just nodded morosely, allowing herself to be ordered about. "I will return to the Dawn Temple and continue searching our scrolls and texts to see if I can find anything else on the subject. If you'll excuse me." Teca stood and exited the room swiftly, leaving a heavy silence in her wake.

"Perhaps . . . if you suddenly veered to the side, he might still run into the web?" Lord Teslar offered weakly, in an uncharacteristic sign of pity for the queen.

"I appreciate the thought, but you and I both know that wouldn't be possible. I'm going to be running as fast as I'm able and to change course like that so suddenly would be an unmistakable giveaway." Evelayn reached up to pinch the bridge of her nose. "Even if I *am* able to master shifting in time, I would have to be able to do it in the blink of an eye if I want to be fast enough to avoid the web." Evelayn didn't look up from the table, and though her posture was still ramrod straight, there was a sense of defeat that hung about her like a second shadow, weighing her down.

Tanvir couldn't bear it.

"Maybe we can help somehow," he spoke up without even truly knowing what he was offering or how it would affect the outcome. "I know you were concerned about him scenting a trap if other Draíolon are nearby, but if you are running that fast maybe some of the most powerful priestesses could glamour Kel and me. We could be waiting in the trees with the web. Evelayn, you just make sure you're far enough ahead of him that you are clear before we drop the web and trap him. It would give you the chance to turn and call down the sun. And you wouldn't have to lose time shifting back." As he spoke the idea took form and solidified into what actually sounded like a plausible possibility. It wasn't sticking to the plan, but if the end result was that Bain was killed, did it matter?

Evelayn met his gaze directly for the first time in days, the rebirth of hope in her eyes practically making them glow. "That . . . that just might work."

"As a backup plan, if you aren't able to master shifting," General Olena cut in.

General Kelwyn was watching Evelayn, his eyes slightly narrowed in consideration. "No, I think Tanvir might be onto something."

Olena looked like she wanted to argue, but General Kelwyn quickly continued, "Your Majesty, I mean no offense, but you are obviously unwell. You must be at your full strength if you wish to defeat Bain, even with the spider silk. You have to survive laying the trap before you can hope to kill him. I think we should make Tanvir's idea our main plan and take the pressure off you trying to learn to shift so quickly. If you are able to do it in the next week, we will adjust accordingly. But otherwise, I think this might work."

Evelayn nodded demurely, but Tanvir could see the relief she was trying to hide. "I definitely agree that it is worth discussing with Teca. If her priestesses can somehow keep Bain from scenting the Draíolon aiding me, this could work."

Tanvir nodded encouragingly at her when her eyes found his once more. And for the first time since they'd returned to the castle, Evelayn smiled at him.

THIRTY-TWO

ER EVER-PRESENT GUARDS HOVERED JUST OUT OF sight, but Evelayn could still feel their presence as she walked down the path toward the lake. Late-afternoon sun dappled the lush forest floor, turning it emerald and golden. Flowers bloomed in riotous bursts of color—a splash of fuchsia there, a broad stroke of burnished gold here, bright blots of blue and purple to her left and right. Even in the shade it was sweltering, but Evelayn welcomed the heat, knowing it meant life and power for her people. All too soon summer would fade and winter would be upon them, which meant the Dark Draíolon's height of power.

This opportunity to possibly end the war during the week of the summer solstice was providence—it could only be fated to succeed.

That's what she kept telling herself, anyway.

Soon the forest thinned, and the glint of sunlight reflecting off water flashed through the foliage. Once, coming here had brought her peace and comfort. But the looming confrontation with Bain and her inability to shift had stolen even that from her. Long before she caught sight of the flock, the constant tension that tightened the muscles in Evelayn's neck and twisted her stomach into such knots she could barely eat or sleep grew even worse.

As she stepped out of the trees into the sunlight, she reached into her skirt for the satchel she'd tied around her waist. Inside were broken bits of leftover bread from this morning's breakfast. She grabbed a handful, and as she took her seat on her usual log, she tossed the bread to the swans who were already swimming toward her.

"Hello, my beautiful friends," Evelayn whispered as the birds began to snatch up the pieces of bread, extending their long, graceful necks forward.

She'd always been fascinated by the swans and had been coming to feed them since she was a little girl holding tightly to her father's hand as he guided her down the path. It had been no surprise to anyone when she imprinted on them on her eighth birthday. So why had she been unable to complete the transformation into a swan since gaining her full power? Kel assured her she would figure it out with practice and time. But she didn't have time, as Teca was fond of reminding her. She only had days left. *Days* before Bain would come and she had to be able to transform and fly out of the trap a split second before he ran into it or rely on the plan Tanvir had come up with instead.

There was no one to help her. Only royals imprinted on animals and had the ability to shift into one when they reached their full power, and with her mother's death, there was no one left to ask for help. She had only Kel and Teca's attempts to explain how it worked in theory, rather than in practice, and her own bumbling failures each day.

The swans finished off the last of the bread and began to slowly swim away, lazily paddling through the still water. Her mind turned— as it always did—to the oncoming ambush on summer solstice. If Caedmon's timetable held true, any minute now her scouts would be bringing her word that Bain's army was on the move—if Bain wished to arrive across from Ristra by sunrise of the following day to draw her battalions out, as they'd been told to expect. The waiting was horrific. Every inch of her body hummed with the need to flee or fight, with no outlet except her training exercises with Kel.

When she wasn't at the lake, they went over the plan again and again, hounding out every contingency, trying to prepare her for every possibility. In the end, no matter how much planning they did and how much everyone tried to help give her the opportunity, it came down to Evelayn killing Bain.

Her troubled thoughts were interrupted by the sound of someone approaching.

"I thought I'd find you here."

Evelayn turned to see Tanvir emerge from the forest, the shadows of the Light Sentries and two priestesses sent to guard her visible just beyond him in the tree line.

"There aren't many other places I would be." She tried to keep the bitterness out of her voice, with little success.

"It will be over soon." Tanvir stopped beside the log. "May I sit beside you?"

Evelayn nodded without speaking, staring out at the swans as they carved lines through the bright sunlight on the surface of the water. He stepped over the log and sat next to her, his presence filling up much more than just the space of his body, making her all too aware of the inches between his hip and hers, his legs and hers.

"Why are you doing all of this? Is it because of what you said? Why did you come find me today?" Evelayn suddenly asked, tired of pretense, tired of waiting and wondering. *This*—whatever was building between her and Tanvir—at least she could pin down. She could examine and try to understand it.

"Why, to enjoy the pleasant conversation, of course," Tanvir teased but Evelayn just glared at him, and the smile on his face died. "What do you mean?"

"Did you notice me before . . . before all this?" She gestured to the diadem that she had to wear from morning until night, and all that it symbolized and encompassed. "I know you said that you . . . in the forest that day . . . that you . . . But I can't help but wonder. Has someone been pressuring you to try and create a connection with me?"

Tanvir's eyes widened, and if Evelayn's emotions weren't drawn so taut, she might have laughed. "*Pressured* me? To . . . to . . ."

"Because they are pressuring me," Evelayn interrupted his unusual stuttering. Perhaps it wasn't what she'd assumed after all then, based on his embarrassment. Or maybe he was just that good. "It's not as if there is a massive battle looming ahead of us, or a fight that I'm terrified I won't win to worry about. I've already been lectured three times this week alone on the fact that even though I am so very young, and it is extremely rare for any Draíolon to choose to be Bound to someone at my age, that as queen I have a duty to provide an heir as soon as possible. That I must procreate as quickly as I'm able, to ensure the royal line carries on, since there is no one else if something happens to me. And you seem to be a nice option, if I were the type to try and orchestrate this kind of thing."

"A nice option?" Tanvir echoed.

"Good family, attractive, strong abilities. Orphaned by the war, so that we have something in common to connect over."

"I'm glad to hear you think I'm attractive . . ."

Evelayn barely withheld a snort. "You know you are. So who was it? Kel? He let you come to get the silk so we'd have time alone—right? And he's championing your plan. Is he the one?"

Tanvir cleared his throat, and glanced over his shoulder, reminding her that they had an audience. "Um, Evelayn . . . I'm not sure *now* is . . ."

She just waited until he shifted uncomfortably on the log.

"But then again, no time like the present to have very important conversations. With an audience." Tanvir gave her a pointed look, but she just glared back. "Look, Ev, I promise you, no one has spoken to me about trying to orchestrate a, um, connection between us. And no one has mentioned the need for you to . . . uh . . . procreate on an accelerated schedule to me either. I know you are young, which is why I haven't made my overtures any bolder than they have been. But I assure you that the interest I admit to having in you is purely selfish. Because I also find you to be attractive—in every way possible. Your mind, your strength, your will, and everything else, too. When I said I loved you, *I* was the only one saying it. Because I meant it."

Evelayn stared at Tanvir. "Oh."

Tanvir shrugged, his expression a comical mixture of contrition and alarm.

"Oh," Evelayn said again, *her* eyes widening this time, flushing hot with embarrassment. "I'm so sorry. I assumed and I . . . oh my. This is . . ." She trailed off and turned away, before he could see the heat rising in her cheeks.

"Please don't," Tanvir said, his voice quiet. "I know you're under immense amounts of pressure, and you have every right to be suspicious of everything and everyone. I picked a terrible time to try to . . . well, you know."

"Create a connection with me?" Evelayn quoted herself, miserably horrified at the accusations she'd made so heedlessly. And after he'd told her he loved her, too. She really was quite adept at making a mess of everything.

"Something like that." Tanvir sounded amused, not angry, and she braved a peek over her shoulder at him. His smile was like the sunshine breaking through a dreary winter morning.

"You're not mad at me for questioning you so . . . bluntly? For . . . for doubting you?"

"Of course not," Tanvir immediately responded. "Now I know you find me attractive. That is far more important than knowing if you love me back or not."

Evelayn found herself laughing, something she hadn't done much of since her mother's death. It was an unexpected gift. Before she could stop herself, she bent forward and pressed her lips to his. He stiffened in shock but immediately softened, wrapping his arms around her and pulling her in to his body. Tanvir's mouth was soft on hers, an unspoken promise of what was to come.

If they survived the summer solstice.

She broke away reluctantly, but Tanvir kept his arms around her, holding her silently as they watched the swans glide across the glassy water.

After a few minutes, Evelayn finally sat up straight, and Tanvir let her go.

"When this is over . . . when you succeed . . . may I formally call on you, Evelayn?" Tanvir glanced down at his hands and Evelayn felt something inside her drawing out, wishing to pull his gaze back up to hers.

"Are you asking to court me, Lord Tanvir?"

"I believe I am, Your Majesty."

Evelayn reached out and touched his hand hesitantly. He looked up, his amber eyes sending a thrill through her veins.

"Yes, you may call on me. If I live to see that day come."

Tanvir turned his hand over so that his fingers slid between hers, sending a wave of warmth up her arm. "You will."

"Do you think I've made the right decision—to trust Caedmon?"

"I do." Tanvir squeezed her hand. "And I will be there beside you. If he plays us false, I will carve his heart out myself."

"If he plays us false, we will *all* be as good as dead."

Tanvir shook his head, squeezing her hand even tighter. "You can do this, my queen. Take all the pain, all the rage and hurt, and channel it. Use the power you have access to and kill Bain. No matter what game any of the Dark Draíolon may or may not be playing, you can succeed. I believe in you, Evelayn."

She squeezed back, her gaze on their entwined fingers. She wanted to see where this led . . . what it would feel like to be courted. She wanted to live in a world where she had to plan festivals and celebrations, instead of battles.

"I hope you haven't misplaced that belief," she said to their hands.

"I haven't."

Evelayn looked out at the swans, now far away, across the lake, and let herself hope.

THIRTY-THREE

T HE FIRST COURSE OF FRESH, SLICED FRUITS DRIZZLED
with a deliciously sweet sauce, and warm, crusty bread, had
only been on the table for a few minutes when the doors at
the end of the dining hall burst open. All eyes turned to the male who
rushed toward the queen with a note clutched in his hand.

"Word from Ristra, Your Majesty," he said breathlessly.

Ceren watched in trepidation as Evelayn stood and took the missive. The little bit of color she'd regained in her cheeks the last few days
drained out again as she dismissed the runner.

The parchment crinkling as she opened the letter was the only
sound in the room; everyone's focus was riveted on the queen.

Finally, Evelayn looked up, her eyes going to Tanvir's first, then
to Ceren, then to the table as a whole. "Bain's army is on the move
toward Ristra and brings a force larger than he ever has before. Our
battalions require immediate assistance." The note crumpled in
Evelayn's fist.

Even though Ceren knew this moment would come, knew that it

would happen at any hour, dread still coated her body like ice and made the little bit of food she'd eaten turn to lead in her belly.

"General Kel, please convene my council at once."

"Yes, Your Majesty." He nodded, then pushed his chair back to stand and hurry out of the room, other members of her council who had been at the meal following quickly in his wake.

Evelayn straightened to her full height and looked over those who remained, including Ceren and Quinlen at her side.

"Do not fear what is to come. I *will* protect my people and my kingdom. *Bain will not succeed*." The words were a ferocious growl, a promise that was so convincing even Ceren felt her own terror ebbing slightly, though she knew the challenge that lay ahead for Evelayn.

"May the Light be with you all," she said, and then inclined her head to her subjects seated at the table.

"May the Light be with you," was repeated back multiple times as she strode out of the room to meet with her council and put her plan into action at last.

Quinlen took Ceren's hand and laced his fingers through hers beneath the table, holding on to her just as tightly as she held on to him.

"May the Light be with you," she whispered thickly when the door had shut, taking Evelayn away from her sight, "and bring you safely back to us."

There was no breeze, no movement to the air whatsoever. The heat swelled up from the ground and pressed down from above, creating a suffocating morass of humidity. Lorcan truly hated summer. It was too hot, but even more than the heat, he hated feeling that slight loss of power that tilted in favor of the Light Kingdom during spring and summer. His father believed that by defeating Queen Evelayn and claiming the Light Kingdom's power for himself, he could put an end to the shifting balance of power and keep it all for himself, year-round.

And though it had seemed far away, so very far away, when this war started a decade ago—when Lorcan was still a youngling—it was now so very, very close. *All* their plans were close. They moved silently through the forest. And though he didn't care for Éadrolan or the heat of summer, Lorcan couldn't help but be grateful to at least be free from the unnatural grayness of the Undead Forest. He hoped never to go back to the accursed place.

They were a silent group moving through the trees toward the appointed place. His father, King Bain, was behind him, as was Lothar. The two priests he'd brought were in front of the princes. Always, even with a limited number of defenders, the king wished to be the most protected. Even more than his own sons. Caedmon was in the lead, guiding them through the path he'd discovered when he'd been sent to scout out Éadrolan for this ambush. The other two generals brought up the rear, protecting the king's back—just in case.

If what Caedmon had told them held true, they were getting very close to where the army would be traveling through the forest to defend Éadrolan from the decoy attack on Ristra. Then it only remained to get into position to spot the queen, fall in behind her, and kill her—finishing Bain's plan and sealing the Light Kingdom's fate once and for all.

Caedmon made a signal from ahead and they all paused. When Lorcan held his breath, he could just hear the muted sound of horses and people moving through the forest in front of them. Caedmon had led them truly and now was their chance. A rush of adrenaline spiked through Lorcan's body as Caedmon gestured again. They stalked forward to fan out and take their positions, the prince's father staying back with the two priests until the queen had been spotted. Lorcan itched to change into his other form—it would be so easy to take to the sky and find her. But he was also vulnerable as a bird and could alert the army to their presence. Most Draíolon knew what animal forms the royals could take, and hawks weren't as plentiful in Éadrolan as they were in Dorjhalon.

Instead, he slipped from tree to tree, just behind Caedmon, the sound of the Light Kingdom's army moving through the forest growing louder and louder. Finally, Caedmon lifted his fist and they all halted. Squinting, Lorcan could just make out the marching figures of the Éadrolanian soldiers. Females and males dressed in the colors of the forest, with weapons strapped to their bodies, moved quickly forward. They weren't marching at full speed, most likely trying to conserve energy for the battle ahead, so he could see their faces briefly before they moved past him. The commanders were on horses, guiding their troops toward their inevitable defeat.

All their plans were about to come to fruition—*all* of them. Lorcan couldn't let himself think too much about it, afraid his feelings or scent would give him away. Hopefully his father attributed it to being excited and nervous about completing the plan to kill Queen Evelayn.

And then he saw her. The queen.

She was surrounded by priestesses (so she'd decided to be a bit more cautious than her mother, he noted), and they were all riding white mares. All of the women's faces were veiled, just as Caedmon had said they would be. When he'd scouted out the palace and tried to discover what routes the army frequented, he'd caught sight of her, and he'd told them she'd been wearing a mourning veil, as were all of her priestesses. Caedmon hadn't been sure if it was an attempt to keep her true features from being readily identified, or if it was just her unique form of mourning. Lorcan had to suppress the urge to attack at that very moment—but he knew better. Only his father had enough power to kill her. And only *she* had enough power to kill his father. If he alerted her to their presence too soon . . .

Caedmon whistled once, a short, quiet trilling sound that expertly echoed the call of a sparrow. The signal for King Bain to move forward with his priests and take his position. Just as they'd assumed, the queen and her priestesses were at the end of the procession. An entire battalion of warriors brought up the rear to protect her from attack from behind. It was more than they'd expected, but still not nearly enough to stop them. Not with King Bain and both of his sons to contend with.

Or so his father thought.

Lorcan felt his father's presence before he heard the soft footfalls of his approach. The power Bain exuded called to the stone in Lorcan's own forehead. Someday, *he* would be the one to wield that power. Someday, he would be the one to rule their kingdoms.

But first, they had to finish what they'd started.

Caedmon had just lifted his hand to make the final signal, when he paused, his head cocked. Lorcan froze as well, his hands halfway lifted, prepared to attack. He'd heard it, too. He spun around just in time to see a handful of Draíolon dressed in dark, close-fitting clothing rushing at blinding speed through the forest, straight toward them.

Evelayn didn't pause when she realized they'd been spotted. Everything had been exactly as Caedmon had promised—the formation of the king and his sons, their location, everything. She only had a split second before the king turned and realized what had happened. She lifted her hand and shot a blast of light at his back. But one of his priests shouted a warning and simultaneously threw a pulsing ball of shadow-flame at her. She had to throw her body to the side, scraping her arm and face on the branches of a tree to avoid being hit. The black flames erupted against the trunk she'd been standing by with a reverberating boom that shook the ground.

Kel and Teca rushed forward, throwing blasts of white-flame and light at the princes, while the other priestesses who had come with her fought the other Dark Draíolon. They'd changed the plan slightly, having other Draíolon attack with her, so if Bain did catch anyone else's scent when he was chasing her it wouldn't strike him as suspicious.

She'd failed at the first attempt—to get him from behind before being spotted. But she knew it couldn't have been *that* easy. It was time to move on to the real plan.

Evelayn hurried around the trees, trying to ignore the sounds of the fighting going on behind her, searching for King Bain. She'd expected him to come for her, but instead she found him standing in front of someone else.

"*No!*" She rushed forward, but it was too late. He had Caedmon trapped.

"Make it worth it!" Caedmon shouted, his eyes meeting hers just before King Bain shot a jet of darkness that blasted through his chest and he crumpled to the ground, dead.

The king whirled to face her, and Evelayn pulled up sharply upon confronting the King of Dorjhalon.

Bain would have been handsome, with his metallic black hair, silver eyes, and the rare coppery sheen to his skin, if it weren't for the rage contorting his face and the gleam of madness in his gaze. Though he was nearing three hundred, he still looked as if he were in the prime of his life. Evelayn knew ruling monarchs could live longer than average Draíolon because of their direct access to the power—some reaching five or even six hundred years old. But he barely looked older than his sons.

"Do you honestly think this will work?" He sneered at her. "Do you truly think *you* can beat *me?*" He shot a blast at her, but it was only halfhearted; she easily dodged it. He was toying with her. So sure of his victory, even with his plans going awry.

Evelayn didn't bother responding. Instead, she looked into his eyes—into the eyes of the Dark Draíolon who had killed both her parents, who had spent ten years trying to tear apart the fabric that held their world together, all because of his insurmountable greed and selfishness. Evelayn looked into his face and saw nothing but endless hunger.

And she did as Tanvir had counseled her. She let all her rage and pain and frustration surge up, calling to the magic until it burned in her conduit stone, begging for release.

"Yes, actually, I do," she finally responded with a smile.

And then she turned and ran.

THIRTY-FOUR

THERE WERE CRASHES BEHIND HER AND SHE COULD only pray to all the gods above that it was Bain following her.

There was nothing she could do to help Kel or Teca or anyone else battling the princes and those behind them, except to defeat the king. Evelayn sped through the forest, the trees whipping past in a blur as she hurried toward the place where Tanvir and the others waited. They would only have one chance for this to work.

Even running as hard as she could, she sensed King Bain keeping pace with her. And she was certain he was a much better shot at full speed than she was. They were almost there—she just had to go a little bit faster. Evelayn pushed her legs forward until her muscles screamed at her, begging for her to slow or stop. The hot afternoon air ripped through her lungs, but she didn't let up. The tree right next to her head exploded, and Evelayn stumbled and nearly fell to avoid the blast of it. He was closer than she'd thought.

Go, go, go, she screamed at herself, launching her body forward again. There was the clearing—almost there—

And then she was hit from behind. She crashed to the ground, pain exploding through her legs.

Evelayn looked down to see black bands encircling her calves and thighs. Bain burst out of the trees into the clearing behind her. Frantic, she blasted away the shadow chains with a jet of light as he rushed toward her. He was going to kill her and it would all be—

But suddenly *he* stumbled and nearly fell as something exploded against his back. He roared in pain—and rage. Evelayn blinked, almost certain it had been *shadow* that had hit him, not light.

There was no time to wonder. Evelayn jumped back to her feet and sprinted away, ignoring the lingering pain from his attack. She glanced over her shoulder to see him barreling after her, Lorcan, Lothar, Kel, and Teca right behind him.

She only had to get him to the other side of the clearing without being killed. Evelayn shot to the right, drawing him toward the forest, and then cut back left just as he sent another blast at her, barely evading the hit. He whirled to follow her, just as Lorcan sent a ball of shadow-flame at her. She threw herself to the ground, but his aim was a little bit off—the fireball exploded just behind her.

She heard Bain curse as she rolled across the earth and onto her feet in one fluid movement. Her entire body hurt, pain pulsing in too many places to count. This was her last chance.

Evelayn sprinted as fast as she had in her entire life toward the edge of the clearing where the trail narrowed once more; the clearing and the forest beyond blurred into a hazy watercolor of greens, browns, and blues. There was the path where Tanvir, Lord Teslar, and the other priestesses waited, not revealing themselves yet in hopes she could still succeed. Bain and Lorcan were both right on her heels. Her conduit stone burned hot in her chest, the power she had access to begging for release, as she somehow found the strength for one more burst of blinding speed.

The moment she hurtled past the appointed spot, Evelayn whirled and lifted her hands. King Bain was right there, his face lit with exultation.

He thought he had her.

And then suddenly, he was ensnared. The webs came from everywhere—the left, the right, even from above where two priestesses clung to branches. It was too many at once. His entire body was trapped for the space of a breath.

Evelayn looked into his eyes once more as she finally released the power and called down the sun. There was a roar, and the sky exploded. Pure sunlight blasted to the earth at the exact moment Bain burst through the webbing with a slash of the shadow-blade he'd summoned, and leapt toward her. There was a split second when the image of his face, contorted with rage, was seared into her mind. And then the light consumed his body.

There was nothing but that blinding beam, the thundering sound of the sun devouring the king of Dorjhalon, and the power flowing through Evelayn's body like a tidal wave she could no longer hold back. She began to vibrate with it; her hands trembled and her stone burned like fire in her breastbone. But she didn't dare let go yet. She didn't know how long it would take to make sure he was truly gone.

And then, suddenly, someone's arms came around her from behind. A gentle, insistent pressure.

"Ev, you did it. He's gone. Let go." A familiar voice murmured in her ear. *"Let go."*

With a gasp, she did as the voice told her, nearly collapsing when, in the blink of an eye, the beam of sun dissipated, leaving behind nothing but a blood-red stone smoking in the charred soil.

"You did it, Ev," the voice said in hushed awe, and this time she knew him. It was Tanvir who held her, who had called her back when she'd almost lost herself in the power.

Lorcan stood on the edge of the clearing, staring at the ground in shock, his brother just behind him.

And that's when it truly hit her. She *had* done it. All the sacrifice and work, all the worry and fear and hours and hours of training had been worth it.

Bain was dead.

THIRTY-FIVE

L ORCAN'S EYES FINALLY LIFTED AND MET HERS. EVELAYN suppressed a shiver. They were the exact same silver as his father's. She knew it was him because she'd heard descriptions of him her whole life. But seeing him in person was an entirely different thing. No one could accurately describe the coldness that etched his handsome face like stone or the arrogant way he held himself, even now, even faced with the loss of his father—his magic. He exuded power . . . even though he was now bereft of it.

She lifted her hands and bound him with shimmering cords of light, despite his having no ability to hurt her. Rather than struggling or protesting, he merely smirked at her, as if he found her diverting.

The others came out from hiding, all celebrating, shouting her praise, but Evelayn only had eyes for the new king of Dorjhalon, and she watched him—calculating. Though she wanted nothing more than to celebrate with her people, to allow her relief to swallow up the fear and tension that had held her captive for the majority of her life, she knew that what happened next was just as important as having killed Bain. Kel and Teca soon appeared, prodding Lothar, who was similarly bound with cords of light, forward to stand beside his older brother.

Though Lorcan had his father's silver eyes, he had his mother's snow-white hair and obsidian-black skin—he was stunning. Lothar, on the other hand, was the spitting image of his father. The metallic glint of coppery skin, with raven-colored hair and slightly darker gray eyes. They were *both* extremely handsome—and extremely dangerous.

"What do you know of the need for balance in our world?" Evelayn finally spoke, still watching Lorcan.

His gaze was unreadable as he looked down at her. She was tall, but he was taller. Much taller. "That depends on what you mean by 'balance.'"

Evelayn tightened the cords around him, letting him feel the force of the power she wielded—reminding him that she had the ability to cut his life short if he wasn't careful.

"You know exactly what I mean."

Lorcan's jaw tightened, and after a pause he nodded, a sharp jerk of his head. She loosened the cords enough to let him breathe again, and he inhaled and exhaled loudly. "If I'm going to be honest with you, I don't know what I believe."

Evelayn glanced over his shoulder at Kel and Tanvir, who stood together, watching their interaction. Kel's expression was unreadable, but Tanvir's eyes were narrowed, as if weighing Lorcan's every word.

Her choices were so limited—and fraught with risk.

If she let Lorcan go, he could try to perform the ceremony to claim the power the Dark Draíolon were now without. He didn't have his father's body, but the stone was still there, lying on the ground. There was the possibility he *could* rule his people in peace in Dorjhalon . . . but there was also the possibility he could take up his father's battle and carry on the war.

Or she could kill him, giving the chance to Lothar. Caedmon had claimed he wanted peace—but he hadn't been sure. Was it worth killing again to find out? And if he'd been wrong, what then?

Or she could hold them both captive until the three days had passed. Lorcan would have to travel to the Immortal Tree to try to regain access to their power—*if* she let him go.

Or she could kill them both and leave the kingdom of Dorjhalon without a king. But where would that leave their world?

She believed what Caedmon had believed—what he'd died trying to regain. There was supposed to be balance. Light and Dark, summer and winter, working together to bring life through its full circle every year. Their world and the world beyond them needed both to survive. There had never been a time when there wasn't a king of Dorjhalon and a queen of Éadrolan to rule together, keeping that balance. No one truly knew what would happen if one kingdom was left without a monarch.

So what did she do now?

Tanvir stepped forward and, with his eyes on Lorcan, quietly said, "You don't have to make a decision now. Take them back to the castle and think on it for a day or two."

Evelayn waved him back, not wanting to appear as though she needed his advice. But regardless, his words aligned with what she'd been leaning toward.

"Take the captives to the castle and keep them bound until I decide their fates," Evelayn finally said, turning away from Lorcan's disconcerting silver eyes. "Send word that their mother, Queen Abarrane, be brought to the castle as well. The rest of the Dark Draíolon are free to resume their lives, as long as they are willing to make an oath of peace with us. Any unwilling to make that oath shall be sentenced to captivity until such time as their power is returned. If at that time they are still unwilling to make a vow to uphold the peace we have regained, they will be sentenced to death."

She paused and looked around at all those gathered, they moved quickly to follow her commands. As Kel and Teca organized the others and roughly guided Lorcan and Lothar back the way they'd come, toward the castle, it finally, truly hit her.

Evelayn looked up at the expanse of azure sky above them and tears filled her eyes. *I did it, Mama,* she thought, hoping that somewhere, somehow, her mother was still watching and was proud of her. She swallowed the emotion down, and when she looked back at Tanvir and Kel and Teca and the rest of those who had helped her defeat King Bain, she was smiling.

"Let the word be spread through both kingdoms—peace has been restored at long last!"

THIRTY-SIX

THE DUNGEONS IN ÉADROLAN WERE QUITE DIFFERENT from those in Dorjhalon. They'd been there long enough for Lothar to be quite certain of it. Just as he was certain that even though the three of them were sharing one cell, his mother and brother were still keeping something from him.

Three weeks they'd been locked there together without one glimpse of Queen Evelayn. Perhaps she had decided to let them rot. So much for her claims of wishing for balance.

In Dorjhalon, the cells were made of obsidian and quartz. The walls were slick and dark and cold. But in Éadrolan the cell was one continuous circular enclosure, carved out of a pure white stone Lothar had never seen before. It never seemed fully dark there; even in the middle of the night their prison almost seemed to glow, the white stone reflecting the tiniest particles of light back at them.

It was nearly impossible to sleep. Or even rest.

So instead, Lothar paced. And listened.

There were three cots set up for them. The bedding was actually quite nice, soft and clean. And their guards allowed them to leave and use the privy, rather than forcing them to use a chamber pot in front of one another. As far as being imprisoned went, the queen had seen to it that they were not treated like common criminals. But they definitely weren't being treated as royalty, either.

"*Cots,*" his mother had sneered when they'd dragged her in, four days after Lorcan and Lothar had been locked up, lifting her hands as if to burn the offensive sleeping situation, only to realize she had no power to draw upon. "She claims to want peace and *this* is how I am to be treated?"

No one answered her, because Lorcan hadn't spoken in days, and because Lothar had nothing to say. Lorcan didn't like it any more than his mother, but Queen Evelayn wasn't the one who had started the war or instigated so much death and suffering. She was orphaned because of his father. How could she not let some of the hatred and anger she was sure to feel bleed into her dealings with them? She had no way of knowing how involved or uninvolved any of them had been in the war or the murders of her parents. Yes, she'd had her revenge when she'd killed his father, and by every right, he should have hated her now, too. But instead, he felt . . . pity. He felt *bad* for her.

Lothar decided to keep his peace, too, because he knew if there was something his mother and Lorcan didn't feel for the new queen of Éadrolan, it was pity.

And so it had continued for days and then weeks, with none of them speaking. Eating in silence when the guards brought them food, and lying on their cots in silence at night, pretending to sleep. But Lothar couldn't shake the suspicion that somehow his mother and

Lorcan were still planning . . . *something*. They'd always assumed he didn't pay attention, that he was too distracted by his books to be of any use to them.

They were wrong.

He scented an unfamiliar Draíolon moments before there was a knock at the door, and then it opened to reveal a tall male with pale blond hair and bright green eyes. He was dressed like a distinguished member of the royal court, not a guard. Lorcan and Abarrane both rose from their cots, where they'd been lounging while Lothar paced.

"I come with an offer from Queen Evelayn. She sends her apologies that it has taken longer than she had hoped to come to a decision, but she finally reached an agreement with her council. They have consented to allow Lorcan to leave and travel to the Immortal Tree to regain his power if he will make a Blood Vow of peace before both courts, and if his brother, Lothar, and mother, Abarrane, remain here as a show of good faith between our two kingdoms and as guarantee of continued peace in Lachalonia."

"*Indefinitely?* She wishes me to stay—"

Lorcan spoke over his mother's screech, cutting her off, "You may tell your queen that we will think on her offer."

The tall Light Draíolon bowed briefly and shut the door behind him with the inescapable sound of the lock scraping back into place.

The moment his scent was gone, the indignation smoothed off his mother's face. Completely serene once more, she glanced at Lorcan, who met her gaze, his expression cold. And then she lay back down on her cot and closed her eyes.

Lothar stared at Lorcan until his brother finally turned to him.

"You're not going to tell me, are you." It wasn't a question.

Lorcan didn't even blink. "I don't know what you're talking about."

Lothar inhaled deeply, letting his brother know he could scent his lie. But Lorcan merely turned his back to him and sat down on his cot, leaving Lothar to resume pacing.

"It's been five days." Evelayn stared at the plate of scones and her cold peppermint tea despondently. "If he truly wanted peace, he would have made the oath and gone to reclaim his power by now."

"I can't pretend to understand what he's trying to accomplish, but he hasn't *rejected* your offer yet, either," Tanvir pointed out.

They sat at a small table in the gardens, having tea. Well, *he* was having tea. Evelayn couldn't eat. She was too worried to do much more than take a sip or two before abandoning her cup entirely, and she didn't even attempt to eat the scones.

The full heat of summer was upon them; her people were enjoying the height of their power and the first peace in a decade . . . but Evelayn couldn't relax. Not yet. Not until balance had been restored, and the problem of King Lorcan and his all too intelligent quicksilver eyes was solved.

"He is a proud Draíolon," Tanvir continued musingly, "raised by one even more proud and domineering than we can imagine. *You* hold all the power right now—he can't do anything unless you *let* him. Perhaps he fears looking weak if he agrees to your offer too quickly."

"Or maybe he's as sadistic as his father and doesn't want peace. Maybe he's just trying to make me sweat."

Tanvir reached out and gently covered her hand with his own, stopping her from picking the tablecloth apart entirely. "Unluckily for him, you are just as attractive when you're sweaty as you are when you're as dry as this scone."

Despite herself Evelayn laughed softly. "Were they that bad?"

"Let's say I will be quite glad when your regular cook comes back from visiting family next week."

Evelayn smiled with a shake of her head, but quickly sobered. "He doesn't care how attractive I am. He wants his power back. And his people *need* it." She glanced across the grounds at the forest to the north of the castle, where far away the border was no longer guarded by her priestesses, and Light and Dark Draíolon were once again able to travel freely and without fear. "But I can't let him do that unless I can be sure he will maintain this peace."

Tanvir's fingers curled around her hand, and he squeezed it reassuringly. "He'll answer. And he'll accept your offer. Lorcan is smart. He knows the only way to get his power back is to make the vow and keep the peace."

Evelayn looked back at Tanvir. "I hope you're right."

"I am. Haven't you learned that yet?"

She pursed her lips at his teasing but couldn't keep from smiling.

"And speaking of being right, I'm looking forward to tonight. It will be just the distraction you need from all of this. I promise." Tanvir lifted her hand to press a kiss to her knuckles.

"And you are always right," she said with a smile.

"Yes, I am."

THIRTY-SEVEN

THEY'D BEEN WALKING FOR QUITE SOME TIME WHEN Tanvir stopped Evelayn. She recognized the scent of the lake even though she couldn't see it—he'd blindfolded her while they were still inside the castle, and then begun leading her to his "surprise."

"Wait right here."

Evelayn nodded, straining to hear anything that would give her a hint of what he had planned. Besides the lake she could also smell flowers—an inordinate amount for where she knew she stood. After only a few moments, he spoke again.

"All right. You can look now."

Evelayn reached up and took off the blindfold and then gasped.

Tanvir stood next to a table, where two chairs were set up across from each other, with yellow ribbons tied around the backs. The white tablecloth was strewn with flower petals as was the entire shore of the lake where the table stood. He was dressed in his formalwear, his brown hair pulled back and a nervous smile on his face. The sun hadn't set yet, but it was dipping below the treetops, painting the entire scene golden with its waning light.

"May I get your chair, my lady?" He pulled one out and Evelayn sat down, still speechless with awe.

After he sat down as well, servants materialized from the forest as if he'd summoned them by magic. Within moments a candelabra was lit in the center of the table, crystal goblets were filled with fresh-squeezed guava juice, and a beautiful dinner of warm bread and butter, honey-drizzled melons, sliced pears, crisp vegetables sautéed with herbs, an aromatic vegetable soup, and roasted pheasant were set in front of them.

Evelayn surveyed the table and then looked up at Tanvir, his golden eyes glowing in the candlelight. "This . . . this is unbelievable."

"I wanted to do something special for you. I hope I succeeded."

Evelayn nodded, unable to speak again. "You did," she finally managed.

He took her hand and lifted it to his mouth, gently kissing each one of her fingers, sending thrills up her arm and straight to her belly. "I'm so glad." He smiled and let go of her hand to pick up his fork. "Now let's eat."

Evelayn was surprised to realize she was actually hungry for the first time in . . . a while. But she couldn't resist teasing him back—at least a little. "Do I dare? I know you weren't impressed with the scones earlier . . ."

"I might have convinced your cook to return a day or two early, for the special occasion." Tanvir winked at her.

"You didn't!"

He grinned.

"And what special occasion did you convince her was so important that she had to cut short her first vacation in three years?" Evelayn asked before taking a bite of the sweet bread. It melted in her mouth, delicious and warm and perfect. She nearly groaned in pleasure.

"Why the night I asked you to be Bound to me, of course."

The fork clanged against Evelayn's plate when she dropped it and stared at Tanvir with her jaw half-open. He was still grinning at her . . . Was it another joke? Was he still teasing? But then his jaunty smile slid away until he was staring back at her, completely serious.

"I was going to wait until after we finished eating—but I can't wait one moment longer. I know it's fast. I know we're young. I know I don't deserve you for so many reasons. But I also know that I love you as I've never loved anyone, and I can't imagine my mornings without waking up at dawn to chase you through the forest. I can't imagine my dinners without your smile to brighten even the worst of days. In short, I can't imagine my life without you beside me now—and forever." Tanvir stood and came over to where she sat. He took both of her hands in his and gently pulled her to stand up in front of him. "I don't want you because you're the queen, or because you've been pressured to provide an heir, or for any other reason except that you love me as I love you. Do you, Evelayn? Do you love me enough to Bind yourself to me?"

Evelayn could barely see him through the tears she struggled to hold back. "Yes," she finally whispered. "I do love you, Tanvir, and I will Bind myself to you."

"You will?" He almost sounded shocked, which almost made her laugh, but then he kissed her, stealing her words and her air as his arms came around her body, pulling her into him. She held on as tightly as she could, meeting his need—his love—with her own, as his mouth moved on hers. But all too soon he broke away to reach into his pocket. She whimpered in protest, and he laughed softly.

"Patience. I have something I need to give you." And then he pulled out the most beautiful ring Evelayn had ever seen.

"Tanvir," she breathed, speechless once again as he slid the ring onto her right hand. It had a thin band with diamonds all the way around it, and an unbelievably clear, pink center diamond, surrounded by small white diamonds set in a way that made it almost look like a flower. She couldn't stop staring at it.

"So . . . does that mean you like it?"

Evelayn nodded so hard her diadem threatened to fall forward off her head. And then she threw her arms around Tanvir's neck, staring at the glittering ring over his shoulder, unable to stop grinning. "I love it. And I love you."

"I told you I'm always right."

Evelayn pulled back with an affronted snort. "Excuse me?"

"I promised that tonight would be a perfect distraction from everything else."

She laughed and swatted at his chest, but that made her ring flash in the quickly dimming light of dusk and she got distracted staring at it again, which made Tanvir laugh.

"We should probably finish this incredible dinner that Cook slaved over all day to make for us," he gently teased, and Evelayn made herself sit down and pick up her fork again. But she kept stopping with her food halfway to her mouth to admire her ring again and again.

"If I didn't know better, I'd think you only said yes for the ring," Tanvir teased.

"And how do you know I didn't?" Evelayn shot right back.

"Because," Tanvir pointed his fork at her right hand, "I didn't show that to you until *after* you said yes."

The forest echoed with their laughter. It was the perfect moment—Evelayn couldn't remember the last time she'd been so happy.

She was so distracted, as Tanvir had promised, she didn't even hear or scent the Draíolon running toward them until he burst through the trees, breathing heavily, startling them both.

Evelayn half stood up in alarm, but Tanvir beat her to it.

"What is the meaning of this?" he demanded. "I gave implicit instructions we were not to be disturbed unless it was an emergency."

The male Draíolon held out a sealed piece of parchment. "General Kelwyn said this constituted an emergency and that the queen was needed right away."

Evelayn's heart sank as she stepped forward to take the missive. It bore General Kelwyn's seal, not quite dry yet. She unfolded the parchment and quickly scanned his message, then looked up at Tanvir's questioning gaze.

"It's Lorcan. He asked for an audience with me—tonight."

THIRTY-EIGHT

L ORCAN ALREADY STOOD IN THE CENTER OF THE ROOM when the queen walked in, followed immediately by Lord Tanvir. Both dressed in finery, flushed, smelling of happiness and frustration and even desire; Evelayn was wearing one of the thin, glittering diadems that marked the queen of Éadrolan's status and—

Lorcan cursed silently. A stunning stone flashed on her right ring finger. An interesting development, to be sure.

He watched them closely, while the four sentries stood around him, maintaining the strands of Light that coiled around his body like ropes, pinning his arms to his sides. A compliment, he supposed, that they deemed him dangerous enough to still require binding him, even without access to his power.

Evelayn faced him and he was struck once again by how beautiful she was. Large violet eyes, lavender-streaked hair, tall, lithe, and so graceful. She moved the way water flowed, smooth and gliding across the floor. But he knew she was also capable of raging like the worst storm imaginable. He'd never forget her blinding speed in the forest when his father had struggled to keep up with her.

"What did you call me here to tell me?" Her eyes were cold and calculating, but he could scent her nervousness beneath the bravado. His lips twitched from a barely suppressed smirk.

"What, no pleasantries? No 'How are you enjoying your stay in our dungeons?' Or perhaps a 'Did you hear the good news of my impending Binding?'"

"How could you possibly—"

"You weren't wearing *that* on your finger when last I saw you." Lorcan cut her off, holding her gaze for a long moment before turning to Lord Tanvir. "What an unexpected turn of events."

Tanvir glared at him, his fury roiling below the surface, a sharp ashes-and-burned-cinders tang in the room. Lorcan wondered if Evelayn recognized just how deep that anger seemed to run in her chosen companion.

"Everyone deserves at least *some* happiness in their life," Lord Tanvir bit out.

Lorcan allowed himself to smile this time. "Ah, yes, but at what cost? I wonder . . . just how much that happiness is worth?"

"Is that a threat?" Evelayn placed a restraining hand on Tanvir's arm when he tensed as though he wanted to attack. Now *that* truly would be an interesting turn of events. "If you called me here to taunt and threaten me, then I bid you good night." She turned with a swirl of sky-blue skirts, preparing to walk away.

"I will make the vow," Lorcan called out.

Queen Evelayn froze, then slowly turned to face him once more, but remained silent, her expression stony.

"I am the king and . . . my people need their power back. In my involuntary forced time for reflection, I have come to realize there is no other way to accomplish that except to make the vow and do as you wish."

Evelayn signaled for Lord Tanvir to stay where he was and then stalked toward Lorcan until she was only a foot away. She had to tilt her head up to meet his eyes. Her skin was luminous, especially with the pulse of her blood brightening her cheeks, pounding at the groove in her throat. "I will only allow you to make the vow if I am assured that you will *keep* it."

"And how do you intend to see to that?" he asked, his voice whisper soft. "A vow is binding. What more do you want from me, Your Majesty?"

She was close enough to touch—if his arms hadn't been bound to his sides. Lorcan's finger twitched by his thigh, itching to stroke the smooth skin of her cheek, to caress the whiteness of her throat, to see if it was as soft as it looked. Her eyes narrowed, making him wonder if she could scent his thoughts.

"Vows are binding, but hearts and wills are not. Will you keep the peace between our kingdoms, Lorcan? Will you help me restore balance to our world?"

Lorcan stood there, staring down at her, a million thoughts and images and plans racing through his mind. She was beautiful—magnificent even. She'd defeated his father. Though he could taste her fear like salt on his tongue, she was resolute and determined. *If only I had met you a decade ago,* he thought.

But she had been but a youngling then, and it wouldn't have changed the reality of his life.

"I will make the vow and bind myself to your terms, *Evelayn,*" he finally said. "And with time, perhaps you will be able to bind my heart and will to your cause, as well. You are not the only one who has suffered at the hands of my father."

Evelayn held his gaze, her chest rising and falling rapidly. And then without another word, she turned on her heel and strode straight to the door. Just before she left, she called out over her shoulder, "I will accept your vow in five days."

Lorcan watched as Lord Tanvir followed the queen, waiting for him to turn, as he knew the Light Draíolon would. And sure enough, he paused to look back at Lorcan, his expression murderous.

"Don't you dare hurt her."

"I'm making a vow, apparently in five days, to that very end."

Lord Tanvir looked like he wanted to say more, but his gaze flickered to the Light Sentries, then back to Lorcan. Finally, he added, "She's been through enough."

"Haven't we all?"

Queen Evelayn's chosen one glared at him for a moment longer, then turned and stormed out of the room after her, leaving Lorcan alone with the sentries, his thoughts, and the lingering scent of violets and determination the queen had left in her wake.

"Evelayn! Evelayn, wait!"

She continued to walk swiftly away from the room and from Lorcan's smirk, his unreadable quicksilver eyes, and his frost-laced scent of pine trees and something heavier, muskier. Was she making a massive mistake? If he made the vow, he couldn't break it. Their magic would bind him.

But he was smart and powerful. And desperate. She didn't feel comfortable around him—she knew she had to tread carefully with the new king of Dorjhalon. Though she'd defeated Bain, there was a nagging feeling, like an itch that always remained just out of reach, that her battles still weren't over.

"Evelayn," Tanvir exhaled, jogging up to her side and taking her hand in his, pulling her to a stop. "Look at me."

She turned reluctantly to face him. Her sentries paused to try and give them some privacy, but remained at the periphery of her vision.

Tanvir lifted her hand—her right hand, where the beautiful ring glittered, even in the dim candlelight—and pressed a kiss to her knuckles. Evelayn closed her eyes, relishing the feel of his lips on her skin, the strength of his grip, his familiar scent of citrus and spice that cleared away the lingering memory of Lorcan's.

"Am I a fool to offer him this?"

Tanvir kissed her knuckles again and then let her hand go. "You are no fool, and if you wish for balance, you really don't have any other choice."

Evelayn sighed and gave him a wry look. "That wasn't very reassuring."

"If you word the oath correctly you can protect yourself and your people. Everyone will get what they want, and we can finally put all of this behind us." There was a ferocity behind his words that took Evelayn by surprise. When he met her questioning gaze, his eyes were haunted; the ghosts of the family he'd lost seemed to enshroud him.

"I have five days. That's plenty of time to make sure I get it right. Then we can finally enjoy peace." Evelayn paused and glanced down at her right hand. "And start planning our Binding announcement and ceremony."

"Peace," Tanvir echoed with a hint of a smile. "I quite like the sound of that. At last."

THIRTY-NINE

T HE CROWD WAS GATHERED IN THE GRAND BALLROOM, both Light Draíolon and even some Dark Draíolon in attendance, though they were hesitant to mingle—most choosing to remain separate. Evelayn stood on the dais, Aunt Rylese and High Priestess Teca just to her right; Lorcan, Lothar, and Abarrane were to her left. Tanvir stood at the base of the dais with Ceren and Lord Quinlen. Though rumors had already begun to spread, tonight was not the time to officially announce Evelayn and Tanvir's betrothal. Evelayn's right hand felt painfully naked without the ring, even though it had only been five days since he'd given it to her.

High Priestess Teca lifted her arm, signaling the time had come to begin, and a hush fell over the crowd.

"Queen Evelayn of Éadrolan will now address us," the High Priestess announced with a slight nod to Evelayn.

She took a deep breath and stepped forward. "We have gathered here tonight to act as witnesses to King Lorcan's vow of peace. Our world cannot continue without balance. Light and Dark work together to create the day and night, to bring the seasons through their full cycles. Together, Light and Dark enable life, in all of its forms. I wish for the Dark Draíolon to regain their power—for balance to be restored. But I can only allow it to happen with an assurance of peace."

Evelayn turned slightly to where Lorcan stood with his shoulders back, his chin lifted, his white hair falling freely around his obsidian-black skin. His silver eyes met hers and the challenge she saw there sent a chill down her spine. *Please let this be the right thing.*

"And so," Evelayn continued, refusing to be cowed, "if you will step forward, King Lorcan, and make this Blood Vow—which is unbreakable upon pain of death—you will be free to go and reclaim your power from the Immortal Tree."

Lorcan stepped forward, all sinewy muscle and raw power, the stone in his forehead still dull, until he was even with her. They turned to face each other as High Priestess Teca took her position between them, one step back.

"Please give me your right hands."

They did as Teca bade. She took Lorcan's hand first and withdrew the sacred silver knife of the Dawn Temple from her belt loop. Raising it high, she intoned, "By the blood of your heart and life force of your body, make you this vow Lorcan, King of Dorjhalon, which you shall never break or suffer immediate death."

Lorcan looked directly into Evelayn's eyes, his gaze unwavering as Teca cut a thin line across his palm with the knife. Crimson blood bloomed where once was unmarred flesh, but he didn't so much as flinch. Refusing to appear weaker than Lorcan, Evelayn lifted her chin while Teca took her hand and repeated the process. When the silver blade slipped through her skin like a hot knife through butter, it burned as though she had been branded. But she didn't flinch. She didn't so much as blink.

"Join hands so that your blood will bind this vow."

Again they did as Teca commanded, clasping right hands together. His skin was cool, his grip firm, but when his blood met hers, heat flared, as though fire were racing up her arm to engulf her entire body. But still they stood frozen, locked in a battle of wills that she wouldn't—couldn't—lose.

"The blood will bind," Teca pronounced. "State your vow Lorcan, King of Dorjhalon."

His fingers flexed against Evelayn's skin as he began to speak, his eyes never leaving hers. She was trapped in that molten silver of his gaze, in the iron force of his will. "I, Lorcan, King of Dorjhalon, do make this Blood Vow, binding even unto death, that I will maintain peace between Éadrolan and Dorjhalon. I vow to respect and honor the power of Lachalonia, both Light and Dark, to help restore the balance my father attempted to destroy. Furthermore, I vow to rule alongside Evelayn, Queen of Éadrolan, and will not come against her or the Light Draíolon to battle. My life is bound to hers—if she dies, I, too, shall pass away. This is my vow."

"So shall it be." Teca grasped their bound hands, but Evelayn was hardly aware of her anymore. There was only Lorcan, his vow, and the searing pain from their clasped hands.

She'd spent countless hours with her council, writing and rewriting the vow, trying to encompass all their fears without making it so specific that he would refuse to make it for fear of accidentally slipping up and causing himself to die. They'd thought it had been perfected.

But as he'd spoken the words, his voice like the velvet night sky, smooth and infinitely powerful, she'd begun to tremble. What had been meant to be a vow of peace had begun to sound like . . . more. It was Tanvir who had suggested having Lorcan's life be tied to Evelayn's—what better guarantee that he wouldn't seek to kill her? But as Lorcan had spoken the words, she'd felt a tug, a sudden thread between them that made her unaccountably nervous. And there was that underlying sense that he was somehow still mocking her—that she was playing right into his hands.

Teca finally released them, but he didn't let go yet.

"I hope you are satisfied, Your Majesty," Lorcan spoke, but this time it was a low murmur, accompanied by a single stroke of his fingers along the sensitive skin on the inside of her wrist.

Evelayn snatched her hand away from him and raised her chin defiantly. "I am."

She turned to face the gathered crowd, her eyes immediately finding Tanvir's. They were darkened with rage, the muscles in his jaw tight, his hands fisted at his sides. But she couldn't do anything about it—yet. "The Blood Vow is complete. Prince Lothar and Dowager Queen Abarrane shall remain here as a guarantee of our joint efforts to restore peace and balance to Lachalonia. King Lorcan, you are free to go and reclaim your power."

Teca produced two white cloths to wipe the blood from their hands, which Evelayn made quick use of, wanting all trace of Lorcan gone. But he ignored the proffered fabric, his fingers closing over the already-healing wound, his eyes still on Evelayn.

"I look forward to being reunited once I have regained my kingdom's power. More than you can possibly imagine." Then he bowed low to her, an elegant folding of his body that should have indicated his respect for her, but somehow still felt like he was merely taunting her. "Until then . . ." King Lorcan took her right hand in his once more and lifted it to his lips, pressing a kiss on her barren ring finger. She didn't dare react with so many watching, but she wanted to slap him. Or blast him off the dais.

Instead, she stood like a statue as he released her, then turned and sauntered down the steps, off the dais, the crowd parting for him as he strode to the massive double doors at the opposite end of the room. Only when they'd shut behind him did Evelayn release the breath she'd been holding, with a relieved exhale.

The tense silence broke as a few Draíolon began to clap and then suddenly they were all cheering and celebrating, while Evelayn stood on the dais, her hand still burning and her whole body trembling.

FORTY

THE FOREST WAS QUIETEST IN THE MORNING, WHEN most of Éadrolan was still asleep. Dew sprinkled the emerald leaves of the trees like tiny diamonds, and the flowers were only half-awake, their brilliant petals stretching open to the slowly rising sun. It had been months since Lorcan made his vow and left to try to reclaim his power. This late in the year the air was crisp with the promise of winter, but Evelayn merely conjured a soft shaft of sunlight to warm the path she walked, heading toward her favorite place in all of Lachalonia. As beautiful as the forest was at that moment, it was nothing compared to how lovely it looked in the height of summer, when there was no need to use her power to warm herself or to coax the flowers to show their jeweled faces.

But at least she no longer had to worry about the consequences of the balance of power shifting to the Dark Draíolon with the return of winter, now that peace had been restored—and Lorcan had made his vow.

The path wound down through the trees, the ground mossy beneath her bare feet as she moved swiftly away from the palace. Her councillors and priestesses knew she still left every morning by herself, usually to go running, but she'd finally convinced them there was no longer a need for anyone to accompany her and disturb the peace she found in the rare solitude she had at dawn. Tanvir usually came with her, and that was protection enough.

Evelayn continued on for a few more minutes and then, finally, she caught a glimpse of the water and a flash of white. She moved slowly now, not wanting to frighten the flock. They tended to be more nervous in the colder months, when predators were more desperate. One swan lifted her head and watched Evelayn as she carefully sat down upon the log, waiting to see if she'd brought them bread this morning. Only when Evelayn remained motionless for a good minute or two did the swan apparently realize she didn't have an offering, and begin to lazily paddle away.

Evelayn watched them for a few minutes, how they interacted with each other and stretched their long necks to duck their heads beneath the water, searching for breakfast. After her father had died, Evelayn had come to this spot every day with her mother, and for a moment she missed her mother so intensely that she felt actual pain—acute and sharp, a stab of loss, an ache of regret.

"I wish you were here for tonight," Evelayn whispered to the air, to the swans, to the soft breeze that brushed at her cheeks. And maybe to her mother, if Evelayn's secret wish was true: that Ilaria was still somewhere nearby—as it had seemed the day of the ceremony when she'd heard her voice. That was the biggest reason Evelayn wanted to visit the swans alone every morning after her run. She'd gotten in the habit of talking to her mother while she was there, and didn't want anyone to hear her. "You would have loved Tanvir."

As the sun rose higher in the sky, warming the earth and the air, Evelayn tilted her face up to let its rays—the power of which she could now harness at will—brush against her skin, and allowed her eyes to drift shut.

Which was why she was *almost* caught off guard when someone rushed straight at her through the trees, moving with extraordinary speed.

Evelayn jumped to her feet, spinning to defend herself against her attacker, only to find herself face-to-face with a grinning Tanvir.

"I nearly got you that time," he said, his eyes sparking with mischief.

There was an affronted trumpeting from the pond, and Evelayn turned to see her swans stretching their wings and taking flight, hurrying away from the newcomer who was altogether too loud and moved too quickly to be trusted. She felt a pang as they flew away, but she didn't want to mar the day by being morose, so she turned to Tanvir with her lips pursed in mock frustration.

"Now look what you've done."

Tanvir glanced at the retreating swans and then back at Evelayn with a slightly repentant smile. "I apologize, my lady. But I couldn't stand to sleep even one more minute knowing that tonight was *the* night—and that I'd find you here alone for at least a few moments."

At his words, her sadness began to dissipate like the dew turning to mist from the warmth of the sun, and Evelayn took a step toward Tanvir. "And why would you wish to seek me out when I was alone, High Lord Tanvir?"

"You know very well why." He reached out to run his hands down her bare arms. The sunlight melted over him, making his bark-brown hair glow as Evelayn tilted her chin up, leaning in to his touch. When he kissed her, she could taste nectar on his lips.

"You seemed sad when you first saw me . . . Were you thinking of your mother?" Tanvir asked a short while later as they finally broke apart, slightly breathless.

Evelayn nodded. "I was wishing she could have been here for tonight."

"I wish she could, too. And your father."

Evelayn reached out to take Tanvir's hand in hers, lacing her fingers between his, just like the first time he'd come to find her on this log, three months earlier, before she'd defeated King Bain. "Your parents, too . . . and your sister."

A dark shadow crossed Tanvir's face, making Evelayn almost wish she hadn't brought up Letha. It was Tanvir's greatest regret—he still felt responsible for his sister's death, even though they'd discussed what had happened many times, with Evelayn trying to persuade him to see that he should not blame himself. He just couldn't forgive himself for losing sight of her during the bloody battle, for the fact that he hadn't been there to fight by her side, to protect her, or to offer comfort as she died.

"Would that they were all here and had been able to rejoice in true peace alongside us." Tanvir gazed out across the pond, as if he could somehow see past this world into the one beyond.

Evelayn squeezed his hand tightly, letting him know that she understood his pain—because she felt the same way.

With a slight shake of his head, Tanvir managed to smile down at her again. "But let's not darken such a bright day with regret or wishes for things that cannot be. No victory ever comes without sacrifice and loss. We've endured the loss. Now let's enjoy the victory." He bent over to press a fierce, almost desperate kiss to Evelayn's lips, which she eagerly returned.

This was why she'd fallen in love with Tanvir—because not only was he kind, but because he seemed to need *her*. Not her crown or her power. Just Evelayn; the comfort she could give him and the friendship and trust they'd developed over the last few months.

Evelayn gently pushed him away a couple of minutes later. "I hate to say this, but I must get back. There's so much to be done before tonight. I'm sure half the court is probably already growing impatient, wondering what's taking me so long."

Tanvir kissed her swiftly once more, then stood, pulling her to her feet beside him. He lifted her hand to his mouth so he could press one last kiss to her fingers. "Until tonight then, my lady."

"Until tonight," Evelayn echoed, wishing she could stay with him all day. *Soon,* she thought. Soon they would have all the days they could ever dream of to be together.

And then before she lost her will to face a long day of preparations, she turned and ran back to the palace, moving as quickly as Tanvir had when he'd tried to sneak up on her. Though she regretted having to leave the pond and the peaceful morning of pretending to be nothing more than just plain old Evelayn behind her, she had no choice.

It was time for her to be the queen of Éadrolan.

FORTY-ONE

"EVERYTHING IS PREPARED AND READY FOR THE GRAND Feast, my lady." Ceren curtsied to her friend, who stood beside the throne, surveying the Great Hall. Her lavender-streaked hair had been intricately braided and arranged around the diadem her mother had worn for so long. The painstakingly wrought swirls of metal that encircled her head and met in a point on her forehead burned silver and white, the gems glittering in the light of the setting sun.

"You know I'd rather you weren't so formal with me, Ceren." Evelayn turned and smiled, her violet eyes bright with anticipation. Ceren was struck once again at the changes in Evelayn since she'd become queen of Éadrolan. She had always been lovely, but now . . . now she was breathtakingly beautiful.

"Well, it feels inappropriate to call you by name when you look so . . . queen-like."

Evelayn shot her a quelling look, but Ceren merely shrugged. It was the truth. The power that Evelayn harnessed made her glow from within. The gauzy silver-and-white dress she'd had created for the special night flowed over her as if it were made of the lightning that she could control at will. The dress had a special opening cut into the bodice to allow everyone gathered to see the pulsing light of the diamond embedded in her chest. She was as delicately pale and seemingly serene as her mother before her.

But Ceren knew that Evelayn held a fire inside her that her mother, Queen Ilaria, hadn't possessed. Many members of the Éadrolan court believed that was why she had succeeded where her mother had failed, despite being so young. Ceren still found it hard to believe that the girl who she'd woven crowns of flowers with, musing over which boy they'd someday fall in love with and Bind to, had truly killed King Bain and ended the ten-year war.

Thousands of candles already burned in the Great Hall, in anticipation for nightfall, reflecting the honeyed light of the sun as it arced toward the earth, preparing to take with it the meager warmth of the crisp autumn day. It was the last day of Athrúfar, the weeklong celebration that marked the end of the harvest and the transition to winter's full power, and the tables were heavy with the spoils of the fields: ripe fruits, sweet breads, roasted nuts, heady wines, herb-crusted fish, and juicy pheasant; there were vegetables bathed in decadent sauces, and all sorts of cakes, pastries, and other desserts, including one of Evelayn's favorites—white-chocolate mousse with fresh raspberries. The musicians had finished setting up in the far corner, and music began to float through the room—an airy, joyful overtone to the increasingly excited hum of the males and females filling the palace.

"Do you think they'll like it?" Evelayn asked, gesturing at the many Light and Dark Draíolon already mingling across the floor below her, something that hadn't happened since the war began, but which Evelayn had insisted on. "Enjoy the celebration, I mean."

Ceren looked out over the growing crowd—the tall, lithe bodies of the adults, the slightly hunched elderly, and the younglings dashing around the legs of their family and friends. Evelayn had wanted every subject of both kingdoms who wished to be present allowed in the palace. Over the last few months, since King Lorcan had left to try and reclaim his power and the peace had held, the two kingdoms had intermingled more and more.

"I'm sure they will," Ceren assured her. She almost reached out to squeeze Evelayn's hand but stopped herself at the last moment, not quite sure if that would be proper in public.

Evelayn flashed her a grateful smile and then continued to survey the Great Hall.

For the first time in over a decade, there were as many Dark Draíolon in attendance at the Great Hall of the Éadrolan Kingdom as Light. The majority of them seemed as eager as Queen Evelayn's people to put the war behind them and forge new bonds of peace and friendship. There had been very few unwilling to make the oath of peace that Evelayn had demanded. Ceren had never seen so many in one place before. She'd *heard* plenty about the Dark Draíolon, the Summoners of Night, Autumn, and Winter, and their penchant for wearing brightly dyed furs and leathers, intricately cut and designed to show off their bodies; but it was different actually *seeing* them mingling with the Light Draíolon, Summoners of Day, Spring, and Summer, who preferred gauzy, iridescent fabrics. Light and Dark together in peace again—finally.

Because of her best friend.

"Go." Evelayn suddenly gave her a little push. "Find someone to dance with. Enjoy the feast. I want to hear all about it when the night is over."

Ceren glanced at Evelayn and thought she caught a brief flash of longing on her friend's face, but then it was gone. As High Queen of Éadrolan, she wasn't able to take part in the revelry, not like she used to. Instead, she had to sit upon her throne and watch as everyone else celebrated the peace she'd won for them.

"Go," Evelayn repeated. "I think I see someone waiting for you." And then her gaze cut to the side. Ceren followed it to see Lord Quinlen standing near the base of the stairs, below the dais the throne sat upon. He wasn't looking at her, but her breath still caught at the sight of his broad shoulders and his pale blond hair.

"All right. But please give me some sort of signal before you make the announcement. I want to be close by."

"I will."

"Promise?"

Evelayn sighed in exasperation. "Yes. Now go. He's not going to wait all night for you."

But still Ceren paused. "You really did it." She gestured at the Great Hall. "All this is because of you. Don't forget this is your celebration, too."

Evelayn shook her head. "Not just me. Many have fought and died to try and win us this peace. It came at a terrible cost."

Ceren knew Evelayn was thinking of her parents and the many, many others who had died. Hundreds of Draíolon on both sides.

Maybe even thousands. "But finally their souls can be at peace, knowing that harmony has been restored. And our children will be able to grow without having to know the fear we did."

"Praise the Light for that." Evelayn took a deep breath. "This is a night to remember those we lost, but also to look to the future. And I believe yours is beginning to get impatient."

Sure enough, Quinlen was now looking up at them—at Ceren—his eyebrows lifted.

Propriety be blasted, Ceren thought, and impulsively bent forward to kiss Evelayn on the cheek. Then without giving the High Queen a chance to react, Ceren hurried down the stairs toward Quinlen and the rest of the Draíolon.

The feast had been in full swing for the better part of an hour when Tanvir finally walked into the Great Hall. Evelayn knew because she'd been watching for him the whole time, growing more nervous with every passing minute that he had changed his mind, that for some reason he had decided it was a mistake. But as soon as he walked in, he looked to the throne and smiled, and her nerves fled at the warmth in his gaze.

As Tanvir wove his way toward her through the crowd, she couldn't tear her eyes away from him. He wore fine linen pants, knee-high soft leather boots, and a silken tunic that came to a V at the tapering of his hips, highlighting his well-muscled chest and arms, his skin turned to burnished honey in all the candlelight. The sash at his waist was the same amber as his eyes, and another matching ribbon tied his long, brown hair back. Many Draíolon's gazes followed him as he made his way toward the throne, but Tanvir only had eyes for

Evelayn, sending a thrill through her body as she tried to remain very still and serene on her throne.

He deliberately held her gaze as he slowly ascended the stairs and came to kneel before her, taking her right hand and pressing a kiss to her fingers, just below the ring she was wearing in public for the first time. His mouth lingered for a moment longer than was proper, sending a shiver up her arm, straight to her heart.

"I apologize for my delay, my lady," he murmured as he stood.

"I'm sure a few of my subjects had begun to wonder at your absence." Evelayn arched a brow at him.

Tanvir's eyes widened with mock affront. "They couldn't honestly believe I'd be frightened off at this point. Because of an intimate party with a thousand of our closest friends?"

Evelayn pursed her lips to keep from smiling.

"If King Bain and his war couldn't tear us apart, your subjects needn't fear that a little thing like announcing our impending Binding like this would frighten me away."

Evelayn found herself laughing with him. Tanvir was right. They'd been through so much in the months leading up to this moment—fighting side by side to defeat Bain, mourning the loss of their parents together, battling through court politics together—if he'd ever doubted his devotion to her, he would have left her side long before now.

"So young to make such a momentous decision."

The smile died on Evelayn's face as she remembered they weren't alone on the raised dais.

Tanvir turned slightly to bow toward the other woman, who had been brought out by her guards a short while before and seated behind Evelayn, to her left. "Queen Abarrane. I hope this night finds you well."

The queen of Dorjhalon tilted her head slightly. "I can't say that it does, quite honestly." Evelayn's guards flanked her on either side, an unused but visible threat in case she tried to cause trouble, but she still managed to look regal—almost powerful—as she sat ramrod straight, not allowing her spine to touch the back of her chair.

"I'm sorry to hear that."

"Lying does not suit you, youngling."

Tanvir's shoulders tightened at the insult, but he managed to keep a smile on his face as he bowed again, a perfunctory little bend of the waist, choosing to remain silent rather than respond. He'd come into his full power years ago, though not nearly as long ago as Queen Abarrane, of course. In point of fact, he was very young by Draíolon standards. He and Evelayn both were. But circumstance had forced them to mature quickly.

Abarrane continued to watch them speculatively. Evelayn hated the gleam in the other queen's eye and wondered again, for the hundredth time, if she'd made the right choice in sparing Abarrane's life as a show of mercy and goodwill toward the Dark Draíolon—and as a way to guarantee Lorcan would keep his Blood Vow of peace before allowing him to go free once more. There were plenty who had questioned her mercy.

She still believed wholeheartedly that Lachalonia needed both Light and Dark power to flourish, and she hadn't seen any other way to regain that balance. Truthfully, she hoped Lorcan succeeded soon. The unnatural shift in the balance of their world that she'd felt since King Bain's death had continued to grow stronger with every passing day, week, and month that the Dark Draíolon remained powerless. And though it was the last day of Athrúfar, it wasn't nearly as chilly outside as it normally should have been by that time of year.

She had no desire to cause the Dorjhalon Kingdom to be destroyed. She only wished for peace—and balance. Evelayn thought she'd come up with the perfect solution, and Lorcan's vow had reassured her that she was right. But now, as she returned Abarrane's stare, she couldn't quite shake a strange sense of foreboding.

Queen Abarrane was close to two hundred, but still as beautiful as any Draíolon in attendance. She had been King Bain's second Binding, after his first died in childbirth, which was why she was nearly a century younger than Bain had been. Her obsidian-black skin was still smooth and her tawny eyes glowed with intelligence—and a faint hint of malice.

Evelayn turned back to the Great Hall, refusing to be drawn into yet another exhausting and mentally challenging verbal sparring match with the much more experienced queen. Surely, Abarrane knew that Evelayn had only done what *had* to be done, for the good of both their kingdoms. Lachalonia would have been destroyed if King Bain had been allowed to continue in his quest to rule over the entirety of it. Of course Abarrane was angry that her husband had been killed, but then, Evelayn wasn't exactly thrilled to have the wife of the man who had murdered her parents sitting on the dais with her, either.

Tanvir motioned to one of the Light Sentries, who quickly moved toward them.

"How may we assist you?"

"Please inform High Priestess Teca that the time has come for the announcement."

When the Light Sentry, a middle-aged man with mauve skin and startling yellow eyes, glanced to Evelayn for confirmation, she nodded, determined to put Queen Abarrane's presence out of her mind. She couldn't change her decision now, and the queen was no threat to her, other than her peace of mind. None of the Dark Draíolon were for that matter, since Lorcan had apparently still been unsuccessful in regaining the Dorjhalon power.

As High Priestess Teca came toward the dais, Evelayn chose to focus on Tanvir and their happiness, not to dwell on the past.

Ceren was still dancing with Quinlen, but more and more Draíolon were pausing, looking at the dais in curiosity as Teca moved with a regal grace up the stairs to stand beside Evelayn and Tanvir. Evelayn kept waiting for Ceren to glance up so she could give her a nod—the signal that the time for the announcement was here—before standing, but her friend was absorbed in her partner, her curled, flame-red hair a beacon on the dance floor. She and Quinlen made a stunning couple; Evelayn was sure another announcement was not far off.

But for now, Teca was looking at her expectantly, waiting for the queen to rise so she could signal the musicians to play a fanfare and begin the betrothal ceremony.

Ceren, look at me, Evelayn thought, willing her friend to notice the expectant hush falling slowly but surely over the gathered Draíolon. Finally, Ceren and Quinlen paused, and her friend glanced up at the throne. Evelayn gave a brief nod, and Ceren grabbed Quinlen's hand, pulling him through the crowd toward the dais. Once they were standing nearby, watching with matching smiles, Evelayn finally looked to Tanvir.

Their eyes met, and she could see her own excitement and happiness reflected back in his gaze.

High Priestess Teca lifted her hands, the flowing white sleeves of her ceremonial robes fluttering up her arms, to signal to the musicians. Within moments, the music cut out and then they played the fanfare that indicated to the crowd to turn to the dais. An immediate quiet fell over the Great Hall, as all the Draíolon faced Evelayn and Tanvir.

"Such pretty, young fools playing at king and queen," Queen Abarrane murmured behind them, but Evelayn ignored her, keeping her smile plastered in place despite the sudden cold shiver that snaked down her spine. She couldn't say why exactly, but she could have sworn there was the hint of a threat in the other queen's words.

Then Tanvir reached for her hand, and from the moment she placed hers in his, there was nothing but the reassuring strength of his grip, and the warmth of his body beside hers as she stood up from the throne, keeping her shoulders back and her chin lifted as they faced the glittering mass of Draíolon side by side. They'd faced far worse together than the bitter, grieving queen, and prevailed. This was their moment of triumph—finally. And no one was going to ruin it.

High Priestess Teca lifted her hands again, but this time as she did, the light of the candles above them expanded, growing brighter and brighter, until the room was glowing as if the very sun itself had been harnessed in the ceiling of the Great Hall and was shining down on them all. Evelayn felt a slight increase in warmth as power was drawn through her stone and out to her people—to Teca. And then there was a huge burst of sparks, raining glittering drops of light down on the crowd, who gasped and then oohed and ahhed together at the display.

"Draíolon of Lachalonia—both Light *and* Dark—today is a day of celebration!" Teca's voice rose and fell in a musical cadence that had the entire hall, even the younglings, hanging on her every word. "At long last, our great and sacred lands have once again found peace!"

A cheer went up from the crowd, and Teca paused until they quieted down once more.

"But peace is not the only reason for celebration this night," she finally continued, and all eyes suddenly fixed on Evelayn and Tanvir. "It is my great pleasure to announce the official betrothal of Evelayn, High Queen of Éadrolan, to Tanvir, High Lord of the House of Delsacht, hereafter to Bind their hearts and souls for this life and the life beyond on the first day of spring in the new year!"

Another, louder cheer rose from the crowd as Tanvir lifted their joined hands up in the air for all to see. Evelayn grinned at her people as four other priestesses walked up the stairs, two carrying the sacred ropes that they would use to entwine their wrists, and two carrying goblets of wine to complete the ceremony.

As the four priestesses stopped beside them, Teca came over and took the ropes, made of gold and silver spun into thread and then braided into an intricate design.

"With these ropes, Queen Evelayn and her chosen king-to-be will pledge their oath to one another for all to see." Teca handed one rope to Evelayn and one to Tanvir.

He let go of her hand as they turned to face each other while everyone watched.

"Please present your left arm, Queen Evelayn," Teca instructed.

Evelayn lifted her left arm in the air, her hand palm-down and her fingers pointing toward Tanvir.

"Please present your right arm, Tanvir, High Lord of the Delsachts."

Tanvir mirrored Evelayn's movement, except his hand was turned up, his eyes on hers, making her stomach dance with the promises in his burning gaze.

Teca continued, "Queen Evelayn and Tanvir of the Delsachts, you may now place the ropes and make your oaths."

As queen, Evelayn went first, wrapping her rope around their arms, binding them together, symbolizing the official Binding that would take place in the spring.

"I, Evelayn, High Queen of Éadrolan, make an oath of intent, to Bind my heart, my life, and my soul to Tanvir, High Lord of the House of Delsacht. He shall be as my left arm, a part of me hereafter and forever more. Flesh of my flesh and heart of my heart." As Evelayn spoke, she couldn't quite keep her voice steady—thinking of all that had happened to finally bring them to this point. Tanvir's fingers brushed against the underside of her arm as he began to twine his rope around their joined arms, interlacing it with hers.

"I, Tanvir, High Lord of the House of Delsacht, make an oath of intent, to Bind my heart, my life, and my soul to Evelayn, High Queen of Éadrolan. She shall be as my right arm, a part of me for so long as we exist. And I shall be at her side, to support her, and love her, hereafter and forevermore." He turned his hand to gently grasp her arm, and she smiled up at him.

An unfamiliar heat spread from the ropes, encircling their arms and then shooting up into Evelayn's body, for a brief moment reminding her of the Blood Vow with Lorcan. She blinked as her conduit stone burned hot against her chest. But then it gradually faded to a pulsing warmth once more, and she banished the memory of Lorcan kissing her hand before leaving, and the sense that though he'd made his vow he was still planning . . . something. She didn't want anything to ruin this night.

"As you have sworn, so shall it be," Teca intoned, taking the goblets—one in each hand—and lifting them up. "Drink and seal your oaths."

Evelayn smiled brightly at Tanvir as Teca handed them each a goblet in their free hands, which they lifted to the other's mouth to drink, symbolizing their reliance upon one another for the rest of their lives and beyond into the afterlife. The wine was stronger than she'd anticipated, burning down Evelayn's throat, then spreading to coat her belly in delicious heat.

"The Oath of Binding is now complete. May the Light bless your forthcoming union!"

The crowd echoed High Priestess Teca's benediction, and then broke into cries of "Praise the Light!" and other cheers. Evelayn stared up into Tanvir's face and couldn't quite bring herself to believe that it was possible to be as happy as she was in that moment.

Someone—who sounded quite a bit like Ceren—suddenly called out, "Kiss! Kiss!" and the cry was immediately taken up and repeated, until it became a chant, echoing through the Great Hall. Tanvir lifted one eyebrow at her, his eyes lit with an unholy twinkle of mischief that made Evelayn's legs feel strangely unsteady.

"We shouldn't disappoint them, my lady. The Draíolon want a kiss."

Evelayn stared up into his face—the face she loved so very much—and grinned. "Then a kiss we will give them. A queen must always keep her subjects happy, above all else."

Tanvir needed no other incentive. He stepped forward, trapping their bound arms between their bodies, and plunged his free hand into her hair, tilting her head up to his. When their lips met, the crowd burst into cheers yet again. Tanvir pressed even closer, his lips moving slightly across hers—a promise of what was to come—and then they reluctantly broke apart.

Evelayn wasn't prone to blushing, but she could feel a brush of heat in her cheeks as Teca stepped forward to undo the ropes, to return them to the Dawn Temple where their most sacred items were kept by the priestesses of Éadrolan.

Once their arms were free, Evelayn stepped forward to address all those gathered.

"Draíolon of Lachalonia, I thank you for joining with me in celebration of our happy news. But even more importantly, in marking this bright new dawn of an age of peace—where Light and Dark will coexist in harmony, side by side. We will work together as was intended in the beginning to—"

Evelayn's conduit stone suddenly flashed ice-cold in her chest, stealing her breath and her words. At the same moment, Queen Abarrane gasped behind her, a sound of surprised pleasure. Many Dark Draíolon around the Great Hall also reacted, jerking or gasping or otherwise indicating that they, too, felt the change.

Her stone returned to its normal warmth, and with it came the sense that the imbalance she'd noticed ever since King Bain's death had finally been righted. This was as it should be—Light and Dark needed each other. Their kingdoms were meant to exist together, to bring complete harmony to their world.

But she could only hope the vow Lorcan had made was truly binding. Because he had finally succeeded. The Dark Draíolon had their power back.

FORTY-TWO

ALL AROUND CEREN AND QUINLEN, THE OTHER Draíolon had begun to murmur—the Light in unease and confusion, and the Dark in excited undertones. Ceren watched as Tanvir reached out toward Evelayn in concern when she stopped midsentence, but she gave a minute shake of her head and he let his arm drop again.

An alarmed buzzing began to build in the Great Hall when the queen didn't immediately continue her speech. But as Ceren watched, Evelayn pulled her shoulders back and lifted her hands to try and regain their attention. When that didn't work, she sent a flash of light out above the crowd. Some of the younglings cried out in surprise, but everyone else rapidly quieted again.

"My Draíolon, balance has once again been restored in our world. King Lorcan has succeeded in regaining Dorjhalon's power!" Evelayn made it sound like a triumph, but Ceren couldn't help glancing around to see if any Dark Draíolon were near her and Quinlen. Could they truly be trusted? "As he has made a vow of peace, I ask you to join in celebrating yet another triumph this night."

Everyone cheered again, but the Light Draíolon's cheers weren't quite as enthusiastic as the Dark. There was a nervous sort of energy in the hall now, where moments before it had been full of joy and happiness at the conclusion of the lovely ceremony.

As Evelayn continued with her speech, Ceren's attention strayed to Queen Abarrane sitting behind Tanvir.

She was smiling.

Anything that caused Abarrane to smile made a hard pit of fear lodge in Ceren's belly.

The rest of the night proceeded without incident, the dancing and feasting continuing for hours, all while Queen Evelayn watched from her throne, Tanvir at her side. Though the initial tension in the room quickly dissipated and the original joviality returned, Ceren couldn't quite shake a strange foreboding every time she glanced up and saw the way Queen Abarrane was watching the celebration with that same little smile curling her lips.

Finally, hours later, when it was closer to dawn than sunfall, Queen Evelayn stood up and lifted her hands, signaling for the music to stop.

"I hope that this feast celebrating the peace between our two kingdoms will be the first of many," Evelayn had just said, when suddenly the three-story-high window on the west side of the Great Hall shattered, blasting shards of glass toward the crowd. The Light Sentries burst into action, rushing with blinding speed toward the broken window as younglings screamed in fear and adults quickly shot waves of light over those closest to the destroyed window to deflect the glass.

Tanvir jumped in front of Evelayn, pushing her back, taking a defensive stance, twin daggers suddenly appearing in his hands. But Evelayn wasn't one to let him stand in front of her while she cowered. Ceren conjured her sword as the High Queen summoned her own weapons—a long sun-sword that crackled with light and a shorter dagger that sparked with lightning in her left hand.

Ceren had just begun to move toward the dais when a hawk as black as night and as fast as shadow dove through the broken window straight toward the queen and her betrothed. In the blink of an eye, a swirl of black smoke twisted through the air, and in place of the hawk stood Lorcan, King of Dorjhalon, dressed completely in black leather.

The crowd gasped and the Light Sentries rushed forward. But Lorcan lifted his hand, and a wall of darkness, writhing with shadows, sprang up around the base of the dais, barricading the four of them— Queen Evelayn, Tanvir, King Lorcan, and Queen Abarrane—from the rest of the Draíolon.

Ceren knew that King Lorcan was older than Evelayn, but not by much, so he, too, was a fairly young monarch. She'd noticed how handsome he was when he'd made his vow; but now his conduit stone was glowing crimson with the power he had regained, which only made his silver eyes even more startling.

He strode to where Evelayn stood stiffly, watching him, took her right hand, and lifted it to his mouth, avoiding the dagger she clutched to press a kiss on her fingers as he had done before leaving months earlier. She yanked it back.

"What is the meaning of this, Lorcan?"

"I see you made it official," he responded, his gaze dropping to the ring on her hand and then flickering to Tanvir.

The sentries were sending blasts of light at the swirling darkness, unsuccessfully trying to break through the shadow wall, but Ceren stood frozen, unable to tear her eyes away from the two monarchs.

"I'm sorry about the window," he continued, "but I never could resist a grand entrance when presented with the opportunity."

Evelayn took a step away from him, closer to Tanvir. "You just regained your power—how did you make it back so quickly?"

"There is so much you have yet to learn, my dear. And I eagerly look forward to teaching you. After you break your Oath of Binding to Lord Tanvir, and Bind yourself to me instead, of course." Lorcan smiled as though he'd merely commented on her dress or her hairstyle, rather than making such an outrageous demand.

Tanvir lifted the sword he gripped, his expression darkening.

"Now, now, let's not get hasty. Someone could get hurt." Lorcan practically growled the last few words and flung a black dart of shadow at Tanvir, which the High Lord deftly deflected.

Evelayn finally moved, so quickly it appeared that one moment she was standing on the dais next to Tanvir, and in the blink of an eye she was behind Queen Abarrane's chair, her dagger lifted beneath the older monarch's chin, threatening to drag it across her throat. Ropes made of light snaked out from Evelayn's fingertips, encircling the older queen, entrapping her so completely there was no possible chance she could use her power to fight back.

"What is it you want, Lorcan?" Gone was the smiling, genteel queen who had been hosting a feast, and in her place was the warrior who had stopped the war. Ceren could easily believe that *this* Evelayn was capable of killing King Bain. She seemed capable of doing anything.

But so did Lorcan as he stalked toward Tanvir, summoning his own twin blades made of swirling shadow and black lightning. "I believe I already made that clear."

Evelayn pressed the dagger against Abarrane's throat, drawing a thin line of blood. "Not another step, or she dies."

The entire crowd watched in silence as Lorcan paused, considering. Tanvir was tensed, ready for a fight. The Light Sentries and priestesses were making barely any progress with the shadow wall. Other Light Draíolon rushed forward to help, hacking at it with sunswords and sending blasts of light and fire at it. The Dark Draíolon throughout the room were edgy, shifting uneasily but not summoning their own weapons—yet.

Ceren hurried forward to join in attacking the wall, desperate to get to her friend—to help somehow. Quinlen followed, conjuring his own weapons.

"I have to say, Evelayn, this is quite the party. I just knew it would be the perfect place to make my grand entrance as the newly invigorated King of Dorjhalon." Lorcan took another step toward Tanvir, and Evelayn pressed the dagger deeper into Abarrane's throat. The other queen made a noise of alarm as her blood began to run a slow trickle down to her collarbone, and Lorcan paused again.

"You made a vow, Lorcan." Tanvir spoke now.

"I made a vow to keep the peace and not to kill Evelayn, true. And as you can see, both Light and Dark Draíolon have gathered here tonight for the festivities, and your queen still stands before you, well and whole." Lorcan shrugged his shoulders.

"Do you know what happens to oath breakers in the afterlife?" Tanvir pressed.

"As I just illustrated, I have broken no oath. Though you're one to speak," Lorcan responded, flippant and unconcerned. Tanvir's gaze hardened and suddenly he leapt forward, a blinding flash of light and fury. Lorcan barely lifted his sword in time to deflect Tanvir's blow.

Evelayn cried out, but there was no stopping the two males as they began to fight in earnest, both moving so quickly that Ceren could barely see what was happening. Blasts of light and darkness and the reverberating boom of their weapons clashing filled the Great Hall. Just when Tanvir appeared to have the upper hand and was poised to deliver a killing blow, Lorcan disappeared into a whirling cloud of darkness, only to emerge in his hawk form, flying around Tanvir so quickly he couldn't react fast enough, allowing Lorcan to shift back into his Draíolon form behind Tanvir, simultaneously sending coils of darkness from his fingertips to encircle the queen's betrothed before he could deflect them.

"No! Tanvir!" Evelayn's cry was a desperate plea, but Lorcan just laughed.

"Oh dear, we appear to be at quite a standoff now, don't we? If you kill my mother, I kill your betrothed." Lorcan shrugged nonchalantly. "Although I believe we can all applaud his gallant attempt to defend his lady. Come along, join me in applauding him." Lorcan's weapons disappeared momentarily so he could clap, turning to face the crowd and gesturing for them to do the same. A few scattered Dark Draíolon clapped, but everyone else stood in stunned silence, except for those still tearing at the shadow wall, desperately trying to get to their queen.

Ceren continued to hack at the writhing shadows with her sun-sword as she watched Tanvir struggle against his bonds; but the chains of darkness made by a royal were unbreakable, except by another royal. And she could tell Evelayn didn't dare move, her knuckles white on the dagger she still gripped against Abarrane's throat.

By the Light, Ceren thought, *will the fighting and terror never end?*

"If you kill him, that is not keeping the peace—you will die, too. What do you hope to gain by all of this, Lorcan?" When Evelayn spoke, Ceren was proud of her friend for keeping her voice haughty—cold even. "Whatever it is, you won't succeed."

"Ah, but I already have." Lorcan's sword reappeared in his right hand, and he stepped forward to press it between Tanvir's shoulder blades. Evelayn remained completely motionless, watching him.

Ceren redoubled her efforts, but it seemed like whenever she started to make a hole in the shadows, more would slither over, filling it back in again. The High Priestess and the other priestesses present were summoning as much daylight as they could, pummeling the shadow wall with all their impressive power—but it was Athrúfar, which meant the Light Power was waning as the Dark Power was coming into its strongest season.

It wasn't enough.

"However," Lorcan continued, "I'm not without reason. In case you didn't hear correctly the first time, I have an offer for you, my dear queen of Éadrolan."

"I don't make deals with oath breakers," Evelayn responded immediately.

"We've already been over this—I have broken no oath yet," Lorcan shot back. "I haven't killed you or broken the peace. And I only ask you to do but one thing."

Evelayn stared at him steadily, seemingly calm and in control, but Ceren knew her well enough that she could tell her friend was frightened.

"Cancel your oath to this unworthy Draíolon and Bind yourself to me instead. Join your power with mine as my queen, so that we might rule our two kingdoms as one, and you shall have your beloved peace."

"Never," Evelayn immediately spat.

Tanvir struggled even harder against his bindings, trying to speak, but the shadows filled his mouth, muffling his words.

"Perhaps you should reconsider," Lorcan said, pressing the sword into Tanvir's back, sending the chains of darkness writhing around his body, like snakes with bodies of black smoke, coiling tighter and tighter, until Tanvir couldn't even move, except to stare at Evelayn, his eyes wide and filled with sorrow.

"Stop it," Evelayn commanded, but her voice was losing authority as she watched Tanvir suffer.

"Say you'll Bind yourself to me and I shall release him. Nice and peaceful, just how you prefer it."

"Never," Evelayn said again, but this time it was a whisper.

"Then you have made your choice." Lorcan's expression became thunderous, and with a flick of his wrist, Tanvir was enveloped in blackness. Ceren's arm fell to her side, the wall forgotten as she stared up at the dais in horror.

"*Tanvir!*" Evelayn finally rushed forward, leaving the queen, to blast a blinding stream of light at the writhing darkness where her betrothed once stood, but it was too late. The darkness broke apart at the onslaught of her power, and Tanvir collapsed to the ground, completely silent and still.

"NO!" Evelayn's scream tore through the Great Hall, a sound that was so full of anguish and fury that even Lorcan—who was still alive somehow despite his vow—took a step back.

And then she sent a blast of light at Lorcan. He barely dodged it in time, so it continued on, tearing a hole through the shadow wall that no darkness was able to refill. The Light Sentries and priestesses quickly converged on the hole, joining their efforts to try and tear it wider so they could get through and aid their queen, alone now on the dais with her two greatest enemies.

"You will consent to Binding yourself to me, or suffer a fate worse than death," Lorcan threatened as he sent a blast of shadow back at Evelayn. She deflected it with a burst of light.

"You can't kill me, or you'll die, too!"

"Ah, but I'm *not* going to kill you. That's the beauty of it." Lorcan attacked again and Evelayn deflected again, but a sudden look of terror crossed her face.

"Something wrong, my lady queen?" Lorcan grinned at Evelayn as they circled each other. Abarrane watched with a calculating gleam from her seat behind them; only the original light-chains on her arms remained to restrain her.

"No," Evelayn said, and shot another stream of light at him, but Ceren could *hear* the fear in her friend's voice now . . . just as the light in the queen's sun-sword seemed to dim slightly.

"Perhaps your subjects are not quite as loyal as you had supposed," Lorcan said, and sent another black tendril of darkness at Evelayn. She cut it apart with her sword, but didn't return his attack this time.

Something was terribly, horribly wrong.

"I believe you are beginning to feel somewhat, shall we say, weak?"

Evelayn lifted her sword up again, but then she stumbled forward a step and the sword winked out and disappeared. The High Queen of Éadrolan stared at her hand as if she couldn't believe it had betrayed her.

"Poison," she said, so quietly Ceren barely heard her, but the word turned everything in her to ice.

"Ah yes, and a very special kind, too." Lorcan sent another tendril of shadow at Evelayn, and though she tried to deflect it, her light flickered and died, and the shadow wound itself around her, trapping her arms at her sides. "Specifically made to block your Light Power completely."

A shocked, terrified murmur rippled through the crowd as their queen—their triumphant, powerful queen—dropped to her knees beside the body of her betrothed. She kept her chin lifted, but she was defeated, and they all knew it.

"Didn't anyone ever tell you my mother was an adept poison-master?"

Abarrane grinned from her seat as she watched her son and the High Queen of Éadrolan.

"She was imprisoned—she was guarded day and night," Evelayn protested.

"But I was allowed to speak with her, and she was still very capable of giving me instructions."

"No one in my kingdom would have done this to me . . . *no one*." Evelayn was emphatic, but Lorcan just laughed.

"Apparently you are quite mistaken about that, my dear."

Quinlen continued to send blasts of light at the wall beside Ceren, but she couldn't tear her eyes away from her friend, terrified she was about to watch Evelayn die.

"I will ask once more. Now that Tanvir is gone, you won't even be breaking your oath." Lorcan walked toward Evelayn, the ruby in his forehead glowing with the power he wielded, while the light in Evelayn's diamond flickered and dulled in her chest. "Will you Bind yourself to me and seal the peace between our kingdoms by joining our power—and our lives—together? We're already bound by the vow I made. This is what is supposed to happen, Evelayn. And you know it."

Evelayn stared up at him, broken and defeated, but still defiant, and Ceren loved her intensely for it. "I will not."

A flash of fury crossed Lorcan's face, and he lunged forward to grab Evelayn's jaw, twisting her face toward his. She tried to jerk away, but his fingers dug into her skin, sending more tendrils of shadow to lock her head into place, forcing her to stare up at him.

"Then you have committed yourself to this fate. I am sorry for it. But there is no other way."

At first Ceren couldn't tell what was happening—it looked as though the shadows were moving across Evelayn's body faster and faster. Abarrane suddenly stood up, breaking free from her bonds, and stepped forward beside her son, hands extended.

The Light Sentries and priestesses were crying out for their queen, so close to widening the hole enough to break through, but they were too slow, and all Ceren could do was watch, frozen in growing horror, as Evelayn began to writhe, her body twisting and contorting.

Lorcan's mouth moved, but Ceren couldn't hear what he said

when suddenly the black bindings became a swirling cloud, hiding the queen from view.

"NO! Evelayn!" Ceren rushed forward, slamming against the wall to no avail. The shadows pressed her back, a cold, swirling force keeping her from reaching her friend before she died, as Tanvir had died.

But when the swirling darkness fell back, Evelayn was no longer there. Instead, a beautiful white swan with violet eyes stood in her place, the diamond conduit stone embedded in the feathers on her snowy breast. Somehow, Lorcan had forced her to shape-shift. The one thing Evelayn had been unable to master. Ceren had never seen a royal force another royal into her animal form against her will.

"Behold your *queen*," King Lorcan sneered, gesturing toward the bird. The swan stretched her wings, preparing to take off, but his mother sent a tendril of darkness around the swan's neck, holding the end of it, almost like a leash, keeping her from flying away.

"Do you see how merciful I am? Allowing her to live, when she showed no such mercy to my father."

Ceren didn't even realize she was still throwing herself against the wall, trying to break through somehow, until Quinlen grabbed her arm and pulled her back.

"There's nothing we can do anymore. Not right now," he murmured to her, holding her in place despite her struggles to break free of his grip. She knew he was right. Even the Light Sentries and priestesses had stopped, standing motionless, waiting.

"And now, watch as I take what she should have given me freely, had she truly cared about peace, as she claimed." Lorcan gestured to his mother, who sent more tendrils of darkness to hold the swan in place.

And then Lorcan took his night-sword, made of shadows and darkness, and cut the conduit stone out of the swan's breast, staining her white feathers crimson with blood as the diamond fell to the ground. The swan screeched in agony, trying to escape her terrible fate, yet unable to do anything but continue her haunting trumpet of pain and despair. Queen Abarrane's dark tendrils tightened even further, refusing to allow the swan to move.

Lorcan bent over and picked up the bloody diamond and held it aloft, his face lit with triumph. "I kept my vow—your queen still lives, and I will maintain the peace. As ruler of *both* kingdoms."

"Kneel before my son—the High King of Dorjhalon *and* Éadrolan!" Queen Abarrane called out.

When only a few Dark Draíolon followed her command, she sent a blast of darkness out at the crowd, causing the younglings to scream again.

Slowly at first, but then faster and faster, the Draíolon—both Light and Dark—dropped to their knees, staring up at the High King of all Lachalonia.

But Ceren didn't look at Lorcan as she was forced to her knees. Instead, she stared at the beautiful swan, still regal and lovely, despite her dark bindings and the bloody hole in her breast.

"This isn't the end," Quinlen murmured beside her. "Somehow, we'll get her back. No matter what it takes."

"No matter what," Ceren echoed as she looked at what was left of her dearest friend, her kingdom's greatest hope, and wept.

ACKNOWLEDGMENTS

THIS BOOK HAD A RATHER INTERESTING ROAD, STARTING YEARS ago when I was playing the suite from *Swan Lake*, by Tchaikovsky, on the piano, and realized I really wanted to figure out how to do a retelling of some sort. I've always loved this ballet and this music, but when I tried to come up with an idea of how to turn it into a story that felt like my own, nothing clicked. I tried three times over the years, but ultimately kept abandoning the partially completed projects because they weren't quite right. Until, finally, in the summer of 2015, Eric C. said the right thing at the right time, and voilà! Inspiration struck and *Dark Breaks the Dawn* finally had the right world, the right characters, and the right plotline to come together at last. So my first thank-you is to him, though he may not even realize what a huge impact his comment had.

Thank you always to my incredible agent, Josh Adams, and the whole team at Adams Lit—especially Tracey and Sam—for always being there for me and for not only believing in my work, but making my dreams a reality. That's some pretty good lemonade with fresh mint!

And of course, so much gratitude to the incomparable Lisa Sandell, editor extraordinaire and dear friend. I'm so grateful we get to work together on another project! And the entire team at Scholastic—you are amazing. I love whenever I get to see you all because it truly is a family, and one I am profoundly grateful to be a part of. Thanks especially to my publicist, Brooke Shearouse, for all her hard work on my behalf. Also a huge debt of gratitude to Elizabeth Parisi for creating the most stunningly beautiful, perfect cover for this book—I may have cried happy tears when I saw it for the first time. And to everyone in marketing, publicity, sales, design, production, copyediting, and all the many departments and jobs that go into creating a book and then sending it out into the world—THANK YOU!

Thank you to Kathryn Purdie for always being there for me, no matter what, rain or shine. I don't know how I'd get through this crazy life without you.

Thank you to Lynne Matson for reading an early sample of this story, and for all your enthusiasm for it—that meant the world to me during a time when I desperately needed it! And thank you to Anne Blankman for reading the early sample AND the finished manuscript, both on short notice. Your feedback is always spot-on! I'm so glad to have such a wonderful agency sister!

Thank you, as always, to my sister Elisse, who is always willing to read for me, and who always helps me figure out how to extract myself from the holes I dig myself into—with my writing, of course. I'd never dig myself a hole in real life (HA!). And thank you to Kerstin for your unflagging support and excitement, and for the occasional DDP or Dole Whip drink. You are so generous and giving, I'm blessed to have you in my life! And thank you to Lauren for always crushing on the boys I write about and for your support as well! I love your reactions to my books. And to Kaitlyn, for being so proud of me and never hesitating to tell me. I truly appreciate it.

A special thank you to Sarah Maas, for being so excited (just from a tweet!) about this book, and for not only wanting to read it, but for your timely and spot-on suggestions, and all your support and friendship in many ways. It means the world to me!

I have met so many incredible people throughout my career (am I allowed to call it that yet?) and would be remiss not to mention those who may not have impacted this book specifically, but have been there for me in so many ways in the last couple of years—talking me off ledges and away from cliffs, commiserating with me, celebrating with me, talking and emailing and chatting and all forms of communicating with me . . . the list could go on and on. Erin Bowman, Susan Dennard, Alex Bracken, Jen Nielsen, James Dashner, Jeff Savage, Jennifer Jenkins, Frank Cole, Ilima Todd, Emily R. King, Erin Summerill, Rosalyn Eves, Ann Cannon, Ally Condie, Martha Brockenbrough, Amy Finnegan, Natalie Whipple, Jennifer Niven, Amie Cousins, Jay Kristoff, and many more. I know I'm probably forgetting some important people, but please know I appreciate you ALL for your friendship, support, and kindnesses to me.

Thank you to the many bloggers, librarians, booksellers, and teachers (especially Jenn Kelly—the world needs more teachers like you!) who have done so much to help spread the word about my books. I wouldn't be here without you all, and for that I am forever grateful! A special thank you to Whitney, Margaret, and everyone at The King's English for all your support and enthusiasm for my books. I might be biased, but I think The King's English is one of the best independent bookstores in the world.

As always, my books would never come to fruition without amazing music to help inspire me. Thank you to the musicians whose art makes it possible for me to create mine. For this book, that especially includes Jaymes Young, OneRepublic, Craig Armstrong, John Paesano, Bear McCreary, Rachel Portman, Jason Walker, Beth Crowley, Mychael and Jeff Danna, and many more.

Thank you to my in-laws, Robert and Marilyn, for always being willing to help out and for your support. And thank you to Brenda and Ray, as well!

To my parents . . . I did most of my edits on this book in a hospital room, praying that my dad was going to survive after a twenty-five-foot fall, and then watching and helping him to recover when he did survive. I also witnessed my mom shouldering burdens that would have crushed any normal person, and doing it with grace and strength. You taught me to work hard and dream big, and I have to thank you for those lessons, both in word and in deed now as I watch you endure this trial together. Just think—by the time you read this in my published book, it will all be behind us!

To my sweet children—I love you more than words can express. As wonderful as this whole "being published" thing is, nothing compares to the best "job" in the world: being your mommy. I adore you four with all my heart.

To Trav, the one who I am blessed to be Bound to forever. I would never have come this far without you. Thank you for EVERYTHING. If I ever succeed at writing beautiful love stories in any of my books, it's only because I'm living one every day with you. (So cheesy, but true!)

And finally, to the readers. Thank you for continuing to go on this wonderful journey with me. Your excitement and passion for my books and stories is what make it all worth it. Thank you, all!

SARA B. LARSON is the author of the acclaimed young-adult-fantasy Defy trilogy: *Defy*, *Ignite*, and *Endure*. She can't remember a time when she didn't write books—although she now uses a computer instead of a Little Mermaid notebook. Sara lives in Utah with her husband, their children, and her puppy, Loki. She writes in brief snippets throughout the day and the quiet hours when most people are sleeping. Her husband claims she should have a degree in "the art of multitasking." When she's not mothering or writing, you can often find her at the gym repenting of her sugar addiction. You can visit her at www.SaraBLarson.com.